Bittersweet Memories

Have a fun read

Bittersweet Memories

By Jannifer Hoffman

Resplendence Publishing, LLC
http://www.resplendencepublishing.com

Resplendence Publishing, LLC
2665 N Atlantic Avenue, #349
Daytona Beach, FL 32118

Bittersweet Memories

Edited by Wendy Williams and Brenda Whiteside
Cover art by Les Byerley, www.les3photo8.com

Print format ISBN: 978-1-60735-390-4

Print Release: April 2012

Dedications

To my special Nieces and Nephews
I love you all

Lily Helfenstein
Michael Nies
Grace Schultz
Mark Kaul
Rick Pfeifle
Rob (Robbie) Pfeifle
Robin Burgher
Brad Martell
Heather Marie Woldt
Greta Kerkvliet
Josh Hoffman
Ryan Hoffman
Katie Kramer
Tara Ann Rau

Also in memory of my first love
Lloyd Nitschke
(1943-1958)

Acknowledgments

Many people helped me along the way
Heartfelt thanks to Gwen Besnett and Jan
Tschida for reading
Chuck Stoetzel who knows Duluth better
than I do
LuAnn Quaschnick, dedicated fan
Randy Klavu for input on dynamite
Ronnie & Sandy Hoffman
And many thanks to my editor, Wendy
Williams

Prologue

Gut-wrenching pain seared through LuAnn's lower body.

"Push," the mid-wife ordered. "Push now."

On the heels of her order, the crack and sizzle of July fourth fireworks split the night sky. How ironic this ill-fated baby should be born on a night that was meant for celebration.

LuAnn bore down, out of breath, pushing and screaming, "I can't do this."

"You should have thought about that nine months ago," the woman standing over her muttered unsympathetically. "Now...push. One more time."

Of course, she should have thought of that, but she couldn't go back. What was done was done. If she'd had a mother, maybe she'd have known about babies and birth control.

LuAnn gave it everything she had, feeling the relief as the stubborn baby slipped from her body. She drew great gasps of air as the newborn did likewise, letting out a wail that sent LuAnn's heart racing with joy and aching at the same time. Over her own moans, she heard the words, "It's a girl."

"Children having children," the mid-wife grumbled as she placed a squirming bundle in LuAnn's arms. "There ought to be a law. Chastity belts like in the olden days."

Tears clouded LuAnn's vision as she lifted her head to look at her tiny red-face daughter. Perfect miniature fingers wrapped around LuAnn's own larger finger as bright brown eyes opened to look at an unfamiliar world. She was the beautiful daughter LuAnn would never get to raise because her father had forced her to sign some papers.

You sign or both you and your kid will be out in the street. I can't afford to raise no kid and you're fifteen years old; you sure as hell can't either.

Chapter One

Almost thirteen years later.

Bart Harridan glared at the note clutched in his shaking fingers. Over twelve years had passed…and now it started all over again. Only one person could be responsible for this. Swearing, he glanced at his office door to make sure it was closed then picked up the phone and dialed a number his lawyer had given him. A man answered after the second ring.

"Yeah, you got Jace Murdock here."

Bart sucked in a breath of air. "Mr. Murdock. I understand you do investigative work."

"Sure, as long as it's legal. What do you need?"

"I need to find someone. And I'm told you know how to be discreet."

"That I do, but I don't like to walk into anything blind. I'd want to know why you're looking for this person," Murdock said.

"Can you meet me downtown, so we can talk in person?"

"Name the time and place. I'm flexible."

"This afternoon. We need to get on this as soon as possible. I'll make it worth your while."

Bart heard a decisive sigh.

"I guess I can clear a block of time for you. Oh and I didn't get your name."

"Bart Harridan. Meet me at Clancy's Bar and Grill at one-thirty. You know where it is?"

"Yeah, Mr. Harridan. I know where it is."

Jace hung up the phone, an uneasy feeling in his gut. Bart Harridan was one of the richest men in Minnesota, certainly the wealthiest in Duluth. He owned a string of hotels that spanned the country, yet he didn't ask to meet in the restaurant of one of his own hotels. Jace made a note to ask Harridan who had recommended him. Oh well, whatever Harridan wanted there was bound to be a hefty commission attached to it.

He'd barely hung up the phone when it rang again. Checking the caller ID, he recognized his sister's number, sighed and answered it.

"Hello, Kayla, what's on your mind today?"

Soft laughter tickled his ear. "Maybe nothing, maybe I just want to call to talk to you."

"And maybe you met somebody you want to set me up with."

"Hey, what are twins for?"

"Yeah, yeah, who is it this time?"

There was a short pause. "Well, she's—"

"Sorry, I'm not interested."

"That's not fair. You can at least hear me out."

Kayla's idea of *hearing me out* was a twenty minute detailed description of attributes for a woman he had no intention of meeting. "When will you get it through your head that I don't need you, *or mom,* to find a woman for me?"

"You're thirty-two years old—"

"So are you, and you don't see me trying to fix you up with every yahoo I meet."

"Huh, I wish you would. I could use a little help in that department. As long as he's as good looking as you are, as tall as you, sensitive like you, loves his mother and—"

"Give it a rest, Kayla. I have to go. I'm meeting someone in half an hour, and I need to get ready."

"A woman?" Kayla asked, a decided lilt of hopefulness in her voice.

"No, and it's a potential client. Good-bye. Love you."

He hung up the phone shaking his head. Ever since his divorce a little over a year ago, both Kayla and his mother had been crusading to get him hooked up again.

Been there, done that, bought the whole damn wardrobe.

* * * *

At 1:25, Jace walked into Clancy's Bar and Grill, wearing jeans and a polo shirt, carrying a small black brief holder. Given Harridan's choice of meeting places, Jace saw no need to wear a suit and tie even if he was conferring with Mr. Bigwig himself. He'd decided jeans fit the occasion just fine.

Jace had never personally met the man, but he'd seen him on the news often enough. Harridan was a large man, oozed confidence and money from every pour, a big political supporter.

Given all that, Jace was more than a little curious as to why a man with connections like Harridan's would hire a smalltime investigator like himself to do a job. Without even talking to him, Jace was willing to lay odds this was something Harridan didn't want the public privy to. He'd said as much when he'd asked Jace about being discreet.

He spotted Harridan in a dark corner, nodded and walked toward him. In person, the man was even more daunting than on television. He must have worked at building that persona since it was common knowledge the man didn't earn his wealth, he'd married into it.

His tanned good looks and muscular build gave evidence of many hours spent both in the gym and on the golf course. Jace recalled a recent article in the Duluth paper announcing his fiftieth birthday.

Harridan stood when Jace approached. He extended his hand, gave Jace a firm shake, motioned him to have a seat then did the same. He had a glass of amber liquid in front of him. *Tap beer?* Jace mused. The man really was going incognito.

"What would you like to drink?" Harridan asked.

"Beer's good," Jace said, taking a seat across the table from Harridan.

Harridan waived to the waitress, pointed to Jace then his own glass.

Jace noted that for a man who usually dressed in Armani suits, he knew how to tone it down if the occasion arose. The waitress set a bottle of Heineken and a glass in front of Jace. When she poured it, he noticed it was the same color as Harridan's drink. So, maybe it wasn't tap beer.

"Who recommended me?" Jace asked taking a sip of the smooth, cold brew.

"That's not important, but he said you did a good job, and I didn't have to worry about discretion."

Even though Jace wondered who it was, he wasn't going to let that stand in his way of taking the job. "That's important in this case?"

"Very. I need to find a woman."

"Your lawyer couldn't find her?"

"No."

Since he didn't expand on his answer, Jace assumed this might be something he didn't want even his lawyer to know. Maybe he'd had an affair, though he wasn't known as a lady's man unless, of course, he knew how to be discrete himself. "Can I ask why you want to find this person?"

"Before I can explain any further, I need to know if you'll take the job. I don't mean her any harm. I just need to know where she is."

Jace sat back in his seat and gave the man a long look. If he was lying, he was damn good at it. At this point, however, he hadn't told him anything other than he meant her no harm. Something just didn't add up. Obviously Harridan wasn't sharing the whole story. He must have suspected Jace was going to turn him down because he spoke again, hastily.

"I'll pay you two thousand dollars now and another two thousand if you find her. You don't need to approach her; in fact I'd expect you not to. You can keep the first two grand whether you find her or not. It needs to be soon though. I suspect she still lives in the area."

Jace leaned forward bracing his elbow on the table. "If I'm going to do this for you, I need a hint as to why you want to find her."

For a moment he thought Harridan would get up and walk out. Then he said, "I need your solemn oath that you won't breath a word to anyone whether you take the job or not."

"You have it," Jace said, becoming more wary by the moment.

"My family's well-being depends on it."

It was common knowledge that Harridan's family consisted of his wife Gladys and only one child. She was about twelve or thirteen. "Now you really have my curiosity peaked. You care to explain that?"

Harridan's face reddened with anger or frustration, Jace couldn't be sure which. "No. And this isn't about your curiosity. This is about my wife."

"I understand. I'm just inquisitive by nature."

"I'm told that's what makes you a good PI, you know how to dig into things. For the record, I'm not trying to keep anything pertinent from you."

Jace would have bet his left testicle that was a bald-assed lie. But what the hell, he was between assignments, and this sounded like an easy no-brainer. Locate this mystery woman, report her whereabouts and he was done.

"Okay," Jace said, pulling a yellow note pad out of his briefcase. "I'll take it on. Give me what information you have."

"I don't have much. I've never met her or seen her."

Jace stared at Harridan, momentarily speechless. That statement blew the hell out of every theory he could have imagined. He sighed. Maybe this job wasn't going to be as easy as he thought. "Well, let's start with a name then."

Harridan shrugged. "She was born LuAnn Randall. I don't know if she ever married. Her mother died when she was about five. Her father's name was Jack Randall."

"You say was?"

Jace could have sworn Harridan hesitated before answering.

"I don't know if he's still living."

"How old is she?"

"Twenty seven, maybe twenty eight."

Huh, he didn't hesitate with that answer. "Was she born here in Duluth?"

"I—don't know."

"Did she ever live here?"

"I think so."

Jace's neck itched. It was just a sensation he got when he was frustrated or irritated with something. He took a swig of beer and stared Harridan in the eye. "This doesn't seem to be getting us anywhere. Why don't we quit the cat and mouse game, and you just tell me what you do know?"

"I already have."

Jace glanced at his scant notes. "You know the name she was born with, her father's name and her age. That's it?"

Harridan nodded. "I'm afraid so."

"No description, no photo, no last known address for either her or her father."

"No."

"I'm assuming you've already checked the Duluth and Minneapolis phone books."

"Yes, with no luck."

"Correct me if I'm wrong, but you have no idea if she was even born in Minnesota. It could have been Wisconsin, North Dakota or even Alaska."

Harridan bristled. "I doubt she was ever that far away, but you're right, I don't know. However I'm sure there was a time when she lived nearby, possibly Wisconsin, but no farther."

"Excuse me for asking, but what is your connection to her?"

"Irrelevant. It won't help you with your search."

"Humor me."

Harridan emptied the beer in front of him. "That's where the discretion part kicks in. If even so much as a rumor gets out, it would be detrimental to my wife's mental health."

"I need reassurance that this woman isn't hiding out for a reason."

"She's not."

Jace took a swig of his own beer. "Can you convince me of that? We've already talked about discretion. You have my word on that."

"I believe you. From what I've heard about you, you're an honest man." He took a deep breath. "My wife is ill. Two weeks ago she confessed to me that she had a child when she was seventeen. The father of the child was already married, and her parents thought she was too young to raise a baby on her own. They talked her into giving it up. She gave it to the child's father when his wife, who was barren, agreed to accept it as her own. Understand this all happened before I knew Gladys."

Jace nodded. "And now she wants to find her?"

"Yes. And I'm sure you can appreciate why she doesn't want the whole world to know about it."

"Just one more question, Mr. Harridan, did you research my background before you called me?"

"Of course."

Chapter Two

LuAnn Barstow watched the giddy second-graders file out of her classroom. They were still cheering as they ran down the hall. The last day of school, she should have been giving herself a mental cheer, but she couldn't dredge it up. The kids looked forward to an exciting, carefree summer while she faced three months of boring loneliness. Maybe this year would be different. Maybe she'd take a trip somewhere—to Yellowstone or Mount Rushmore.

Still trying to build up some enthusiasm for the upcoming summer vacation, she grabbed the eraser and started clearing the blackboard.

"LuAnn, what are you doing?" It was her closest friend, Barb from the third grade room across the hall.

LuAnn smiled. "Getting things ready for next year."

"You are pathetic. Come on. A bunch of us are going down to Rango's for pizza and a celebration drink. Join us."

"You know I don't do that sort of thing."

"What *sort of thing*—have fun?"

"Don't you have to go home to your husband and kids?" Barb had a wonderful husband and five-year-old twin daughters.

"It's only three o'clock; they're with the sitter 'til five. Besides Rich is picking them up, and I have the whole evening free if I want. Being married isn't the same as going to jail," Barb added, laughing.

Barb walked up to LuAnn, took the eraser out of her hand and pulled her toward the door. "I'm not taking no for an answer. Patsy's brother, Ron, is joining us. Ron's a teacher over at Sandburg High. He's a good guy, perfect for you. We want you to meet him."

LuAnn snagged her purse from the top of her desk. "You guys might as well stop trying to set me up. You know I don't—"

"*Do that sort of thing,*" Barb mimicked. "Yeah, yeah, I know."

"Besides, I've been in class all day. I'm a mess. And I have to go home and water my flowers."

"You're a mess all right, LuAnn, but it's not your appearance. Someday I'm going to get you drunk enough to tell me why you're so sour on men. You've been divorced what, eight months? And I haven't seen you so much as go out on a date."

LuAnn scowled. "I'm not sour on men."

"Glad to hear it. Let's go."

* * * *

Back at home, Jace checked his meager notes. He didn't have much to go on, but then how hard could it be to find LuAnn Randall in a city the size of Duluth with less than a hundred thousand population. Add thirty thousand for the neighboring city of Superior, Wisconsin, and it still wasn't that many. On the other hand if it was that easy, Harridan would have either done it himself or turned it over to one of his own people.

It was possible; however, this might be so private he didn't want anyone near him to know about it. Could she be hiding from him? Harridan had said he meant her no harm, but that could be a bogus statement. To satisfy himself he went online and checked the local phone listings himself. He found two LuAnn Randalls; one had a husband so Randall was her married name, the other was old enough to draw social security.

Then there was the question of why Harridan had specifically picked a disbarred lawyer to do his investigating. Was it because of his track record or in spite of it?

Jace was hardly proud of losing his license to practice law in the state of Minnesota or of spending two nights in the county jail for contempt of court. Did Harridan view that as an asset? If so, why? He intended to find out before he turned LuAnn Randall over to Harridan, assuming he was able to locate her.

After doing an internet search for LuAnn and coming up with nothing useful, he Googled her father Jack Randall. His obituary came up. He had died eleven years earlier. Both his parents and wife Lucinda had preceded him in death. He left one daughter, LuAnn. He'd spent fifteen years employed at Otis Elevator but wasn't working at the time of his of death. It mentioned that he was a Duluth resident. Jace made a note to check the elevator company—maybe there was a life insurance policy naming LuAnn as the beneficiary. If he had a pension, it might still be making payments to her. Or, even if it had been eleven years, some of the long-timers might remember him.

Jace rechecked his notes. According to Harridan he needed to find LuAnn quickly because *his family's well being depended on it*. But he'd been very adamant about discretion. Could it have something to do with his daughter Chelsea?

He realized he'd written the daughter's name down, not because Harridan had mentioned it but because Jace remembered it from a court case. Harridan had been arrested for popping a reporter who had sneaked into the backyard and taken a photo of Chelsea. He'd also destroyed a three thousand dollar camera. Jace made a note that Harridan was not above breaking the law to protect his daughter and keep her out of the public eye. That was about a year ago when Chelsea was eleven or twelve. The case came up at the same time he himself was in court defending a drunk driver. A case he'd won but had him doubting the criminal justice system.

Jace shook that depressing memory off just as another thought hit him. If Bart Harridan had an affair with Lucinda Randall, it's possible he could have fathered a child by her. Maybe Harridan was looking for *his* long lost daughter. Huh.

My family's well being depends on it.

Is it possible Chelsea is ill and needs a transplant from a sister? That made sense. And as far as being secretive, Harridan normally guarded his family from the public eye.

Jace glanced at his watch. It was going on four o'clock. If he left now, he could make it to Otis Elevator's downtown office before they closed. Plus it was Friday night and maybe he could find out where they hung out after work. It was a lot easier getting information from a man after a couple of drinks had loosened his tongue.

As he walked out the door, his cell phone rang. Caller ID told him it was his buddy Devon Bailey. They'd gone from grade school all the way through law school together. The difference now was Devon still practiced law.

"Yeah, Devon, what's on your mind?"

"Fishing. We could get a few hours in yet this afternoon, if you have time."

They were joint owners of a thirty-two foot cabin cruiser docked at the Harbor Cove Marina on Park Point. "I wish I could," Jace said. "I'm working on a case. How about tomorrow? Fishing's better in the morning anyway."

"You got it. But we need to get back by one thirty because I have to be home for a graduation in the afternoon. How about we meet there at eight?"

"Sounds good to me."

"In the meantime I'll go over and replace the downrigger that broke last weekend. While I'm at it, I'll bring a thermos off coffee and stock the fridge with liquid refreshments. You can supply the food."

"You got it. See ya at eight."

* * * *

Bart Harridan came home to find his wife waiting for him in the den. She stood at the bar pouring expensive French brandy into a highball glass. By the looks of the half-empty bottle and her blood-shot eyes, it wasn't the first. She sloshed ice in the glass. It was four o'clock in the afternoon, and she was still in her nightgown.

They'd married right out of college twenty-four years ago. Gladys was actually kind of cute back then, with a petite figure and exotic dark eyes. She was even okay in bed. But the reason he'd married her was her daddy was in poor health and worth a bundle.

Bart, an only child, had had to work to put himself through school. His own father had a menial job at the paper mill and was more interested in watching football or basketball, or any other game he could tune in, anything that didn't include spending time with a son who abhorred sports.

"Where the hell have you been?" Gladys snarled, tottering over to a chair, drink in hand.

"I had a business meeting. Isn't it a little early in the day to be drinking?" He walked up to the bar and poured himself a straight shot. The very sight of his soused wife sickened him. She'd long since lost the appeal he'd once had for her—about the time her daddy passed and left her his millions nearly fifteen years ago. Thinking about the lie he'd told Murdock made him want to laugh. He almost wished Murdock would spread the rumor.

"Where's Chelsea?"

"Where else. In her room listening to god-awful music."

"Maybe if her mother wasn't always drunk she'd come out of her room once in a while."

Gladys made a short cackling noise that sounded like laughter. "I'm not her mother."

His hands itched to curl around her skinny, ugly throat. "Dammit Gladys, watch your mouth. She could hear you."

She gave a wry smile and raised her glass to toast him. "Here's to the father of the year award winner."

He glared at her. "You're the only woman I've ever known I could truly call an asshole." Her laughter followed him out of the room. He went straight to his office, slammed the door behind him and poured a scotch from the bottle in the drawer. If there was any way he could murder that woman and get away with it, he would. But the first person they went after was always the husband. Even if he hired someone to have it done, they could still ferret him out.

Thinking about hired help, he pulled out his cell phone and dialed a number. When his man Armon Kastansa answered with a curt hello, Harridan said. "What's he up to?"

"Not much. Went straight home, and he's been there until a short while ago. Right now he's walking into a building down on Michigan Street. There's several businesses there so I don't know who he's seeing. Want me to follow him inside?"

"No, just stay on his tail but keep out of sight. The last thing we want him to know is that he's being followed."

Bart had met Armon in the gym where they were both working out some twelve years ago. Armon apparently knew who Bart was and had approached him for a job. Kastansa wasn't the brightest color in the box, but he was meticulous in his work, unquestionably loyal and best of all, he had absolutely no conscience. He'd proven that on the first job Bart had given him—taking care of Jack Randall.

Chapter Three

It wasn't the first time she'd heard them argue and certainly not the first time she'd seen her mother drunk. But it was the second time Chelsea had heard her mother deny that Chelsea was her daughter. The first time had been three weeks ago. She'd suspected it for some time though. Ever since she began to compare her own mother's behavior to that of her friends' mothers. They talked to their daughters, even hugged and kissed them. They also kissed and hugged their husbands.

But that never happened in this family. No one hugged or kissed anyone. At least her father was somewhat nice to her. That left her with one conclusion, she was the result of one of the many affairs her mother accused him of having. Chelsea suspected a woman must have gotten pregnant and didn't want the baby, so Bart Harridan brought his daughter home expecting his wife, Gladys, to welcome the child with open arms. Unfortunately for Chelsea, she was the unwelcome child.

Chelsea brushed her tears away quickly, replaced them with anger and cranked her stereo up loud enough to make the shingles rattle. It wasn't fair. None of it was her fault. Why was she the one to suffer for their mistakes? Why couldn't they be like every other family she knew?

Nobody bothered to tell her to turn the music down. She didn't even like this particular CD; she'd only bought it to irritate *them*. She stood it as long as she could then turned it down herself. No one else seemed to care if she ruined her hearing.

* * * *

Jace walked into the Otis Elevator shop at 4:25. At the same time a tall, thin, forty-something man jingling a set of keys in his hand stepped out of an office. Four other closed doors surrounded the huge cavity of the mostly empty room. He wore green coveralls bearing an embroidered Otis logo above the name, Gardner.

"Sorry," Gardner said. "Unless you have an emergency, we're closed for the weekend."

"Nope, no emergency. Just looking for information on a former employee."

"Who you lookin' for?"

"Jack Randall."

"Hell, he died ten, eleven years ago."

"Did you know him?" Jace asked.

"Can't say I did. I've only been here six years. Got transferred from Fargo, but I remember a couple of the guys talking about him. He quit when he won a lottery or something."

Jace wasn't quick enough to hide his surprise.

Gardner laughed. "Guess you didn't know that, huh?"

"Guess not. Any of the older guys around who might remember him?"

Gardner started walking toward the door sorting through his keys. "Oh yeah, several. Bill's been here the longest, but there's at least two or three more."

Jace followed him. The man was obviously anxious to lock up. "I don't suppose you could tell me where Bill lives?"

"Don't need to. You can catch the whole lot of them two blocks up at the Pioneer Bar. Most of them stop there for happy hour on Friday nights…left about half an hour ago. I'm only here yet because the wife called with a list of groceries for me to pick up on my way home."

Jace thanked Gardner for his help and decided, since it was only a couple of blocks, to hoof it to the Pioneer Bar.

It was dark inside and noisy, with a blue-collar crowd celebrating the end of the workweek. The room was long and narrow, with a packed bar embracing half of it. He spotted the familiar green coveralls toward the back between the bar and the busy pool tables. They were at a high table, some holding beer bottles. A couple had drinks that could have been cola or hard liquor. Each one had a second drink in front of them untouched, compliments of the Pioneers' happy hour no doubt. All were munching on the free hors d'oeuvres advertised at the front door.

Jace sat at the only open stool at the bar and ordered a beer. While waiting, he glanced around the room appearing to be interested in what was going on. He received two bottles of Bud Light, both opened. Picking up one, he slid off the stool and sauntered over to the Otis table. There weren't any stools empty, so he simply elbowed in. Five sets of eyes turned on him.

"Hey, guys," he said. "I couldn't help but noticing the logos on your coveralls. You all work at Otis?"

He received four friendly nods and one hostile glare from a wiry little man at the end, Saul, according to his nametag. Jace did a quick survey of the other nametags.

Bill spoke. "Yup, we all have the privilege of keeping the public from plummeting to their deaths."

Saul grunted derisively.

Ignoring Saul, Jace smiled. "I used to know a fella that worked there, Jack, Jack Randall. Anybody know him?"

Bill laughed. "Oh yah. He was a character."

"That's a mild way to put it," a man named Chris muttered. "If you were his friend, you were one of a kind."

They all laughed except the stone-faced Saul. He shoved his empty beer aside and picked up the happy hour freebie.

Jace was getting the picture on Jack Randall, and it wasn't pretty. He had the feeling he'd get more information if he dropped the friend bit. "He was more of an acquaintance than a friend, I guess you'd say."

"He wasn't a pleasant sort," Bill said, "but nobody deserves to die that way."

That perked Jace's interest, but if he supposedly knew Randall, he'd know how he died. "What was the outcome of that anyway?" he asked.

"Smoking in bed," Chris answered grimacing. "Burned to a crisp."

"Jeez, I didn't even know the man, but that's brutal," a fourth man, Reed, said. "Maybe I'll give up the smokes. Can't smoke anywhere any more anyway." He picked up a corn chip, dipped it in salsa and shoved it in his mouth. "Didn't he win a lottery, or something?"

That brought an audible snort out of Saul.

Bill chuckled. "Saul, you're just pissed because he didn't give you any of it. Apparently cousins weren't on his list of benefactors."

Jace made a mental note. *Saul was Jack's cousin.* That bought him the opening he was looking for. "Whatever happened to his daughter, LuAnn? I lost track of her after Jack died."

"Don't have a clue," Bill said.

Chris shook his head in agreement. "Me either."

"You might ask her grandmother," Bill suggested.

Jace masked his enthusiasm. "You mean Lucinda's mother?" he said, thankful he recalled Jack's wife's name from the obituary. Obviously it wasn't Jack's mother, since both his parents had preceded him in death.

"Crazy old bat," Saul muttered scowling.

That comment told Jace he was on target. "Where is she at?" he asked.

"None of your business," Saul snapped. "Why the hell you so interested anyway?"

"Last I heard she was in an assisted living place over in Superior," Bill said, ignoring Saul. It seemed Saul wasn't any better thought of than his cousin Jack.

"I've seen you somewhere," Saul piped up. He took a long pull of beer, staring hard at Jace.

Jace decided this might be a good time to make a hasty exit. He'd probably gleaned all the information he could out of this crowd. He stood up. "Well, gotta go. Thanks for the visit—"

"I remember where I saw you," Saul said, his loud voice drawing the attention of everyone nearby.

Jace had one thought. *Oh shit.*

"You're that lawyer," Saul went on, making no effort to tone it down. "The one that got the woman off who wacked her husband."

"I'm not a lawyer anymore," he said.

"I read about that case in the paper," Bill said, saluting Jace with his beer. "I even remember his name, Marley Jacobs. He was pounding the hell out of his wife. Good job, man."

"You can't just shoot a man for that and get away scot free," Saul grumbled.

Bill's eyes narrowed on Saul. "Any man who hits a woman deserves to be wacked as far as I'm concerned."

Saul signaled the barmaid and ordered two more beers then turned on Bill. "That's 'cause you're a henpecked pussy."

"No," Bill said with ill-concealed anger. "It's because I love and respect my wife."

Jace sensed an undercurrent of animosity between the two men, and he was pretty sure it hadn't started with this conversation. He needed to make a quick exit, so he clapped Bill on the shoulder. "Thanks, Buddy, I appreciate the vote of confidence. Obviously I agree with you. I gotta run.

* * * *

LuAnn followed Barb into the crowded interior of Rango's Pizza Bar. They joined a group of at least fifteen people, most already started on their first round of drinks and pizzas. A couple of men moved over to make room for them. One, Kelsey Grayson, LuAnn recognized from school. He was thirty-eight years old, single and the athletic director. She had turned him down numerous times when he'd made a pass at her. Of course he flirted with all the women, even the married ones. LuAnn took the brunt of it since she was the only unmarried female on staff younger than he was.

LuAnn maneuvered around Barb, forcing her friend to take the seat beside the vicarious Grayson. Barb knew how to handle him. LuAnn quickly dropped into a seat next to a man she didn't know. He was pleasant looking with arresting light gray eyes. He certainly looked safer than Grayson with his suggestive eyes and touchy, feely fingers.

He smiled at her and held out a hand. "Hi, I'm guessing you're LuAnn. I'm Ron Bennet."

LuAnn groaned silently. Just her luck to sit beside the very man Barb was trying to hook her up with. No wonder Barb allowed her to make the seat switch so easily. Ron was good looking in a suave sort of way. He wore khaki pants and an open-at-the throat pale grey polo shirt. It matched the color of his eyes, and she wondered if that was intentional. Men didn't normally think about those things. Maybe his mother shopped for him.

She took Ron's hand, giving him a deliberately limp shake and a cool hello. She looked around for a spot at another table, but the place was jammed.

"You're not happy to be here, are you?" he said.

His candid remark took her by surprise, and she felt a little guilty. "You're right. I'm not. I was planning to go home and water my flowers."

Ron gave her a strange look then burst out laughing. "You're serious aren't you?"

He had a nice healthy laugh, and it made her smile. "That sounded lame, didn't it?"

Still chuckling he said, "At least you didn't give me the old I-need-to-wash-my-hair routine. Your hair is nice by the way."

She flushed. No one had ever said that to her before, and she didn't know how to respond. Two weeks earlier she'd let Barb talk her into highlighting it. Shrugging she said. "My dad always said it looked like dirty dishwater."

"Fie on him. I like the contrast of coloring. It reminds me of honey. You must spend hours in front of the mirror to get it to curl like that."

"It's naturally curly. I hate it, but there's not much I can do about it unless I *do* spend hours trying to straighten it every day. Either way, with the humidity, the curls just spring right back."

He watched her for a minute then said, "You don't like talking about yourself, do you?"

Again she felt her cheeks heat up, but she smiled. "You're very perceptive for a guy."

"I suppose if I say you have a pretty smile, you'll jump up and leave, so I won't say it."

"Good. I'd appreciate that. Barb tells me you teach at Sandburg High."

"Yup, English and Literature."

"Do you like it?"

"Sure, the kids are great. Well, most of them anyway." He laughed. "You always have a few rebels that give you a challenge."

"I get the feeling you like challenges."

"Now who's the perceptive one?"

"Look, Ron, don't take me on as one of your challenges. You'll be disappointed."

"How can you be so sure?"

"I'll be up front with you. I don't date. So your time and energy is wasted on me."

* * * *

Jace's phone rang while he was walking the two blocks back to his Ford Fusion. He looked at the caller ID and saw it was his mother. *Jeez,* he moaned. She must have been sharing notes with his sister. He snapped the phone open.

"Yeah, Ma, what's up?"

"Where are you, Jace?"

"Downtown, just heading home."

"Good, you can stop in for supper. I made your favorite—pork chops."

She knew exactly how to get his mouth watering for her cooking. "Who's all going to be there, Ma?"

"Just Kayla, and your father, of course."

"None of her friends?"

"Nope."

"Okay, I'll stop, but I'll have to eat and run. I have work to do."

"Wonderful, see you in a few minutes. It's almost ready."

He could picture her smile as he hung up. It didn't take a lot to make her happy. She was in her glory when she could feed people.

He started the car, glancing in his rearview mirror. The street was empty with the exception of a black sedan parked behind him about a half block away. When it made a quick u-turn and disappeared, Jace shrugged and put his car in gear making his own u-turn to exit the dead-end street.

Jace pulled up in front of his parents' three-story house on Superior Street. It always gave him a burst of nostalgia coming back to the place he'd spent his childhood. He looked up at the third story window, the loft that had been his personal sanctuary growing up with three sisters. Going up to the front door, he noticed they'd put in a new sidewalk and painted the trim since he'd been there two weeks ago. After a quick knock he walked into a kitchen filled with delicious smells.

"Hello, anybody home?"

"We're in the sitting room," his mother, MaryAnn, called.

Heading through the kitchen, he stopped to check out the aromas coming from an electric frying pan.

MaryAnn appeared in the doorway. "Don't you dare touch that cover," she scolded. "You'll ruin the dumplings."

"I thought you said we were having pork chops."

She stood on her tiptoes to press a kiss on his cheek. "We are honey. Don't worry; we have special guests that wanted dumplings. Come in and sit down. Everything will be ready in about twenty minutes."

He walked through the dining room into the sitting room warily. He still didn't trust his mother and sister to not have a female surprise waiting for him, especially when he noticed the table was set for six. He gave his mother a warning glare to which she grinned.

He breathed a sigh of relief and delight when he spotted his older sister, Wanda's two kids.

Ten-year-old Donna jumped up and threw her arms around his waist. "Uncle Jace!"

Jace gave her a monster hug, kissing her on top of the head. "Hi Chicken Little. How are you?"

"I'm good."

"Where's your mom?" he asked, glancing around the room.

"Her and Daddy went out on a date," she groused, giving him a mischievous look. "But Grandma made dumplings so it's okay, and Grandpa's teaching Donnie how to play checkers."

Jace greeted his father and eight-year-old nephew. "Who's winning?" he asked.

"Grandpa is," Donnie grumbled. "But it's only the second game."

Jace laughed. He knew his father. Donnie would have to learn the game before Harold would give him an edge. He took a seat on the sofa next to his twin sister and gave one of her dangling locks a tug.

"Hey, Brat. How goes it?"

Kayla sent him a pouting frown. "My friend, Sharon is very disappointed that you wouldn't at least meet her."

He smiled. "That will spare her from the greater disappointment she'd have after she met me."

"You are incorrigible, you know."

"So I've been told."

Chuckling, Harold did a double jump on two of Ronnie's movers. "So, Kayla," he said. "What time is Sharon picking you up?"

"Dad!" Kayla shrieked. "Don't tell him that." She looked at Jace and shrugged sheepishly. "I needed a ride. My car's getting brakes."

"Uh-huh."

Kayla spent the next ten minutes raving about Sharon until even Harold was rolling his eyes.

"Dinner's ready," MaryAnn chirped from the doorway.

"Did you know about this?" Jace questioned his mother, taking a seat beside Donnie.

"What?" MaryAnn asked innocently. "That Kayla's brakes needed fixing? Well sure. It's very dangerous to drive with squealing brakes."

"Don't get so bent out of shape," Kayla quipped. "You can just say no."

"All right. No."

"Sharon's a nice girl," MaryAnn put in adding, "save room for apple pie."

Jace gave her a skeptical glare. "So were Sandra and Linda and Marcie and—what was that skydiver's name?"

"Monica," Kayla muttered. "Okay, so she was a little off the wall."

"A little," Jace exclaimed. "She had twenty-two tattoos and three ex-husbands."

"She does not have twenty-two tattoos," Kayla insisted.

Jace spooned dumplings and potatoes smothered with creamy white sauce onto his plate. "Well, I'm assuming she had some hidden I didn't see."

Harold chuckled, and both his wife and daughter sent him piercing glares.

"I have to admit she wasn't the best candidate for you," Kayla said. "But in my defense I hadn't actually met her. Linda found her for you."

Jace groaned. "And you wonder why I get a little turned off by your selection of *candidates*. What time is Sharon picking you up?"

"Around eight-thirty."

"When's the last time you saw Dustin?" his mother asked making a clever attempt to change the subject. She knew what would draw his attention away from Kayla's *dating service*. If he hadn't known she really cared about Dustin, it would have irritated him since the subject of the son who wasn't legally his child was depressing.

Jace released a deep sigh. "Three weeks ago. She only lets me have him if she has a hot date and can't get a sitter who's willing to stay overnight. And it's always on her terms."

"That's awful," MaryAnn said, passing him the platter of pork chops.

He shrugged. "Yeah on one hand, on the other hand I got to spend a whole night and day with him."

"That's a sorry case," Harold said. "Too bad you couldn't adopt him when you were married to that witch."

"Doesn't it bother you that she's dating?" Kayla put in.

Jace savored and swallowed a mouthful of food before he answered. "Not in the least. My only regret is losing Dustin."

"He called you Daddy," Kayla said.

Eight-year-old Donnie in his youthful innocence said, "Why don't you get married and have kids of your own."

Chapter Four

LuAnn let herself into her cozy little house. The two-bedroom bungalow was all on one floor, except for a dark damp basement, but it was all hers. She loved it. The furniture was unremarkable but comfortable, and it fit in her budget. She masked the shabbiness with live greenery. Young plants were inexpensive, and under her watchful care they flourished until her home resembled a jungle. She loved the feeling.

Not for the first time since leaving the pizza bar, she chastised herself for giving Ron Bennet her phone number. He'd been so sweet she'd let down her guard for a moment. When he called—if he called—she'd have to let him down lightly. His gentleness should have encouraged her, but somehow she just wasn't interested. Maybe Barb was right. Maybe she was sour on men. And now she'd given her phone number to a man she had no intention of seeing again.

Sighing, she filled her watering can to take care of her beloved plants. As she did so her thoughts wandered to her disastrous marriage.

Roger Barstow had been sweet and gentle too when she'd first met him. They'd only known each other four months when he'd talked her into getting married. She'd said yes because she wanted a normal life so badly: a house, a husband and most of all children. But he seemed to change almost immediately after they'd said their vows. When he walked out, he'd accused her of being frigid.

Maybe it had been a mistake to insist they get married before they went to bed together. The truth was she'd enjoyed the kissing and petting but as it turned out, not the intimacy of sex. Maybe she *was* frigid.

After Roger, she'd vowed never to put herself through that again. She'd kept his name only because she wanted to sever all ties with her father. Just thinking about him put her nerves on edge even after all these years. *Twelve years,* she thought, and still her arms ached for the baby girl she'd quickly named Becca in the five minutes she'd been allowed to hold her.

"You're too young," he'd griped as he coerced her into signing those papers. "We can't afford to buy diapers and all that crap you need. Besides, you don't know a damn thing about babies and neither do I. Let somebody raise it that knows what they're doing."

It wasn't but a month later when he won that lottery. They had money; they could afford whatever they needed. She begged him to help her find the baby, but he flatly refused, saying it was better off where it was. She never knew how much money he'd won, but according to the way he squandered it, there must have been over five hundred thousand dollars. It took him less than two years to go through it all. Four months after he'd announced they were broke, he died in a fire while smoking in bed. She was a senior in high school. The expensive house he'd purchased had extensive smoke damage and was foreclosed on. LuAnn went to live with her maternal grandmother. During the next year she went through all her father's papers hoping to find out where her baby had gone, but there was nothing.

In a little over three weeks, Becca would be thirteen—a teenager.

She heard Max, the neighbor's gray and white cat, mewing at her patio window. Max made regular visits to her house looking for the treats she kept handy. She let him in, scooped him up in her arms and let her tears soak into his soft coat.

* * * *

Home at last, Jace headed straight for his office and his waiting computer. It was after nine o'clock, and he had a lot to do. Sharon had shown up half an hour early, whether by plan or accident he didn't know, but he'd been obligated to stay and talk to her or appear obnoxiously rude. Nice woman—too nice—to the point of being overbearing.

All he could think about was getting home and doing more research looking for LuAnn Randall.

The first thing he did was pull up an obituary for Lucinda Randall. She was born Lucinda Ilene Downer and died leaving her husband Jack and five-year-old LuAnn. At that time they were listed as Duluth residents. Also surviving was her mother Emma Downer of Superior, Wisconsin.

Bill had said he thought she lived in an assisted living facility in Superior. Jace found no obituary on her, so that probably meant she was still there. Resorting to the Duluth/Superior phone book, he looked for Assisted Living Facilities. After wading through numerous ones located in Duluth, he found ten with Wisconsin area codes and addresses in Superior. Making a note of each one with phone numbers and addresses, he turned off the computer and called it quits for the day. It was too late to make any calls today. He could do it tomorrow from the boat with his cell phone.

* * * *

"Who's the father?" Jack Randall demanded, standing over her like a police interrogator. "Who is it? I'm going to make that son of a bitch pay."

LuAnn cringed. She couldn't tell him. Wouldn't tell him. But he kept at her. He'd never let it rest. So she lied.

"I don't know."

LuAnn flinched when he raised his fist. "Whore!"

LuAnn came awake instantly, a scream lodged in her throat. The dream seemed to have lasted only moments, and yet she was drenched in sweat. The sheets were damp and in a twisted mess. Her face was wet with salty tears.

She knew the nightmares would come. They always did if she even so much as thought about dating. She never should have given Ron Bennet her phone number. Maybe she'd get lucky and he wouldn't call.

* * * *

Jace arrived at the marina at ten minutes to eight. He hopped aboard the thirty-two foot Bayliner carrying his cooler, thinking about getting the engine warmed up when he saw Devon pull up in the parking lot. He waved a greeting to his friend. "Hey buddy, looks like it's going to be a beautiful day for fishing."

"Yeah. Great idea coming this morning," Devon called from the dock. "I hope you brought something good for breakfast. I'm starved."

Jace laughed. "We have McDonald's Egg McMuffins. You navigate I'll cook."

Devon stepped on board lugging his tackle box. He stopped and looked back at the parking lot. "Who the hell is that guy tailing you?"

"What guy," Jace asked, his gaze following Devon's. "Where?"

"Huh. He must have taken off. He was between us coming over the bridge, driving so damn slow I gave him the horn."

"What kind of car?"

"A black Buick LaCrosse."

"It was probably some asshole who didn't know where he was going."

"Yeah, most likely," Devon said indifferently. "He just irritated me."

"Could have been a sightseer."

"At this hour. Alone. I doubt it."

Jace laughed. "Get the tow lines. I'll fire up the engines."

Fifteen minutes later they were heading through the channel toward the wide expanse of Lake Superior. Once they reached their favorite fishing spot and had dropped the lines, Jace pulled out his cell phone and note pad.

"Watch my lines for me, will you? I have a couple of calls I need to make."

Devon chuckled. "Big case?"

"You might say that."

"Why the hell don't you try to get your license back? You're a damn good lawyer, and your talents are wasted on this PI business."

Jace shrugged. "I'm thinking about it."

"You know as well as I do that Judge Porter was out of line having you disbarred. He could have given you a six-month suspension or let it go altogether. The guy's a nut case."

"Yeah well, he's the most powerful nut case in the state."

"Still, how he managed to convince the board that you were guilty of some horrible misdeed is beyond me," Devon said, adjusting his pole in the downrigger.

"I gave false evidence, Devon. I *was* guilty."

"Guilty of what? Keeping an abused woman out of jail for killing a no-good piece of trash like Marley Jacobs? I'd have done the same thing."

Jace gave his friend a wry smile. "I know that, and you know that, but a lot of people felt she should have done time, saying she could have divorced him."

Devon snorted. "They obviously don't understand the abused-wife syndrome. These guys brow beat their wives until they don't know which way is up, much less how to get out of an abusive marriage. And how many of those bastards go through restraining orders and kill their ex-wives. As far as I'm concerned, she did the right thing."

Jace laughed. "That's how I felt. Porter seemed to have a vendetta against me from the start of that trial. It's strange too because I've never had trouble with him before."

"I think he was on the take."

Jace shook his head. "I've actually thought of that, but I don't see how. Jacob's entire family was living from hand to mouth, besides Porter makes more than me and you put together. Why would he put a brilliant career in jeopardy for money he doesn't need?"

"All I can say," Devon said, reaching for his coffee thermos, "is I have my eyes and ears open."

"It's not all bad," Jace said. "I'm enjoying this little sabbatical. Ever since I got that damn drunk driver off last year, I've been discouraged with the justice system. I'll dive back in when I'm ready."

"Good. And just remember if you get a hit while you're on the phone, the fish is mine."

"You have to get it in first," Jace said as he dialed the number for the first assisted living facility on his list. He'd already decided he couldn't just come out and ask if Emma Downer lived there. They likely couldn't or wouldn't tell him.

The phone was answered on the second ring. "Hello, Cedar Ridge, Candy speaking."

"Hi Candy, I wonder if I could speak to Emma Downer."

"Hmm. Is she a resident or a caregiver?"

"Resident." He heard some paper shuffling.

"Sorry, I don't have anyone by that name."

"Okay, I must have the wrong place. Thanks." At least he found out she wasn't there. He called two more numbers with the same results. As he dialed the fourth, his rod tipped.

Slamming his phone shut, he raced to grab it before Devon could get there. Twenty minutes later he pulled in an eighteen-pound lake trout.

"You lucky son of a bitch," Devon grumbled. "You always get the first fish, and while you're hanging on the phone yet."

"It's called multi-tasking, my friend. Don't worry. I'll let you pull in the next one."

Still laughing he took care of the fish then went back to his phone. Two more strikeouts. He only had three names left on his list. The next call was to Harmony House.

A cheerful voice came on the line. "Good morning, this is Gretchen. How may I help you?"

Jace saw his rod tip. Devon had his hands on it grinning. "I'd like to talk to Emma Downer please."

"It's almost lunchtime, so Emma's in the dining room. She always goes an hour early to make sure she's on time, so she wouldn't be answering the phone in her room. Can I take a message?"

Jace's mind did a mental *bingo*. "No thanks, I'll just call later or maybe I'll just stop in and visit her." Out of the corner of his eye, he watched Devon struggling with a fish he had on the line.

"I'm sure she'd enjoy that. Emma hardly gets any visitors. Should I tell her to expect you?"

"No, not necessary. I'll just see her when I get there."

"All righty, goodbye then."

Jace hung up the phone, noted the address he'd written down then went to help Devon net the fish he'd hooked on Jace's line.

"What are you grinning about?" Devon asked. "This one's mine."

"I got a hot date lined up for this afternoon."

"Ha! Can't be too hot if it took six calls to get a woman desperate enough to go out with you."

Jace grabbed the long handled net. "You better concentrate on that fish or you're going to lose it. Keep the rod up, give him some play."

"Shut up and get ready. It's here."

Slipping the net under the played out trout, Jace gave a hoot of laughter. "Looks smaller than mine," he crowed, bringing it on board.

"Damn if it isn't," Devon said. "That's because it was on your line. I need to catch my own fish on my own line."

"Go take care of your fish, then refill my coffee cup. I'll re-bait the hook."

Sometime later they were sitting back, each with a beer in hand, waiting for the next bite.

"How's the PI business going?" Devon asked.

Jace hooked his feet in the rail and leaned back in his chair. "Slow but coming along. Good thing I had a healthy savings built up."

"You get your calls finished?"

"Yup. Work's done."

"Who's Emma Downer? Your hot date."

Jace gave him as skeptical look. "You might say that. How are Dorothy and the kids by the way? Haven't seen them in a while."

"Billy's going to be a freshman next fall, and Heather will be in sixth grade." He went on embellishing some of their accomplishments, adding that Dorothy was considering going back to school to get her nursing degree.

Jace was thinking about Devon, only one year older than he was, being all domesticated with a happy family life while he seemed to be floundering.

"She's having an affair," Devon said matter-of-factly.

It took all of five seconds for Jace's feet to hit the deck as he sat up straight to stare at his friend. "What?"

Devon laughed. "Just checking if you were paying attention. You seemed to be off in another solar system. Why don't you find a woman, get married and settle down. Isn't your biological clock ticking or something?"

Jace shook his head. "You about gave me a heart attack there."

"You need kids, Jace. You always talked about having half a dozen. What do you hear from Dustin by the way?"

Jace snorted. "It's been three weeks since I've seen him. I'm at Karen's mercy. He was less than two years old when I came into his life. I love that kid, and there's nothing I can do for him."

"Her ex is still in his life?"

"Yeah. And since he's the legal father, I'm out in left field on a wing and a prayer."

"Is he keeping up with his support payments?"

"As far as I know. Right from the get-go I offered to take over his payments if he'd allow me to adopt Dustin."

"He never asked for scheduled visitation rights in all the three years you were married to Karen, did he?"

"No. At the most he saw Dustin once a month, sometimes every other month, and then he didn't actually spend time with him. It was more his parents' idea. They wanted to be involved in Dustin's life, so Craig would just dump him off there and pick him up later and bring him back home. I'm sure his main objective was to piss me off."

Devon gave Jace a concerned look. “You do realize that if anything happened to Karen, he would get custody?”

Chapter Five

By noon they'd caught their limit of fish, had docked and secured the boat and Jace was headed home. He quickly showered and changed to get rid of the fish smell then headed over to Wisconsin to the Harmony House. It was one-thirty when he got there. He hoped the lunch hour had ended.

He walked into a large two-story building that looked like an old-fashioned boarding house. The well-kept surroundings, including perfectly manicured lawn and hedges, flower beds and various pots bursting with germaniums, porch swing and wicker furniture gave the place a friendly, homey feeling. It lived up to its name on the outside anyway.

Inside he found Gretchen, according to her nametag, the same woman he'd spoken with on the phone, manning the counter.

"Hi Gretchen. I'm here to see Emma Downer. I called this morning."

Gretchen looked him up and down and gave him a brilliant smile. "Oh yes, I remember you. I think Emma is in the activities room, she likes to work on the jigsaw puzzle up there." Gretchen pushed a logbook toward him.

"You'll need to sign in and don't forget to sign out again when you leave. We need to keep track of all the visitors and how long they stay."

He put down his name, date and time and who he was visiting then smiled at Gretchen. "Where do I find the activities room?" he asked.

She pointed across the small lobby to the elevator. "It's on the second floor. Three doors down on the left. It's right across from the lunchroom. You can't miss it. Emma doesn't get many visitors, so I'm sure she'll be happy to see you. However, if you know her, you'll know what to expect," she added with an expressive giggle.

That certainly prodded his curiosity. Jace hesitated then asked, "Has her granddaughter been to see her recently?"

"Yup, LuAnn comes nearly every week usually on Saturday or Sunday."

"I suppose she works during the week," Jace prompted.

"Yeah, I think she teaches."

"Oh, do you know where?"

Gretchen glanced at his entry in the logbook. "Nope, and come to think about it, she came on a Monday once and mentioned she'd come straight from school. I suppose she could have been attending classes instead of teaching. I guess I just assumed she was a teacher."

Jace chocked that up to memory, thanked her and headed across the lobby. Stepping into the elevator, he saw a sign that read *Serviced by Lagerquist*. He wasn't even sure why he noticed it, probably because of his visit to Otis the day before.

On the second floor he walked down the hall to a room that said *Activities and Crafts*. Inside the large room several people were watching a big-screen TV while others were in a far corner working on various crafts at an oblong table.

Two women were sitting at a round table working on a half-finished puzzle. Three other chairs were empty. A collection of single and partially assembled pieces covered the rest of the table. It appeared to be a picture of dolls sitting on shelves. Both women wore colorful cotton housedresses. One, who appeared as round as she was tall, sported an apron over her dress. He guessed the apron lady to be in her early eighties, the other, diminutive and slightly stooped, looked a little older. Both glanced up at him curiously when he took a seat across from them.

"Nice picture," he said. "My grandmother used to collect dolls."

Apron lady grunted while her companion gave him a smile that suggested she'd left her dentures in her room. Jace remembered Saul calling Lucinda's mother a *crazy old bat.* He guessed the grunter was her.

"I'm looking for Emma Downer," he said.

"What you want with her?" Apron lady asked while smiley giggled.

"I'm looking for her granddaughter, LuAnn."

"Oh, she's a tramp," Smiley chirped.

"Shut up, Nelly, you don't know nothing," Apron lady barked. Obviously she was Emma.

"Well, you told me she was," Nelly said, frowning.

"That's none of his business."

Now that was an interesting exchange. Nonchalantly picking up a puzzle piece, Jace put it in place. "Can you tell me where she lives?" he asked.

"Who the hell are you?" Emma snapped adding, "And who wants to know?"

"My name is Jace Murdock, and I'd like to know."

"Whaddaya want with her?"

"I have business to discuss."

"If you're looking for money, you may as well get lost. She doesn't have none."

Nelly giggled again then quickly stopped when Emma gave her a frosty glare.

"I don't need her money. I just have to find her."

"Why?"

Emma Downer was one tough nut to crack. He had to give her something, but he certainly couldn't tell her LuAnn's biological mother was looking for her. "I can't tell you that, it's confidential," he said. "But it will be worth her while, I can tell you that much."

Emma flashed Nelly a warning glance. "You ain't the first man been sniffing around looking for her," Emma said carefully picking up a cluster of puzzle pieces she'd assembled and sliding them in place. "I'll tell you the same thing I told the other one. Go to the mall with your questions, they have an information booth."

This time Nelly managed to hide her snickers, but her twinkling eyes gave her away. Jace was thinking he'd have better luck questioning her when Emma wasn't around.

"How long ago was the other man here?" he asked.

She ignored him.

He asked her a few more questions, but she'd totally clammed up. When she made a point of twisting her fingers in her ears obviously turning her hearing aids down or off, he decided he may as well leave.

He stood up, gave her a token goodbye which Nelly acknowledged with a smile and left.

Gretchen was nowhere in sight, so he signed out and quickly flipped back a couple of pages studying the names. He hit pay dirt the Sunday past. She'd signed in as LuAnn B. She'd come to see Emma Downer—and stayed twenty minutes.

That told him she was no longer LuAnn Randall. She must have gotten married. As he walked out he had another thought. Given the fact that she didn't sign her last name and her grandmother was so ornery and close-mouthed, he wondered if she was hiding from someone or something. On the other hand, since she was a regular visitor everyone likely knew who she was. It seemed every step he gained was followed by a frustrating step backwards.

Outside he found a man sitting on a battered Harley Davidson parked next to his Ford. It was Saul. He was smirking and obviously waiting for Jace. A smoking cigarette dangled from his lips.

"Get anything out of the old bat?"

"What are you doing here?" Jace asked, choosing to ignore his comment.

"Waiting for you."

Jace didn't even want to converse with the man, but since he'd struck out with the grandmother he was back to square one. "Why?" Jace asked as if he didn't already know.

"You wanna know where LuAnn is. I can tell you."

"And what's that going to cost me?"

"Five thousand."

Snorting a disgusted laugh, Jace opened the door of his car. "I'm not that desperate to locate her."

Saul came to his feet, arms folded over his chest. "You tell me what it's worth to you."

Jace hesitated, shrugging. "Twenty bucks."

Saul snickered. "You're going to an awful lot of trouble to find information that's only worth twenty bucks to you. Why do you want her anyway? She doesn't have any money."

Jace was starting to wonder why LuAnn Randall's relatives believed the only reason anyone would look for her was to get money. Something just didn't feel right about this case and Bart Harridan or not, he was determined to find out what it was.

"What makes you think I want money from her?" Jace asked.

Saul sat back on his motorcycle chuckling. "Some people think her old man stashed some of his lottery money and she's the only one who knows where it is. And don't give me that shit about being his long lost buddy. Jack didn't have any friends that I know of, and if he did, they sure as hell didn't come from your side of town. So what's your gig? Why are you looking for her?"

"That's none of your business," Jace said, his mind already working around the stashed lottery bit and wondering what Harridan knew about it. The man was already richer than sin, so that didn't make sense.

"How about a grand?" Saul countered. "That shouldn't be a hardship for a rich guy like you."

"I'm not that desperate. I have fifty bucks on me, take it or leave it." He started to get in his Fusion, going for a bluff.

"All right," Saul said quickly. "I'll take it. But that only gets you the answer to one question."

"Good enough," Jace said taking out his wallet. He extracted a fifty-dollar bill and handed it to Saul. "I want her address. And don't even think about lying to me."

Saul gave him a hostile glare as he snapped up the money with grime darkened fingers. "Fifteen twenty-two South Danube Street. And you better not be up to no-good. I think a lot of LuAnn."

"Yeah, I can see that. She means so much to you you're willing to sell her out for fifty bucks. What a guy."

Jace got in his car and pulled out of the parking lot without a backward glance. Even though he was happy for the information, the sight of Saul nauseated him. What if LuAnn really was hiding out and that asshole was willing to hand her over to anyone with cash in his pocket. He was starting to sympathize with this faceless woman who seemed to be alone in the world except for a cantankerous old grandmother and a distant reprobate cousin. Did she even know she was the result of her father's affair? Or was Harridan feeding him a line of bullshit?

Jace intended to find out before he turned LuAnn over to him.

Once he'd left Saul and Harmony House behind him, Jace stopped at the side of the road to program his GPS. According to the map that came up, Danube was a short street a little over ten miles south of the retirement home. He glanced in the rearview mirror before pulling back out on the road and spotted a black Buick LaCrosse parked a block behind him.

Son of a bitch! Somebody *was* following him. And it wasn't Saul.

Ignoring his *recalculating* GPS, he took the first right and drove until he saw the car make a right behind him. He made a quick left, then another, then a right into an alley, made a u-turn and waited. Sure enough the Buick whizzed past. Jace pulled out behind him, got close enough to read the license plate then took a quick left hoping the guy hadn't spotted him. Apparently he hadn't since the car was going hell bent for leather, obviously trying to catch up with Jace.

Well damn. Who the hell was following him? He pulled back out heading away from the Buick and going in the direction of LuAnn's house, keeping a wary eye on his rearview mirror.

He found her house without any problem. It was a small one-story with pale green siding and darker green shutters. Flowers surrounded the front and sides as far as he could see. He drove past, turned around and parked across the street a couple of houses down. He opened his cell phone and punched in a friend's number who worked at the police department.

"Logan Rydell here. My caller ID tells me I'm talking to Jace. What's up buddy?"

"Not much, except that I need a favor."

"Sure what is it? Your sister isn't finding enough dates for you to choose from. Want me to get Maggie on it?" Logan laughed at his own joke.

"That is so not funny. Hey, I'm on an interesting case and just discovered I have a tail. I got the license number. Any chance you can check it out?"

"Sure, what's the number?"

Jace rattled off the number along with the make of the car.

"I'm on my way home. I'll call you as soon as I get a handle on it."

"Okay thanks." Jace snapped his phone shut, thinking about knocking on LuAnn's door, just as a Ford Mustang pulled into her driveway.

A sharp looking young man dressed in khaki slacks and polo shirt stepped out of the car and walked up the sidewalk to the door. Must be Mr. B., her husband. Mr. B. hesitated then knocked—obviously not her husband. Jace wasn't sure why, but that made him breathe easier. Although, he decided, it could be a boyfriend. Or a salesman albeit empty handed.

The man knocked several times as though insisting someone should be home. After a few moments he returned to his Mustang, backed out and drove away. That's when Jace noticed a drape on the wide front window move. If it had been a dog, he'd have stuck his nose though the drapes or barked. So…she was home but didn't want to open her door to this particular person. Was she afraid of him? Maybe she *was* hiding.

Technically, Jace had done his job. He could go back to Harridan, tell him he'd found LuAnn, collect the balance of his four grand and be on his merry way. If he hadn't spotted the guy tailing him, he might have done just that. But something fishy was going on, and he wanted to find out what it was.

Hoping he'd have better luck than Mr. Mustang, he left his car where it was and walked up to the door past a mailbox with no name on it. He rang the bell and waited. Not ready to give up, he knocked, with no results, then rapped his knuckles solidly on the door a second time to get her attention.

Out of the corner of his eyes, he watched the drapes; they weren't moving. A peephole on the door didn't appear to have movement either.

He leaned against the door and called out, "LuAnn, I know you're home. Please open the door. It's important that I talk to you. LuAnn…my name is Jace Murdock. I'm a private investigator. Someone hired me to find you. I don't want to turn you over to this person without talking to you first. I don't know what you're hiding from, and I don't care other than I want to make sure I'm not doing you an injustice."

He gave a huge sigh then spoke to the door again annunciating loud and clear. "I'll be at the Applebee's on Tower Avenue tomorrow at noon. Please meet me there. Help me out here so I can do the right thing. I'll leave my card under the mat, and you can look out the window again to see what I look like as I walk away. Please be there."

Jace made a point of not turning around to see if she was watching. It seemed something had her scared, and it made him highly suspect of Bart Harridan's real reason for wanting to find her.

When he got back to his car, his phone was ringing. It was Logan.

"Yeah, buddy, what did you find?"

"Your car is an Alamo rental. No way can I find out who rented it without going up to the airport and flashing my badge. Maggie has company coming so I can't do it tonight, but I'll get up there first thing in the morning if that'll work for you."

"Sure, just give me a call when you know something. And thanks, I owe you."

Logan laughed. "You've helped me out more times than I can count. I'll see you next Saturday."

"You bet. Wild horses couldn't keep me from watching you get hitched. How's your grandmother doing?"

"Feisty as ever. I'll be talking to you tomorrow."

* * * *

LuAnn went to the kitchen window to watch him drive away. She couldn't see his face, but he was quite tall with broad muscular shoulders and had a backside that certainly filled out his jeans nicely. Jace Murdock. The name sounded vaguely familiar.

What was he talking about anyway? Who was trying to find her? Certainly nobody cared enough about her to hire an investigator. Then her heart skipped a beat. Could it be her daughter? But how? She was only twelve. Granted she'd know about internet, as smart as kids were these days, but could she hire a private detective? Doubtful.

I'm such a damn coward. If I'd answered the door, I'd know. If only he hadn't come right on the heels of Ron's visit, she might have let him in, but she was still in the no-thank-you-I-don't-want-to-date mode. But Jace Murdock was not there to ask her for a date. Now she'd have to wait until tomorrow to find out what he wanted to talk to her about.

She heard a sound at the back patio door and saw Max waiting for his treat. The one male she eagerly invited into her home. She let him in and picked him up, squeezing his soft furry body. He rubbed his face on her chin giving her the affection she needed as she tried to calm her nerves and not get her hopes up because of the elusive promise from a stranger knocking on her door. *Someone hired me to find you,* he'd said. Who else but her daughter would want to find her?

Blinking rapidly at the moisture pooling in her eyes, she held Max up in front of her. "What do *you* think, Max, should I meet Mr. Murdock tomorrow?"

Chapter Six

On his way home Jace was conscious of his stomach growling. He hadn't eaten since breakfast on the boat, and it was nearly six o'clock. He didn't feel like going home and cooking, so he stopped at a little Chinese takeout place that was famous for its ginger chicken.

Coming out of the shop with his delectable smelling bag, he happened to look up and spot one of Harridan's hotels just a block away. On a whim he tossed his bag in the car and walked to the hotel. Something at the retirement home had sparked his interest, and he just now remembered it.

Inside he walked toward the elevator and punched the *up* button. When it arrived, he waited for two smartly dressed people to get off then stepped inside and pushed the third floor indicator. That was actually more time then he needed to spot the little sign. *Serviced by Otis Elevator.* He wasn't surprised—just curious. Otis was the largest elevator company in the area, with probably the quickest response time. That wasn't what interested him though. It was the fact that Bart Harridan might have known Jack Randall. That thought put a whole new twist to this venture.

His mind racing a mile a minute going over all the possibilities, he hurried back to his car. On the way his cell phone rang.

"Hi, Jace, it's Karen."

He groaned, thinking about his ginger chicken getting cold on the seat beside him. His ex-wife only called when she wanted something.

"Yeah, Karen what do you need?"

"Well, honey," —not a good sign. She only called him honey when she was desperate— "I know it's awfully short notice, but I just got invited to this...ah...elite party, and I can't get a sitter for Dustin." Jace's heart rate accelerated. "I have to leave in half an hour and that includes getting ready. Any chance you could pick him up?"

Hell yes. "I think I could manage that," he said, trying to keep the elation out of his voice.

"Good, I do have to leave soon though."

"I'm on the way. I can be there in twenty minutes."

"Thanks, you're a doll. Oh, and he hasn't had supper yet."

"No problem." *No surprise either.* Small wonder the kid was underweight.

He hung up and made a left turn that would take him to her house up on Miller Hill. He wondered what happened to Dustin's *other* father. Maybe she was going on a date with him, or maybe he was in jail. Hell, Jace didn't care. Why look a gift horse in the mouth? His day just went from shit to sugar with one lucky phone call. An added bonus was he knew his mother would be thrilled to keep Dusty while he met with LuAnn tomorrow.

* * * *

"What do you mean, he spotted you?" Harridan barked into the phone.

"He went over to Superior," Armon Kastansa said. "There wasn't a lot of traffic, so it was tough to stay out of sight."

"What was he doing over there?"

"He went to the Harmony House retirement place and was in there about half an hour. Afterwards he talked to a guy on a motorcycle in the parking lot. Then he headed for south Superior and suddenly he started making lots of quick turns. I figure that's when he spotted me."

"Why would he even be watching for a tail?"

"I'm guessing this morning when he went fishing I got squeezed between him and another guy on the lift bridge. Turns out the other guy was going on the boat with him. I saw the man looking back at me, so I hightailed it out of there and stayed out of sight until they came back around noon. I think he was the one who got suspicious and warned Murdock."

"What the hell is he doing fishing when I told him this was urgent?"

"I couldn't tell you that, Mr. Harridan."

"Damn. Get back to the rental shop and get a different car. Then go to that retirement home and see if you can find out who he was visiting."

"Yes, sir. I'll see what I can find out."

"And tonight put a bug on his car so we can follow him easier."

"He keeps his car in the garage, and he has a high tech security system."

"Shit. Okay, follow him tomorrow and see if he makes a stop long enough for you to plant it."

"Will do."

Harridan hung up the phone and reread the note he'd received two days ago.

Leave ten thousand dollars in a brown paper bag in the south trash container in the park behind your house. If I see police or anyone else in the area, I won't pick it up and then the anti goes to twenty thousand. Put it there Monday night at nine p.m. then get in your car and drive away and stay away for an hour.

If I don't get the money, you will be exposed and your daughter's life will be in danger.

It was typed on white paper. And he was certain there'd be no fingerprints even if he did take it to the police.

Not for the first time, he wondered why the blackmailer was only asking for ten grand. Or was it just the beginning, a test of sorts. He or she didn't actually say what they would expose, but equally disturbing was the threat to his daughter.

It wouldn't bode well for him if she was harmed or kidnapped and he hadn't contacted the police or met the demands. And he damn sure didn't want to hire a curious guard to watch her around the clock.

The most obvious thing hanging over his head was her adoption. And the only possible living person who could know about that was LuAnn Randall. He should have taken care of her at the same time as Jack. But why wait all this time to hit on him. The only explanation was that she's just recently discovered Chelsea's whereabouts. So much for motherly love, she'd rather blackmail him than contact her daughter. Chip off the old block.

But how had she found out? Gladys? His loving wife could have blabbed anything when she was drunk, which was far too often. Granted she didn't know the details of his deal with Jack Randall, but that wouldn't stop her from spouting off that Chelsea wasn't her child.

Hell, he hadn't even wanted a kid. He'd done it for her. She'd started drinking about the same time she found out she couldn't conceive. He'd thought a baby would help her change into someone who wouldn't be an embarrassment to him.

Instead of being happy about having a daughter, the ignorant woman believed Chelsea had come from one of his affairs.

Nothing could be farther from the truth. He didn't even know Jack until he'd overheard him talking to his partner while down in the pit where they were working on one of the elevators.

They had a huge convention going on at the hotel, and he'd walked downstairs to see what was taking so long to make the repairs. He heard Jack grumbling about how he was going to have to force his fifteen-year-old daughter to get an abortion. That's when Harridan got the idea to approach Jack Randall.

Since the baby was born at home by an attending midwife, it was easy to write their own birth certificate. He should have probably cleared that with Gladys first, but hell, he thought she'd be so excited to have a baby she'd be willing to go along with anything. He couldn't take a chance on telling her the truth; she was too loose-lipped.

To complicate matters, it only took Jack Randall a year to go through the half a million bucks Harridan paid him. Then the idiot wanted more. Harridan gave him another fifty thousand, but for a man with a spending addiction, that didn't last long. Harridan had no choice but to rid himself of the problem.

Getting Jace Murdock to find LuAnn had been a stroke of genius on his part. Murdock, however, was slacking off too much. If he didn't come through by Monday, Bart would have to pay the blackmailer. He could handle that, but he was determined not to make a second payment.

* * * *

Chelsea lay on the floor making notes in her diary. Her room was directly above her father's home office, and two years ago she'd discovered if she held her head against the return air duct she could hear his telephone conversations. He had a loud booming voice naturally, but when he talked on the phone it went up an octave—like he thought everyone in the world was hard of hearing.

She'd first started really paying attention to his conversations after her mother claimed she wasn't her daughter. Gladys—as Chelsea had began to think of her—was always ranting about something, but if Gladys Harridan wasn't her mother, who was? At one time Gladys had said Chelsea was the result of an affair her father had had. It made sense since she could not remember ever getting so much as a hug from her mother, but on the other hand her father didn't hug either. Chelsea wished she had a dog to cuddle up with when she felt lonely—which was all the time.

At least trying to figure out what her father was up to gave her something interesting to do. She checked her notes from yesterday. Her father had called a Mr. Murdock, an investigator to help him find someone. After he'd come home from his meeting with Mr. Murdock he'd called Armon Kastansa, his personal guard, and told him to follow

Mr. Murdock. Chelsea disliked Armon Kastansa; he looked like a big ugly ape, and he always stared at her funny with his beady close-set eyes. She didn't even like being in the same room with him which didn't happen often anyway. She was always shooed up to her room when he came, and she couldn't hear them clearly because they seemed to keep their voices down whenever they talked in person.

Today he was upset because Mr. Murdock went fishing. Man, she went fishing with Patty and her father once. Was that ever fun. They never did anything fun in this house. Sometimes they went to Dad's hotel to eat, but that was so fancy-shmansy, mucky-muck she hated it. Why couldn't they go to McDonald's like other families? Dad was always warning her about not embarrassing him. He was constantly picking on Gladys for that, too. Sometimes she felt sorry for Gladys.

* * * *

"Why can't I call you Daddy anymore?" Dustin asked twirling chow mein noodles around his fork.

For a second Jace was speechless, his heart heavy. "Who says you can't?"

Dustin shrugged his thin shoulders. "My other dad. He said, since you aren't married to Mamma anymore you can't be my daddy. But I have three grandmas, why can't I have two daddies?"

In spite of the murderous thoughts he had for Dustin's *other* dad, who never was a father to him outside of supplying sperm, Jace managed to give him a cheery smile. "I don't see any reason why you can't. In fact, we'll make it our little secret. You can call me Daddy anytime you want as long as I can call you Son."

Dustin gave him a little-boy grin. "Deal." He held up his hand so Jace could give him a high five.

"Speaking of grandmas, I know your grandma, Mary Ann, would love to see you, so how about I take you there while I meet an important client for lunch tomorrow."

When Dustin made a small pout, Jace felt like crap because he knew Craig used his parents as a way to rid himself of Dustin every time they were together. But Jace had to meet LuAnn, providing she showed up. "And when I get back, if we have time, we can take a drive out to the farm and see the horses."

That brought his head up, as Jace knew it would. "Really? Do you still have my helmet?"

"Of course I do."

"You think Grandpa Harold will play checkers with me?"

"I'd be surprised if he didn't."

"Okay, it's a deal then." Dustin lifted his hand for another high five.

* * * *

The next morning Jace learned his mother was serving at a church luncheon, and his father was off to play golf. His sister Kayla wasn't answering her phone, and his sister Wanda had left with her husband and kids on a day trip to visit Gooseberry Falls on the north shore.

He was contemplating his situation when the phone rang. Caller ID told him it was Logan.

"Hey, Logan. Damn, you're quick. It's not even ten thirty."

Logan laughed. "I'm not just quick, I'm good."

"Halleluiah, what did you find?"

"The Buick LaCrosse was rented by Armon Kastansa. It was also exchanged yesterday afternoon for a different model. I don't know the details on the new vehicle."

Jace frowned thoughtfully. "Well, hell, he knows I spotted him so he's changing cars."

"Why is he tailing you anyway?"

Jace moved to the window so he could keep an eye on Dustin who was throwing a ball for the neighbor's dog. "I can't help but think it has something to do with this new case I'm working on. A guy hires me to find someone, so he has me tailed? Doesn't make sense."

"Huh, sounds like he doesn't trust you."

"Then why hire me?"

"Smells like bad fish if you ask me. Who's the guy?"

Jace glanced at the clock not wanting to be late for his lunch appointment. "A big name in town. I promised him absolute confidentiality. It seemed like a simple open and shut case. Now I'm starting to wonder. In fact, I already located the person."

"Let me guess. You aren't ready to expose her?"

"I never said it was a woman."

Logan's deep chuckles filled the phone. "You didn't have to. I have a sixth sense about these things."

Dustin came running in the house, and Jace held the phone aside to tell him to get cleaned up they had to leave soon.

"Sounds like you have your kid there. Good for you."

"Sure is. I don't see him often enough. I'm meeting someone for lunch, so I have to get moving."

"A woman?"

"Yes, but it's not what you're thinking."

"I wouldn't take any bets on that if I was you," Logan said, laughing. "Let me know how it works out. By the way, I'll run a background check on Kastansa tomorrow if you want. See if he has a rap sheet."

"I'd appreciate it. Thanks."

Chapter Seven

What did one wear to meet an investigating stranger? Certainly not something provocative. LuAnn gave a mental laugh—she didn't own anything provocative, except underwear.

She had made up her mind to meet him even before she retrieved his card. She'd already convinced herself that the only person who could be looking for her was her daughter.

Her hands shook as she donned a red tank top with a stripped red, white and blue, short-sleeved cotton top. After discarding the idea of jeans, she decided on the navy blue slacks she'd found on sale at Herbergers.

She brushed out her long, curly brown hair, eyed the frosted streaks critically, then gathered the sides to the back of her head securing them with a red clip. The rest cascaded down her back.

Her stomach gave a nervous lurch as she glanced at the clock. Applebee's was only fifteen minutes from her house. She didn't want to be early, but then again she didn't want to be late either, best to be there promptly at noon. The thought of having contact with her daughter after all these years had her heart doing flip-flops.

Slipping into her navy flats, she reflected on the fact that Becca, as she called her, would be thirteen in exactly twenty-five days—a teenager. Getting past the fourth of July was always painful, but this one would be particularly difficult since she knew thirteen was a major milestone in a girl's life. LuAnn had firsthand knowledge of how stressful that age was without a mother's guiding hand. Did Becca have a thoughtful mother who would explain the facts of life to her? Was she happy?

LuAnn blinked away the moisture that always flooded her whenever she thought about Becca and surveyed herself in the full length mirror. She wondered why she didn't just get rid of that mirror; she never liked what she saw in it.

* * * *

As Jace pulled into the Applebee's parking lot, he glanced once again in the rearview mirror. There was no sign of a tail, but then he couldn't be sure since he didn't know what kind of vehicle to watch for.

He caught a glimpse of Dustin's jubilant face in the back seat. Dustin was small for his age, so he still needed a booster seat. He didn't mind though because it enabled him to see out the window easier.

Jace had no choice but to bring him along. Maybe it would turn out to be a good thing. Maybe having an almost six-year-old with him would make LuAnn open up. Staring out the window of her house instead of answering the door had him confused. Was she that leery of strangers? Was that other visitor a stranger too? He had already begun to wonder if she was hiding from something or someone. All the more reason to talk to her before he turned his info over to Harridan. He couldn't bring anything up on the net about her because he still didn't know her last name.

"Do you remember what we talked about?" he asked Dustin as they got out of the car.

Dustin hiked on his backpack that was full of drawing paper, crayons and books. "Yes, sir, kids need to be seen and not heard."

When he raised his thin arm in a well-executed salute, Jace laughed and ruffled his shock of red hair. "You have a good memory, Son."

Dustin's grin widened. "Thanks, Daddy." He slipped his small hand into Jace's as the hostess led them to a booth. "Okay, Son, here's the program. Take out your drawing tablet and colors then after I introduce you concentrate on your pictures and ignore whatever we're talking about."

Slipping into the far side of the booth to make room for Jace, Dustin immediately began taking his things out of the backpack. "Are you going to say some bad words?" he asked laying his paper and colored pencils out on the table.

"I certainly don't plan to, not in front of a lady."

"Don't worry, if you do I won't listen to them."

Dustin's tone was so serious Jace had to stifle a laugh. He took out his cell phone, checked for calls then turned it off. He didn't want any interruptions while he talked to LuAnn. Looking around the restaurant, he noted all the occupied tables and booths held families or couples. Only one had a lone man. A big burly gruff looking character who'd come in shortly after they did. He'd taken a seat across the room and spread a newspaper out it in front of him while talking on a phone.

She walked in the door at exactly twelve noon and stood surveying the room. Her gaze fell on the hairy guy with the newspaper, but she hesitated and continued looking.

Jace wasn't prepared for what he saw. She had a figure that models would envy and was neatly but conservatively dressed in patriotic colors. Rich brown hair with golden highlights was drawn back at the sides and left to cascade in long curls down her back.

If she wore any makeup at all, it wasn't apparent on her flawless face. She was one of those rare women who seemed to have natural beauty with no effort at all.

When her arresting almond-shaped brown eyes swept past him, he waved. Her gaze paused briefly on Dustin until Jace nodded to her.

Jace stood up as she walked toward them. Interestingly enough, her attention vacillated between him and Dustin. Maybe it was the schoolteacher in her, or maybe she hadn't expected to see a child with him. Well, certainly she wouldn't have expected that.

He extended his hand. "You must be LuAnn."

She gave him a surprisingly brilliant smile, and she placed her cool hand into his. "Yes, and you would be Jace Murdock, but who do we have here?" she asked, gesturing toward Dustin as she slid into the booth across from them.

"This is Dustin—my son." He didn't want to hurt Dustin's feelings by calling him anything other than son.

LuAnn smiled at him. "Hello, Dustin. How is it you got to come along today?"

The boy beamed. He looked up at Jace as though asking permission to speak. Jace gave him a slight nod.

"Grandma was busy, and I couldn't play checkers with Grandpa."

She gave Jace a mischievous glance then turned back to Dustin. "So how old are you?"

"Five. I'll be six in a month. I can go to first grade then."

"I understand you're a teacher," Jace said. "You must have a special connection with kids."

"You might say that. I do speak the language," she added, laughing.

It was a pleasant lilting laugh.

A waitress appeared with a notepad and menus. "Can I start you off with some drinks?" she asked, laying out a menu in front of each of them.

When LuAnn ordered the raspberry tea, Jace said, "I'll have the same."

"And you, young man?" she asked Dustin.

"Lemonade," he replied giggling.

"He doesn't like ice," Jace said.

"You got it. I'll be back shortly to take your orders."

Dustin looked at the menu frowning. "I can only read the McDonald's menu."

"You must go there a lot," LuAnn said.

Dustin nodded. "Only with my mom or my other dad. Daddy doesn't like it."

LuAnn raised questioning eyebrows at Jace.

"His mother and I are divorced," Jace explained, not really wanting to go into it any farther at this point.

"Yeah," Dustin said sadly. "That's why I don't get to see Daddy very often."

Jace sighed inwardly. "It's complicated," he said. "Dustin why don't you get started on that picture you were going to draw for Miss—" He looked apologetically at LuAnn, "I'm sorry, I don't know your last name."

"Barstow. It's LuAnn Barstow."

"Can you draw a picture for Ms. Barstow?"

Dustin gave her a serious smile and arranged his pencils. "Sure, I'll draw you a picture. Are you having a hot date?"

LuAnn's mouth dropped open, and she gave Jace an accusing look. Her cheeks took on a rosy hue.

Jace pinched the bridge of his nose stifling a laugh. "All right, Dustin, you better explain that comment because I don't have a clue."

Dustin lifted his narrow shoulders. "Well, when Mom gets all pretty like you, she says it's because she has a hot date."

LuAnn glanced at Jace and laughed. "I believe that's one of the nicest compliments I've had from a male in a long time. Thank you, Dustin."

Dustin looked up at Jace a bit sheepishly. "I guess it's time to be seen and not heard, huh?"

* * * *

"Applebee's. What the hell is he doing there?"

"Eating I imagine," Kastansa said with an air of indifference.

"Who's with him?"

"A good looking chick," Armon Kastansa told Harridan. "And I'm too far away to hear what they're sayin'. And he has a kid with him too."

"A kid? He doesn't have any kids. Whose kid is it?"

"How the heck should I know?"

"How old?"

"He looks to be about four or five. He came in with Murdock. The woman came a few minutes later. I think they know each other because they're all laughing and having a hi-ho time."

"It's seems to me," Harridan groused, "that the asshole is doing everything but his job. She could be his girlfriend. When they leave, follow her. Get her license number and her address. I want to know who she is. You think you can handle that?"

Kastansa didn't like Harridan's attitude, but the man paid well and with cash. He didn't want to lose his cushy job so he answered with a snappy, "Yes, sir, Mr. Harridan. I can handle it."

* * * *

By the time their order came, LuAnn had decided she hadn't had so much fun in ages. Dustin was a delight, and Jace's reaction to everything he did was priceless. It was almost as if the man had limited knowledge of soon to be six-year-olds.

She still hadn't figured out why he didn't see his son very often and who the *other dad* was, but she hoped to find out.

When Dustin drew a picture of half a cow announcing it was a halfer, LuAnn laughed until she had tears in her eyes while Jace explained to his son that a *heifer* was not half a cow just one that hadn't had a calf yet.

As much as she was enjoying herself, she was anxious to find out about Becca, which is what she'd convinced herself this was all about. She finished her oriental chicken salad thinking of an opening. The opportunity presented itself when Dustin headed for the restroom after convincing his father he was old enough to go by himself.

"Please," she said finally. "I'm anxious to know who is looking for me."

He gave her a searching look. "At this point, I can't tell you. It's a sensitive matter for my client, and he wants total confidentiality. My concern is that he's not being honest with me. Do you have any reason to expect someone has reason to harm you?"

She only gave that a moment's thought and shook her head. "No. None whatsoever. I lead a pretty boring life. Besides, all my friends and acquaintances know exactly how to find me."

"This person didn't know your married name. He asked me to find LuAnn Randall. That probably means it's someone who knew you before you married."

She felt her heart drop. "It's a man then."

"Yes. But he's doing it for a woman or so he says. Are you okay with me asking you a few personal questions?"

She thought a moment then shrugged. "Sure, why not. I'm not hiding anything." That wasn't entirely true, but the thing she was hiding was the very reason she wasn't going to bare her soul unless he brought it up first.

He got up to let Dustin back in his seat then went on. "The first thing I'd like to know is if you've seen your birth certificate?"

That threw her for a loop. He wanted to know about her birth certificate—not Becca's. "Yes, of course I have. Why?"

"Who is listed as your mother?"

A spark of annoyance crawled up LuAnn's spine. "That's an odd question. My mother is/was Lucinda Randall. She died when I was five."

"That would be Lucinda Downer, Emma's daughter?"

"Yes. Where are you going with this? I don't understand."

"Bear with me here. Does the birth certificate have an official stamp?"

"Of course, well, at least I'm sure it does. I haven't actually looked at it in a long time, but it's in my dad's old filing cabinet at home. Are you implying she isn't my real mother?"

"According to the information I got from my client, yes."

"That's preposterous. Who is this idiot, and why is he interfering in my life?" She tried to keep the irritation she felt out of her tone in deference to their juvenile companion. Dustin had finished his chicken strips and was avidly back to drawing. If he was paying any attention to their conversation, she couldn't tell. She recalled his comment earlier about being seen but not heard and hoped he was too young to understand what they were talking about.

Jace sympathized with her. He was starting to wonder about Harridan's motive himself. It wouldn't be the first time a client had lied to him.

"I can't tell you that. I've promised full confidentiality. But I can tell you one thing, he's a very influential man here in Duluth. If you heard the name, you'd recognize it. I can promise you, he won't get any information from me until I'm convinced about why he wants to find you."

"I wasn't hiding."

"Like I said before, I'm sure the only reason he couldn't locate you on his own was because of your name change. I know you said you have nothing to hide, but I really need your help figuring this out." Jace suddenly remembered a thought he'd had when he originally met with Harridan. The possibility that he'd had an affair with Lucinda and LuAnn was his daughter.

"What about your father?" he asked.

"What about him?"

"Is he listed as your father on your birth certificate?"

"Oh, for crying out loud," she said, giving an impatient huff of air. "Of course he is! I even look like him."

Jace gave an incredulous snort. "I seriously doubt that."

"I'm talking about hair and eye color, they're identical. Is this really what this is all about? My parentage?"

Jace couldn't with any stretch of imagination picture those beautiful brown eyes on Jack Randall. "I'm afraid so," he said. "You sound skeptical. What did you think it was about?"

"I—I don't know. I'm just…surprised, that's all."

More like disappointed, Jace thought. He knew a lie when he heard one, and she was up to her pretty little ears in something. "Give it your best guess," he prodded. "You obviously had some expectations about why I wanted to see you."

The waitress showed up with a pitcher of ice tea to refill their glasses, and Jace could tell by LuAnn's furrowed brow that she was using those few moments to come up with an answer.

"I was curious, that's all."

Another lie. "Who was the man knocking on your door just ahead of me yesterday?"

Her face turned a lovely shade of pink. "I don't see why that's any concern of yours."

"Was it someone you knew?"

"Yes."

"Someone you could trust?"

"Yes. What are you suggesting now?"

Jace drew a deep breath. If he wasn't careful, she'd get up and stomp out the door. "I'm concerned about you. A man wants to find you, and he obviously lied to me about the reason. Another man you know knocks on your door, and you don't answer it. Makes me curious."

She drew a deep breath then took a sip of iced tea. "Look, he's a friend of a friend. I met him last night, and I foolishly gave him my phone number. He must have used that to look up my address in the phone book. I'm not interested in dating, and I tried to explain that to him. I don't know why I'm telling you this. It really is none of your business."

Jace wanted to ask her why she wasn't interested in dating. But that certainly wasn't any of his business. Maybe, he reasoned, she felt the same way he did. He could identify with the I-have-a-friend-for-you-to-meet routine.

"You're right," he said softly. "Sorry. If there's nothing further you can tell me, I'm not sure where to go with this. I'd like you to check your birth certificate when you get home to see if it has a valid stamp." He reached for his wallet, pulled out a business card and handed it to her. "This has both my cell phone and my home number. Please call me if you see anything amiss or if you think of something you forgot to mention."

"Are you going to turn my name over to your client?"

"Not if I'm convinced he's lying to me, and that's the direction things are leaning at this point. But if I don't, he'll find someone else who will, and I have a bad feeling he's up to no good. I also think he's having me followed which doesn't make any sense at all. Unless he suspects I won't follow through, in which case he may already know where you are."

"You're starting to frighten me."

"Good. That means be careful. Call me if you need help. I feel like I helped get you into this mess so…until we can figure out why he really wants to locate you, you have reason to be concerned."

"How did you find me?" she asked. "My grandmother?"

Jace gave a harsh laugh. "Heck no, she told me to go to the information booth at the mall. It was Saul. I believe he's your father's cousin."

LuAnn rolled her eyes. "Oh yes, my favorite upstanding relative." She gave a dry laugh.

"He's for sale cheap. I got your address for a measly fifty bucks."

"That's all he asked for?"

"He asked for five thousand."

LuAnn's eyes narrowed angrily. "Shades of my beloved father."

That statement gave him the opening he'd been waiting for. "Does that mean you were at odds with your father?"

She blew out a hissing breath. "You might put it that way."

"How exactly would you put it, LuAnn?"

She gave him a sharp perusal, hesitating. "I don't see how that could possibly have anything to do with someone looking for me?"

"I don't know. You tell me."

She pressed her lips together and glanced at Dustin as though she hoped he'd interrupt them so she could avoid answering. Dustin was busy concentrating on a horse he was drawing, paying no attention whatsoever to their conversation.

"It was a long time ago," she said finally.

"When your mother died?" he prompted.

"No. But he was never a good father as far back as I can remember. He treated me like his personal slave. I cooked our meals from the time I was six."

She was leaving something out. Jace was sure of it. "You were—what—about fifteen when he won the lottery? Did it get any better after that?"

The glare she sent over the table told him he'd touched on forbidden ground.

"How do you know about that?" she asked in a gruff voice.

"The guys down at Otis Elevator."

She made a rude sound. "I guess that explains how you know Saul."

"Yes, and they also clued me in about your grandmother. Saul was waiting for me when I left Harmony House yesterday. He wasted no time telling me money could buy any information I wanted."

He could tell she wanted to swear, but bit it down when she glanced at Dustin.

"What are you drawing now?" she asked him, clearly needing to drop the subject of Saul and her father.

"Horses," Dustin answered proudly. "Daddy has horses on his farm." He pointed to each of three horses with people on them. "This one is me and this one is Daddy and I made one for you too. Do you like horses?"

LuAnn smiled. "I love horses."

"Can we go riding today?" he asked Jace.

"We'll see. If we don't make it out there today, next time you visit for sure."

Dustin gave LuAnn a sad look. "Yeah, maybe next time."

LuAnn glanced at her watch. "That reminds me, I have to go see my grandmother. She needs a prescription filled, and I have a few questions I'd like to ask her, so I better get going. Thank you for lunch though. It's been fun. It was nice to meet you too," she said to Dustin.

She seemed anxious to leave. Jace came to his feet and took her proffered hand. "Please check that birth certificate when you get home and give me a call. My client wanted an answer ASAP."

She hesitated. "What are you going to tell him?"

"Do you want him to find you?"

"I—I don't know, especially since I don't fully understand why he wants to see me."

"Like I said before, I don't think he'll give up. He seemed quite determined, and he has the resources to do it. Call me later—and be careful."

Chapter Eight

LuAnn left the restaurant with an unsettled feeling. Jace Murdock had managed to frighten her, and she, more than ever, wanted to know who was looking for her and why. Worst of all, she couldn't imagine it having anything to do with Becca, and that thought dashed her hopes of finding her daughter. But who else cared enough about her to hire a private detective to locate her? He said the man was influential, and she'd recognize the name. Was Jace Murdock just toying with her? That's what it felt like.

Did he have some ulterior motive? Like her father's supposedly hidden money. That was a joke. Jack Randall couldn't hold on to a dime longer than it took to flush a toilet. She didn't know how much he'd won in this mysterious lottery, but it had seemed to be quite a lot. They'd moved into an expensive house, got new furniture, a new Cadillac and in an uncharacteristic gesture of goodwill he'd even bought her a car, used, but he'd let her pick it out. Maybe he'd had a spurt of conscience for making her give Becca away when all they'd have had to do was hold out six months and they could have afforded to keep her.

She stopped at Harmony House intending to question her grandmother. This business of her parentage was making her antsy. Like she told Murdock, her likeness to her father was unmistakable, but she didn't look anything like the pictures of the mother she barely remembered. Had Lucinda actually given birth to her? Even if the birth certificate was stamped, those kinds of things could be faked. Grandma Emma would certainly know the truth— if LuAnn could get her to talk about it.

* * * *

Jace paid the bill at Applebee's, and as he and Dustin walked to the car, he checked the calls on his cell phone. There were two messages from Bart Harridan. No surprise there. He turned his cell phone back on, and it rang immediately. It was Karen.

"Where are you?" she demanded even before he finished saying hello.

"I'm at Applebee's. What's the problem? I thought you didn't want him home until tonight."

She made a rude sound. "I need him home real quick. I forgot my father has this big sixtieth birthday bash this afternoon, and if I don't bring their only grandchild with me, I'll be in deep doo-doo. How quick can you get him home?"

Jace knew he didn't dare argue with her. He was too dependent on staying in her good graces if he wanted to see Dustin again. At least until she had the next *hot date* and no free sitter available. "With road construction between here and there it'll take a good half hour," he told her, cursing the fact that he had no parental rights.

"That'll work. Thanks. Oh, and can you stop at the liquor store and pick up a bottle of that good brandy Dad likes. I forgot to get him a birthday present." She hung up without waiting for his answer. She knew he'd do it, and he wouldn't make her pay for it. All part of the keep-Karen-happy routine he danced around to get to see his *son.*

He gave Dustin a sympathetic smile and explained the situation, promising to give him a ride on the horses on his next visit. He'd see to it that he kept that promise too.

* * * *

"Of course I remember her being pregnant," Emma Downer snapped. "She was big as a house."

The relief flooding LuAnn's mind was short lived when Emma went on chattering more to herself then to LuAnn. "Or maybe that was the one she lost. I'm sure that jerk of a husband of hers did something to her because when I went to see her at the hospital she had a black eye." Emma harrumphed. "Said she fell against the dresser. Likely story."

"She had a baby that died?" LuAnn asked incredulously.

"Yup, a boy, born dead, went full term too."

LuAnn had a difficult time digesting that information. "Was it before or after me?"

Emma's wrinkled brow furrowed. "Heck I don't remember. Those days all run together in my head sometimes."

Taking a deep breath, LuAnn asked, "So, do you remember her being pregnant with me?"

Emma shrugged. "Well I suppose, you're here ain't you?" She gritted her teeth and turned to stare out the window, mumbling more to herself than LuAnn. "Wasn't much older than you were when your belly started swelling. I told her not to marry that fool. But she wouldn't listen to me. Of course it was too shameful, she had to marry somebody. At least you didn't marry no fool, but that's not saying much since you didn't bother marrying anyone at all. Like mother, like daughter, I say, a shameful lot the two of you."

LuAnn decided it was time to leave, she'd heard that speech before. But the fact that her mother lost a baby was new information. She intended to go home and have a close look at that birth certificate then go through some of her father's things to see if she could find their marriage certificate and anything else that might shed some light on this crazy chaos Jace Murdock had dropped in her lap.

She went straight to a pharmacy and filled Grandma Emma's blood pressure prescription—because Grandma didn't trust any of *those people*—then she dropped it off at Harmony House's front desk.

That finished, she got in her car and instead of heading home decided to go to the Miller Hill Mall. It was Barb's birthday on Tuesday, and she wanted to pick out something unique for her. Barb already had everything in life that mattered, a cute little three-bedroom house overlooking

Lake Superior, an adoring, hunky husband and two great kids. Those were all the things LuAnn had wanted at one time in her life, at least the kids, but sometime in the last few years, she'd stopped dreaming about having children. She just didn't see herself as good mother-material, not after giving up Becca. It seemed like if she had another child it would be a betrayal to the daughter she'd given away.

She spent more time shopping than she intended, realizing it was because she dreaded going home. The project that awaited her, going through her father's file cabinet, was not something she looked forward to.

* * * *

Bart Harridan was extremely irritated. Why wasn't Murdock answering his phone? He never should have hired the man, but it was a way to kill two birds with one stone, literally. He had big plans for the trouble-making lawyer who'd messed with one of his own, but first he needed to find LuAnn.

Whether he found her or not, he'd have to go to the bank tomorrow and withdraw ten grand to pay off the blackmailer. If LuAnn met with an unfortunate accident before she could pick up the money, he could simply retrieve it himself. But he couldn't take a chance and not put it out there—what if it wasn't her? Who else though, that brainless cousin of Jack's, Saul Randall? Not likely. If he knew anything, he'd have been asking for money long before this.

Whoever it was, he didn't have the option of not paying. If the police got involved and the truth about Chelsea came out, he'd be in deep shit. Gladys would probably jump at the chance to blab to the world; especially since the dim-witted woman believed Chelsea was actually his daughter. If she found out the truth, she'd jump at the chance to turn him in.

His phone rang. Caller ID said it was Kastansa. "What's going on?" he growled before Kastansa could say a word.

"She stopped at the Harmony House, the same place Murdock visited yesterday."

"Did you find out who he was seeing?"

"I tried but the little wench at the front desk wouldn't tell me anything."

"Where did Murdock go when he left the restaurant?"

"He headed west, but I don't know where he went. You told me to follow the broad."

Harridan ground his teeth. Kastansa had been in his employ almost twelve years and the only good thing about him was he followed orders—to the tee. The man was dumb as a brick if he had to make a decision on his own. Unlike Murdock who was too smart for his own good and went directly against his orders about contacting LuAnn, and he was convinced that's who he was having lunch with. To make matters worse, he had yet to inform Harridan he'd found her.

Kastansa was blabbing about some insignificant trivia until he suddenly announced, "Okay, she just came out. Want me to keep following her?"

"Yes, and if she gets home call me immediately with the address. I'm guessing it's her—and if it is, Murdock is pulling a fast one on me."

"They sure were friendly at lunch. Laughing and talking like they were old buddies."

"That SOB is going to pay for double-crossing me. Did you get anything useful from his house?"

Kastansa chuckled. "Oh yeah, I found a hammer on a table in the backyard, and I'm betting it's got his fingerprints all over it and best of all his name is carved into it."

"A hammer? That's perfect. I trust you used gloves to pick it up."

"You bet. It's on the seat beside me, real handy when I need it."

"Don't do anything until we're sure it's LuAnn."

* * * *

Chelsea lay on the floor scribbling like crazy in her dairy. She wanted to make sure she got down every word he said. He was so pissed at Jace Murdock, he was talking loud and clear today. And he was teed at some woman named LuAnn too. It was the first time he mentioned the name of the person he was looking for. But what was with the hammer?

She looked up to find her mother staring at her from the door. She hadn't knocked as usual. Chelsea quickly slammed her dairy shut and shoved it under the bed out of sight.

"Are you going to get this room cleaned up or not?" Gladys sputtered, spilling some of the liquid from her highball glass onto the carpet.

"Yes, ma'am. I'll get right to it." Chelsea got up off the floor and began making her bed.

"For crying out loud its two o'clock in the afternoon. You know you're supposed to straighten your room in the morning when you get out of bed. I will not tolerate sloppiness."

Well, maybe you should look in the mirror, Chelsea wanted to say. Instead she just grunted.

"And don't give me any sass, young lady, or I'll see to it that you're grounded for a week."

Gladys must be into reading her thoughts. "Yes, ma'am. Sorry."

Gladys stood there glaring until Chelsea had finished with the bed, put two pairs of shoes in the closet and placed her neatly folded pajamas in the nightstand drawer. Then she quickly collected her dirty laundry, dropped it in the bathroom hamper and turned to give her mother a bright forced smile. "There, see all done." She was finding it harder and harder to think of this woman as her mother. Somewhere, she was sure she had a real mother who loved her.

Chelsea held her breath until Gladys stoically backed out of the room and pulled the door shut behind her. Being grounded would seriously put a damper in her plans. Her friend Betty's father had promised to drop them at the mall tomorrow.

Dad had already given her permission. He didn't seem to care what she did as long as she stayed out of his hair and didn't cause a scene anywhere—that would get her grounded in a hurry for sure.

He'd even given her fifty dollars spending money. She intended to buy a little recorder so she could tape his conversations when she wasn't in her room.

* * * *

After delivering Dustin to his ex-wife along with a forty-dollar bottle of brandy, Jace headed out to check on his quarter horses.

On the way he took several turns watching his rearview mirror without detecting a tail. Harridan had called again in the last half hour. The man was persistent. Why was this case so urgent anyway? Harridan hadn't bothered explaining that.

Jace had already decided to call him back and opt out of the job. He wasn't looking forward to it, but he couldn't in good conscience turn LuAnn over to him without knowing the truth about why he wanted to find her.

His sixty-acre plot of land twenty miles west of Duluth was self-sufficient. A spring-fed pond supplied water for the horses, and giant oaks provided shade. For protection against winter weather, he'd built a small pole-barn. If he couldn't make it out every other day or so, the neighbors looked in on the horses. They had two teenage daughters who loved animals and paid regular visits. Plus, Kayla enjoyed riding, so she often brought her friends out.

A small cabin, on an adjoining five acres that still belonged to his parents, provided a rustic escape when he wanted to get out of town.

Jace vowed to get Dustin out there on his next visit.

* * * *

When LuAnn finally pulled into her garage, it was eight o'clock and threatening clouds lingered in the west.

Max was at her patio door waiting for his treat.

She let the cat in, picked him up and carried him with her to her bedroom to change clothes. Rummaging in the basement was not the place to wear her best slacks. Sitting Max on the bed, she gave him his bacon bits then kept up a one-sided conversation with him while she donned a pair of old Capri jeans and a Minnesota Twins t-shirt she'd bought at a yard sale.

Max finished his snack and watched her silently.

"Come on," she said, scooping him up. "You might as well keep me company. I don't like that dreary basement." Her father's belongings, salvaged after the fire, were all down in her storage area. She rarely looked into them unless she needed something in particular because she just didn't care enough about him to bother. Even though she dreaded it, she was curious enough to bother with it now.

She stuck her cell phone in her pocket along with Jace's card—in case she found something interesting enough to call him about—and headed for the stairs.

Closing the basement door behind her, so Max couldn't escape, she switched on the bare-bulb light and went straight to the back of the cavernous room and the old metal file cabinet that had belonged to her father. The air smelled musty. One window at the back provided additional light during daylight hours, but the dark clouds had brought on an early darkness.

A flashlight, she realized, might have been a good idea. All she really needed though was to find her birth certificate, and she knew where that was. Then she'd hunt for their marriage document and a birth certificate for the baby that had died. Maybe she'd get lucky and locate them all in the same file.

She put Max on the floor. "Here, you go check out if there're any mice down here while I look through this stuff." When she opened the first drawer, she got a distinct whiff of smoke that lingered in everything he owned even after all these years. It brought back memories that she didn't cherish. She wondered if the smell was still there or if her imagination conjured it up.

* * * *

Harridan stared at his computer screen chuckling. "Excellent job, Kastansa. That address shows a LuAnn Barstow living there. She must have married. No doubt in my mind it's her though, not after she met Murdock for lunch. The bastard is double-timing me. You haven't seen a man, like a husband, hanging around have you?"

"Not since I've been here. She let a cat in, that's all."

"Good. Don't go in until dark. Use the hammer to do what you have to do and leave it behind. You have any problem taking care of business there?"

"No sir, none whatsoever."

Harridan hung up the phone chortling and rubbing his hands together like the Joker when he foiled Batman. He'd be rid of LuAnn, and Murdock would finally get what he deserved.

Just to be on the safe side, he'd plant the money anyway. If it wasn't picked up, he'd know he got the right person, and he'd retrieve it in the morning. The trash was emptied every Monday and Thursday always in the morning. Obviously the blackmailer had checked on that, too. Plus Monday was a slow day at the park. The barrel wouldn't have much in it when he deposited the money.

* * * *

Chelsea wondered who LuAnn Barstow was. And what was her father planning to do in her house? Was he supposed to use the hammer to break a window? And what kind of business did he have to take care of there?

She wished there was some way she could warn Mrs. Barstow. Maybe she could find her number in the phone book.

Chapter Nine

Keeping a wary eye on the storm clouds moving in, Jace pulled up in front of his house just as he got a call from Logan.

"Hey buddy, I found your man. Name's Armon Kastansa. No history in Minnesota but plenty in Chicago. Arrested but never convicted. Seems there was big money involved every time to get him freed. This is a man who is willing to do anything for money, so he connects himself to men who need dirty jobs done and have the cash to pay for it. Not exactly an upstanding citizen."

"It sounds to me," Jace said, "like just the kind of man my client would have in his employ." *At least on the sly,* he thought. Harridan took great care to stay off the radar screen on anything that could cause a scandal. Rumor was the man had political ambitions. It sounded more and more like LuAnn Randall Barstow could stand in his way. So what was the connection? Possibly her ex-husband—if she was divorced. They hadn't gotten into that. But if Harridan knew her husband, ex or not, he'd have known LuAnn's last name.

"Check your e-mail," Logan was saying. "I located a picture of him. It's about ten years old, but you might get an idea what he looks like."

"Great, at least I'll know who I'm watching for. I just got home. I'll go in and bring it up. Again thanks, I owe you big time."

"I owe you, Jace. You were instrumental in getting Chad off the drugs while I was gone for two years."

"That's not a debt, Logan, and even if it was, it'd be your brother's not yours. Enough said."

"Right, 'nough said. Go check out the photo, maybe you've already seen him. Good luck."

A few minutes later Jace opened the attachment and a man's face stared back at him. Younger and less facial hair but there was no mistaking—he'd been the lone man in the restaurant today.

Son of a bitch. That's why nobody was tailing him when he left Applebee's—the bastard had shifted gears and was following LuAnn. And she'd refused to give Jace her phone number.

He had no choice but to drive out to her house and warn her.

In view of the weather, he drove his ten-year-old Chevy Silverado. He kept the seldom-used pickup in a garage behind his house. Peeling rubber as he pulled out of the driveway, he debated calling 911, but there was still an off chance that Harridan was telling the truth. After all, he hadn't made a direct threat at this point. Jace was going on his gut instinct. Plus even if Armon Kastansa had a less than stellar reputation, he couldn't be certain Harridan had hired him.

But on the other hand...

* * * *

LuAnn located her birth certificate in short order since she knew where to look for it, but her heart sunk when she examined it. Her parents were named just as she was sure they would be, but the document had no embossed seal signifying that it wasn't a copy. She folded it up and stuck it in her hip pocket, thinking maybe if she kept looking, she might find the original.

She'd gone through half the drawers finding nothing else of interest when she heard her phone ringing upstairs. Immediately after, a loud crash, like glass shattering on the floor, sounded directly above her. Rushing blood sent her pulse racing as she recollected Jace Murdock's parting words, *be careful.*

Attempting to still her nerves, she rationalized that the wind had picked up. It could be a tree branch slamming against a window. It wouldn't be a first time. She decided to go up and check it out when she heard a thump that definitely came from inside the house.

Feeling a growing sense of panic, she glanced at Max who was staring at the door at the top of the stairs. When she heard footsteps on the wood floor in the kitchen where the door to the basement was, her mouth went dry. The house was small. It would only take a person a couple of minutes to determine no one was upstairs and head for the basement, especially if they'd seen the light from the outside through the small window.

She pulled Jace's card out of her pocket along with her cell phone and dialed the number with shaking fingers.

He answered on the first ring with a curt hello.

"Jace, its LuAnn. I'm in my basement, and I can hear someone upstairs walking around in my house."

"Do you have a way to get out?" he asked quickly.

"Yes, there's a small window."

"Then go. Now! Run to the Holiday Station at the end of your street. Wait for me. I'll call 911 and be there in a few minutes to pick you up."

"No! No police." She knew he'd wonder why she didn't want the Superior Police Department contacted, but she had no time to explain.

Stifling a scream, she slammed her phone shut, stuck it back in her pocket and positioned her small stepladder under the window. She then stretched and turned the overhead light bulb out of the socket burning her fingers in the process. The bulb crashed to the cement floor making enough noise to alert anyone upstairs attuned to sounds.

She grabbed Max, climbed the three steps on the ladder, then struggled a few precious moments with the rusty lock and swung the top- hinged window open. She flung Max out into the rain at the same time a sudden shaft of light from the top of the stairs warned her someone had opened the door.

A vile curse that sounded male came from the top of the stairs then she heard the quick clatter of his tread as he bounded down the wooden steps. Panicked noises came from her throat as she hoisted her upper body out the window leaving her feet dangling. Using her arms she struggled to wiggle free of the small window. A heavy flying object hit her lower leg bringing on a sharp pain. She ignored the pain as she managed to get one foot out to brace on the outer frame and attempted to push herself the rest of the way out into the rain. Something grasped her ankle. She screamed and kicked back with her free leg, connecting with something solid.

A gruff shriek railed out behind her, and her ankle was free. Without looking back she scrambled to her feet and ran, rain pelting down her face. It was almost two blocks to the Holiday Station.

She had made the length of the first block when a white pickup careened in front of her on the street as she was about to cross. The pickup stopped so short she nearly ran into it. The driver's side door swung open, and a man burst from behind the wheel.

Blinded by rain, LuAnn screamed, dodged his reaching arms and tried to run around the back of truck. She could see the lights to the service station. If only she could make it far enough so someone could hear her screams.

He called out her name, and then he tackled her around the waist, hauling her to a stop. Soaked to the skin, rain hampering her efforts, she kicked and scratched, fighting and screaming with everything she had in her. A hand clamped over her mouth, silencing her, and the last thing she remembered before everything went black was the sound of her helpless suffocating moans as he dragged her into the pickup.

* * * *

"Kayla? I need your help. I'll be there in five minutes." Jace hung up his phone, finding it difficult to steer and hold on to LuAnn in case she woke up and tried to jump out of the truck. His sister's place was twenty minutes closer than his. He hoped to get there before his passenger regained consciousness. He hated having to muffle her screams, but they had been loud enough to shatter windows, and if her assailant had followed, he could pop out of the driving rain at any moment. He had to get LuAnn away from there fast before he could be followed.

Becca!

LuAnn awoke suddenly, a scream lodged in her throat. Some sixth sense told her to hold it in. The memories of the rain and the white pickup rushed back at her. A man came out of the vehicle. He'd grabbed her, holding his hand over her mouth when she screamed. She'd hit and clawed franticly at him until she'd passed out.

As her mind cleared, she realized from the glowing lights of the dash she was laying on the front seat of a moving vehicle, probably the pickup. She needed to make an escape plan. Her leg throbbed like hell, but she'd run this far on it, and she could run farther. Thankfully she wasn't bound or gagged. Without moving, she narrowly opened her eyes to familiarize herself with her surroundings.

The rapid swish of wipers and pounding on the roof told her the rain was still going full force. She didn't know how long she'd been out, but it only seemed to be a few moments. The top of her head rested against her assailant's thigh, and he had one hand firmly pressed on her arm holding her down as he drove with the other. If she tried to get up, there was no way she could get away from him, besides she couldn't jump out of a moving truck. Her best bet was to wait until it stopped. Until she knew what was happening to her or found a chance to escape, she planned to remain unresponsive.

* * * *

Kayla had her garage open and was standing in the doorway looking frantic. When Jace cornered the driveway, she stepped aside and motioned him into the empty stall.

"What's going on—" Her question fell off when her gaze fell on his wet, limp passenger.

"Close the overhead then get the door. I need to get her inside to tend to her." He reached in and lifted LuAnn out to carry her up the three steps into Kayla's kitchen.

Kayla followed close behind. "She's bleeding," Kayla cried. "Is she shot?"

"Lord, I hope not. Where can I put her?"

"In the spare room, it's closest, first on your right."

Kayla raced ahead of him and threw her grandmother's quilt back to expose the top sheet. "Hold on I'll get some towels." She ran to the adjoining bathroom returning an instant later, arms loaded. "Why didn't you take her to a hospital?" she asked as she spread a couple of large towels on the bed.

"We were in a downpour. I didn't know she was hurt. I thought she just fainted." He laid her violently shivering body on the bed. "I'll explain later. Let's see how badly she's hurt."

His sister went straight to the foot of the bed to examine LuAnn's bleeding leg. "She has a large bruise starting and a shallow cut in the skin that doesn't look serious. If something blunt hit her hard enough to break the skin, she's going to have a mighty sore leg. I'll get some antiseptic and bandages."

Jace looked down at her feeling helpless. She was still shivering, and her skin felt cold and clammy. He checked her pulse and found it strong, but they had to get her dry. When Kayla returned a moment later with a first aid kit, Jace asked, "A faint doesn't usually last this long, does it?"

"No, usually just a few moments as far as I know. Did she fall or hit her head on something?"

"Not unless it was before I found her, and she was running strong then. We need to get her wet clothes off, Kayla."

Chapter Ten

LuAnn's eyes flew open; she didn't know who Kayla was, but she'd recognized Jace Murdock's voice. He was *not* going to take her clothes off. "I can do that myself," she said shakily.

Jace frowned down at her. "How long have you been awake?"

LuAnn swallowed, her throat felt dry and raspy and her lower leg ached something awful. Whatever that housebreaker threw at her must have had some weight to it, or a sharp edge. She shuddered thinking it might have been a large knife. "I woke up in the truck just before we got here. I didn't know it was you who'd abducted me, so I was thinking about how I could escape. You put your hand over my mouth. I—I thought you were…that man from the basement."

Jace swore softly. "I'm sorry, but you were screaming hysterically. I didn't know where the guy was, and we were only a block from the service station. Since you didn't want me to call the police…and then you fainted. By the way what do you have against the police?"

LuAnn swallowed trying to clear her dry throat. "I…can I have some water?"

"Of course," Kayla said quickly. "I'll get it."

"Where am I, and who is she?" LuAnn asked when Kayla left.

"You're at my sister Kayla's house. You were cold and shivering, and it was closer than my place."

Kayla came back with a glass of water. "You better sit up to drink this."

LuAnn braced herself on her elbows, trying to get to a sitting position, wincing at the stabs of pain coming from her leg. Jace helped lift her and stuffed a couple of pillows behind her back.

Kayla handed her the water and stood quietly watching as she drank. Over the top of the glass, LuAnn noticed the questioning look she gave her brother.

"I was just going to take a look at your leg," Kayla said, "but maybe we should get your wet clothes off first. I can throw them in the dryer."

LuAnn swiveled a concerned look from Kayla to Jace as she handed the empty glass back.

Kayla's lips twitched. "I guess you better wait outside," she told her brother.

Before he left the room, Jace nodded solemnly. "Call me when you're finished. We need to talk."

After he left, Kayla handed LuAnn a dry towel. "I'll get some things for you to wear until yours are dry. We're about the same size. Then I'll take a look at your leg." She disappeared through the door closing it firmly behind her.

As LuAnn shed her wet t-shirt, she thought about Jace's parting words. She knew what he wanted to talk about, and she wasn't looking forward to it. But right now all she wanted to do was get dry and warm. Even her underwear was soaked, but she decided to leave it on. The lacy, black bra and matching skimpy panties were a birthday gift from Barb two months ago. LuAnn deliberated over why she'd decided to finally remove the tags and wear them to meet Jace for lunch. Shrugging that thought off, she dried her hair as best she could then wrapped the towel around her upper body and stood up, balancing on one foot to remove her wet Capri's.

The door opened, and Kayla came in, hesitating. She obviously noted the look of concern on LuAnn's face.

Kayla smiled. "It's okay. He won't come in until we tell him to. He might be a rascal of a brother, but deep down he's a gentleman—well, most of the time anyway. You really aren't his girlfriend, are you?"

LuAnn paused, staring at Kayla. "Whatever gave you that idea?"

"He's been divorced over a year, and I've never seen him with another woman—at least not one of his own choosing."

That surprised LuAnn. He was an exceptionally attractive man in a rugged sort of way. The type you see in outdoor magazine ads, manning a gun or fishing pole in his long-fingered hands. When he'd walked away from her house yesterday, she'd only seen him from the back, and she recalled liking what she saw. Barb had once asked her, kiddingly, if she'd ever met a man that *turned her on*. Maybe Barb wasn't kidding because for some odd reason she had the feeling Jace Murdock turned her on.

LuAnn sucked in a breath of air when she put pressure on her leg.

Kayla rushed to help her. "Sit down on the bed," she instructed. "I'll slide them off for you."

LuAnn sat down, more than glad for the help. "What do you mean, 'one of his own choosing'?"

Kayla eased the Capri's off laughing. "Mom and I are always trying to set him up, but lately he's become a total grump about it."

"I understand where he's coming from there. My friends are always trying to find a man for me. They just won't believe I'm not interested."

"Why not?" Kayla asked handing her a mid-sleeved pullover sweater and a pair of denim shorts.

LuAnn thanked her and slipped the sweater over her head. "It's hard to explain, but I had a bad marriage, and my life is good without the complications of a man."

"I hear you there," Kayla said laughing.

LuAnn tilted her head at the sound of erratic music coming from the other room. "Is that a radio playing?"

"No," Kayla said. "That's Jace banging on my piano. He does that when he's thinking. Only God knows how anyone could think the way he plays. Mom forced us both to take lessons, but he never took to it, only knows a few songs. I'll go throw these wet things in the dryer while you finish dressing. Then I'll have a look at your leg. It doesn't seem to be bleeding any more, but I can put some disinfectant on it and a bandage. Be right back." She hesitated at the door. "Can I tell Jace to come in? He's playing an awful lot of sour notes out there. I think he likes you."

LuAnn closed the snap of the shorts Kayla had given her. "I doubt that. I have a feeling I'd make any man play sour notes. I'm just a financial investment to him."

Kayla raised her brows. "Hmm, I guess I'd like to hear that story. What happened to you tonight anyway?"

"Somebody broke into my house. I—I think he was trying to kill me."

"Oh my God. Why?"

"Maybe you should ask your brother that question. He knows more about it than I do."

* * * *

Jace pounded on the piano, keeping an eye on the bedroom door, waiting for his sister to reappear. When she did, his fingers stopped moving. He turned to her expectantly, only to be pinned with a narrow gaze. "Who is she?"

"Her name is LuAnn Barstow."

"She said she thinks someone was trying to kill her tonight…and you know more about it than she does? Feel free to tell me this is none of my business, but you did come to me for help, so I'd like to know what is going on. What kind of a relationship do you have with this woman?"

"You might say, none. I just met her a few hours ago."

Kayla's gaze widened in disbelief. "I thought you had Dustin with you today?"

"I did. He had to go home early. Karen's father was having a birthday party. Can I go in and talk to her now?"

Kayla threw her hands in the air. "Fine, but I'd like to bandage her leg."

Jace nodded. "I'll talk to her while you do it. Then you can see I'm not trying to hide anything from you."

"I'll get my first aid kit." Kayla turned to walk down the hall, calling over her shoulder, "She's dressed so you can go in."

Jace gave a soft knock on the door and walked in. LuAnn was fully dressed, sitting on the bed with her feet up. She was examining her battered leg. And he noted, other than the bruise, she had exceptionally nice legs. Then he had to wonder why that would even enter his mind.

"How are you feeling?" he asked.

"Other than my leg aching, and shaking from the inside out, fine. At least I'm dry and somewhat warm, thanks to your sister."

Jace sat down on the end of the bed close enough so her foot made contact with his thigh when she stretched out to lie back on the plumped pillows. "Can you tell me what happened?"

She took a deep breath. "After I left you I—"

Kayla walked in then stopped when she realized they'd been talking. "Do you want me to leave?" she asked looking at LuAnn rather than her brother.

"No," LuAnn said. "Please stay."

Kayla glanced at Jace. "I wanted to treat her leg."

He motioned her in. "I told you it was okay. Just keep this between us for the time being."

Kayla nodded, pulled up a chair and began assessing the damage to LuAnn's leg.

"Go on," Jace prompted LuAnn. "What happened when you left Applebee's?"

LuAnn glanced warily at Kayla then said. "I went to see my grandmother, and she asked me to get her prescription—"

"You said you intended to question her. Did you learn anything new?"

LuAnn lifted her shoulders and drew a deep breath. "I asked if she remembered my mother being pregnant."

"And?" Jace prompted when she didn't continue.

"She said she did, and that my mother was as big as a house when she gave birth." She sighed then went on, "It made me feel great until she added I had a brother who died at birth and she wasn't sure which pregnancy she was remembering."

"I take it you didn't know about the other pregnancy."

LuAnn shook her head and brushed a shaking hand through her damp hair. "No, I didn't. Anyway, after that I got her prescription and delivered it to her nurse. I went out to the mall to pick up a birthday present for my friend, Barb."

"What time did you get home?" Jace asked.

"Around eight. I'd already eaten a fast-food burger at the mall, so I let Max in and went to my—"

"Who's Max?" Jace interrupted.

"My next door neighbor's cat. I take care of him when Tom, that's my neighbor, goes out of town on business, so Max comes to my house for a treat nearly every night. Then, as I was saying, I went to my bedroom to change clothes and went down in my basement to look for the birth certificate you wanted to see."

A flinch of pain crossed her features as she watched Kayla apply antiseptic to her wound.

"Sorry," Kayla said, sending her patient a sympathetic smile followed by a curious glance at her brother.

"Did you find it?" he asked.

"Yes, It was…oh my gosh… It was in the pocket of my jeans."

"I took everything out," Kayla said quickly. "It's lying on top of the dryer. Give me a moment to finish wrapping this, and I'll get it. Can you hold her leg up?" she asked Jace.

He complied, finding the feel of LuAnn's warm leg in his hands surprisingly pleasant. "How serious is it?"

"It's mostly just a nasty bruise. The cut shouldn't need stitches. You took a hard hit whatever it was from."

"I don't know what it was. He threw it at me when he was coming down the stairs."

Kayla taped the bandage then smiled. "All done."

"Thank you, Kayla, it feels much better."

"You're welcome. I'll go get those papers if you like."

"Please do," Jace answered. After Kayla gathered up her things and left, LuAnn related the rest of what happened, up to running into him in his white pickup.

Kayla came back and handed the damp piece of folded paper to Jace. She set LuAnn's cell phone on the nightstand then returned to her chair.

Jace's gaze flicked to LuAnn as he unfolded the damp birth certificate. "I already looked," LuAnn said. "It's a copy. I was still searching hoping to find the original when I heard the intruder upstairs."

Jace examined the document then folded it up and placed it on the dresser. "I guess this neither proves nor disproves anything."

All was quiet for a moment while he sat thinking. Finally, he looked up at LuAnn and asked, "Who is Becca?"

Chapter Eleven

LuAnn felt her face heat up. Her heart rate did triple time. "How…how…I don't understand?"

"In the pickup you woke up momentarily, shouted out the name, and then you were out again."

She took some deep steadying breaths. She wasn't ready to tell him about her daughter, but she had to tell him something. "You'll think I'm crazy."

"Tell me anyway."

Kayla was frowning.

LuAnn's gaze focused on the bright handmade squares of the quilt beside her. "Becca doesn't exist. She was…a fantasy. I gave her up when I was fifteen." She'd stuck as close to the truth as she could, keeping her eyes averted, not wanting to see the incredulous look on Jace's face.

"You kept an imaginary childhood friend until you were fifteen?"

Damn, she shouldn't have told him her age. "It…it wasn't what you're thinking, and I don't feel like explaining, besides it's irrelevant."

Jace gave her a long searching look. After a moment he sighed. "All right, we'll leave that one for now. How about you explain why you didn't want me to call the police when you're home alone and a stranger is creeping around in your house—"

LuAnn's mind drifted back to the events of the last twenty-four hours. What if it was Hank Jamison looking for her? Until Jace mentioned calling 911, she hadn't considered that Jamison might look for her. But why would he hire an investigator when he was Superior's Chief of Police. If he wanted to find her, surely he could do it on his own, and he'd likely have done it long before this. But she couldn't possibly reveal her connection to Hank Jamison without explaining about Becca. Was there a chance this was all someway connected to Becca?

Suddenly she realized Jace was still talking.

"—you should have called 911 before you called me. I live thirty minutes away. If I hadn't already been within a mile when you called, I'd never have been able to help you."

That brought up a question that lingered on the back of LuAnn's mind. "Why were you so close anyway?"

Concern etched his features, and he gave her an empathetic look. "You're not going to like the answer to that."

* * * *

Harridan reached in his drawer, pulled out a bottle of Scotch and poured a double shot. He shuttered at the long draw he took. "How the hell did she get away? Where is she?"

"Damned if I know. It was raining like a bitch. She climbed out the basement window and took off. I couldn't fit through it, so I had to run upstairs and go out the door. By the time I got to the back of the house where the window was, she'd disappeared."

"Well, damn it to hell. Did she get a look at you?"

"I don't think so. By the time I found her, she had her head out the window. I got there and grabbed her foot, but she kicked back at me and hit me in the face—I think my nose is broke. After that she scrambled out the rest of the way and never looked back that I could see. I threw the hammer at her, and think I got a good hit 'cause she screamed like a wounded banshee."

"You left the hammer there?"

"Yup, and they won't find my prints on anything I can guarantee you that."

"Where is Murdock?"

"According to the GPS bug I planted in the wheel-well, he's at home. The car hasn't moved tonight. He did use it to go to Applebee's, and then he drove twenty miles or so west out of town. I don't know where exactly. Like I said last time I called to give you the broad's address, she went shopping all afternoon, so all I did was sit around and wait for her."

* * * *

Jace decided to try bargaining with her to get some answers. He kept silent while LuAnn shifted on the bed waiting for him to explain.

"That doesn't make any sense," she said impatiently. "Why wouldn't I like the reason you were close by?"

"I know who broke into your house."

"What? Who?"

Out of the corner of his eye, Jace saw Kayla's gaze swivel back and forth between him and LuAnn. If this hadn't been such a serious matter, he would have found it comical. "You haven't told me why you didn't want the police involved."

"What does one have to do with the other?"

Jace pulled his knee up on the bed shifting his body so he faced her. "I can't answer that without some help from you. Something's going on here, and unless we can get to the bottom of it, whoever is after you may not give up. I need all the facts, if I'm going to help you."

LuAnn looked clearly agitated. "My issue with the police happened a long time ago."

"Then why are you so reluctant to talk about it?"

She blew out an exasperated puff of air. "I once dated the Superior Chief of Police's son. It…it didn't end well. Now who broke into my house?"

Jace waited, but she didn't elaborate. "That's it? You dated his son, so now you'd rather be attacked in your house than call the police."

"Yes. So unless he is your mysterious *client*, it can't have anything to do with this."

"He's not my client. Was your breakup so terrible he'd want to do you bodily harm?"

LuAnn rolled her eyes. "No! We were kids. It was a long time ago."

"According to your birth certificate you're only twenty-eight. Can't be *that* long ago. You want to tell me what happened?"

"No. I do not! And I think I just figured out why you were in my neighborhood. It must have been you who broke in my house. It's all starting to fit together. I kicked the man in the face when he grabbed my foot, and you have a scratch on your forehead. Do you really even have a client, or are you after something yourself?"

Jace stared at her for a long moment, until Kayla spoke up. "You better tell her who broke into her house because I'm starting to believe her."

He ignored his smirking sister and the urge to actually laugh as he touched the dried blood on his forehead. "For the record you *did* put that scratch on me." He held out his hands where there were similar marks all the way up his arms. "You also did these when I tossed you in the pickup while I was *abducting* you. I tried to tell you who I was, but you were hysterical and fighting like a she-cat."

LuAnn grimaced. "Sorry. I guess I was a little out of it."

Jace smiled at her. "I guess. When you first came into Applebee's this noon, do you remember the lone man sitting across the room with the newspaper in his hands?"

"Yes, I remember," LuAnn said, nodding slowly. "He was a big guy with a lot of hair on his face and the only person sitting alone. Since I'd only seen you from the back, I thought it might be you until you waved from the other side of the room."

"His name is Armon Kastansa, and he's been following me since I was hired to find you."

"How do you know that was him?" LuAnn asked frowning. "And how do you know his name?"

"I gave his license plate number to a friend of mine who works on the Duluth police force. After he had the name, he looked up his record. He's a bad dude. I didn't get the photo until I got home tonight, and since I didn't have your phone number, I was coming over to warn you. I was just about there when you called."

LuAnn looked confused. "So, do you really think he was trying to kill me?"

"I can't say for sure, but it looks that way."

"But…why?"

"That's what I'm trying to figure out." He turned to look at Kayla. "Would you be interested in getting me a beer?"

Kayla stood up. "Sure. How long would you like it to take me?"

"A few minutes." Jace grinned. "You're pretty smart for a girl."

"I shared a womb with you. I can read you like a book. Would you like something too?" she asked LuAnn.

"A beer sounds good—lite if you have it."

When Kayla left, Jace turned back to LuAnn. "I'm convinced my client hired Kastansa to tail me. To me that means he gave up his right to privacy. His name is Bart Harridan."

LuAnn gasped. "My God. He's the wealthiest man in town. What does he have against me?"

"That's what I'm trying to figure out. The story he gave me was that you are his wife's daughter, born when she was seventeen and before they knew each other. His wife is supposedly ill and wants to meet you."

LuAnn's eyes widened. "That's why you were asking about my birth certificate."

"Exactly. My instructions were to find you and tell him where you lived. I was to have no contact with you whatsoever."

"But you did contact me. Why?"

"I didn't trust him. Something about his story was off. Then when I noticed I was being followed, I really became suspicious. Assuming he made up the story about his wife looking for her long lost daughter, can you think of any other reason he might want to contact you? Or have you killed?"

LuAnn shook her head slowly, swallowing hard. "No. I've never even spoken to the man or his wife. The only time I've seen them is on television. I don't understand."

"Let me throw something else your way. Your father and Saul both worked for Otis Elevator. Otis services Harridan's hotels."

LuAnn gripped her hands in her lap. "My father worked at a lot of places while he was with Otis. He worked there at least twenty years."

"Until he won that lottery," Jace supplied.

"Yes, as a matter of fact. That's when he quit."

"Is there anything you can think of concerning your father that could be traced back to you in a negative way?"

"Not that I know of, besides he died a long time ago."

Jace thought she answered a little too quickly. She didn't even think about it. That meant either there was absolutely nothing or she was hiding something. He'd bet on the latter. Everything seemed to stem from *a long time ago.* Jace tried to think. Something wasn't adding up, but he couldn't figure out what it was.

Kayla's knock on the door interrupted his disjointed thoughts. "Yeah, yeah, come on in." Balancing three open beers, she handed one to him, one to LuAnn and sat back on her chair sipping on the last one. "Get anything resolved?" she asked.

"No," Jace and LuAnn answered in unison.

"Do you both realize it's almost eleven o'clock? I for one have to go to work tomorrow. I have at least five appointments, and there's usually some walk-ins."

"What kind of work do you do?" LuAnn asked. Not only was she curious, but she also wanted to get away from the depressing barrage of questions.

"I'm a veterinarian."

Jace gave a humorous snort. "She didn't even have to go to school. She practiced on me."

LuAnn took a sip of her beer enjoying the coolness in her dry throat. "When you said you shared a womb, I presumed you were twins. I'm a teacher so I know a lot about kids. It must be the twin factor because most boys wouldn't go along with their sisters playing doctor."

"It wasn't playing," Kayla scoffed sending an affectionate glare at her twin. "I patched him up every time he did some stupid reckless stunt. I even put stitches in his thigh when he fell off his moped, so Mom and Dad wouldn't find out."

"Oh, my memory is clear on that," Jace said groaning. "It hurt like a son of a gun. She poured Dad's favorite whiskey over it. And I didn't *fall* off the moped. I missed the board on a fantastic jump I was trying to make. You did a good job for a ten-year-old. She even boiled the thread and held a burning match on the needle to sterilize it."

"You put stitches in when you were ten-years-old, using whiskey for anesthesia," LuAnn repeated incredulously. "That must have hurt something awful."

"I was a tough kid," Jace said, puffing out his chest.

Kayla laughed. "He bawled like a baby, but he wouldn't let me stop. If Mom and Dad had found out, they'd have put his moped on vacation for at least a year. There were numerous other times he needed my skills. When we were twelve, he tried to jump a picnic table on roller blades. He had bones sticking out of his wrist, and he wanted me to fix it."

"Ouch, that hurt even worse," Jace said, grimacing. "Dad took away my blades for a month. Good thing I had those lawn mowing jobs so I could buy a secret pair."

"Yeah, and you made me be an accessory every time. You were a walking disaster. You even conned me into pushing that horrible mower while you were hurt."

"Hey, I paid you. Besides it was self-propelled. All you had to do was guide it."

When Kayla made some derogatory remark about him still owing her, Jace gave her a chiding answer.

LuAnn enjoyed listening to their childhood antics. It was something she'd always missed. Sighing she said, "Obviously you had parents who loved you and cared what you did."

"That we did," Kayla said softly, giving LuAnn a sympathetic smile. "You look very tired, LuAnn. Maybe you should both stay here tonight."

"That would be wonderful. Thank you so much, Kayla. I really didn't want to go back in my house tonight." What she didn't say was that it might be a long time before she was comfortable going home.

"Yeah, good idea," Jace agreed. "LuAnn appears to be safe here, and maybe we can come up with something after sleeping on it. I have some calls I can make in the morning, do a few inquiries."

Kayla sent LuAnn a bright smile. "I've never seen him quite so protective."

Jace grunted. "I feel responsible. I got her into this mess."

"I don't doubt that for a minute, but you can explain tomorrow," Kayla said. "Right now, I'm going to bed. LuAnn, I'll get you some PJs and your clothes, they should be dry by now, and Jace, I'll put some bedding out on the sofa for you."

"Oh my gosh," LuAnn replied. "That reminds me, I need to call my neighbor and see if Max came home. Maybe he could go over and check if my doors are locked and what window was broken."

"Don't tell him where you are," Jace cautioned. She nodded, reached to retrieve her phone from the nightstand and quickly punched in some numbers. "At least the phone didn't get too wet. It seems to be working," she mumbled. "Tom? Hello, it's LuAnn."

Jace only listened half-heartedly while LuAnn asked about the cat, which strangely, seemed to be her top priority—small wonder she and Kayla had hit it off. Apparently Max had come home dripping wet but fine. She then asked Tom to go over and make sure her doors and windows were locked, including the one in the basement. She told him he'd need a flashlight as the basement light had shattered. Jace decided Tom wasn't a curious sort because he never asked any questions—at least none that he heard LuAnn answer. Before she hung up she told him that unless something was amiss, he didn't need to call her back. She'd call him in the morning.

The first thing Jace was going to do in the morning was call Logan. He wanted to know a little more about the Superior Chief of Police, and then he was going to call Bart Harridan. Hell, maybe he'd just give the man LuAnn's address and collect his money, play ignorant and see what his reaction would be.

Before he went to bed though, he planned to take a stroll around the house, make sure they didn't have any unwanted visitors lurking about.

Chapter Twelve

"So now you've lost track of both of them," Bart Harridan all but shouted into the phone at Armon Kastansa.

"I've been parked across the street from Murdock's place for the last three hours just like you told me to do. His car is still in the garage, and no lights have been on in the house."

"Does he have another vehicle?"

"Hell if I know. I ain't seen him drive anything but a blue Ford Fusion, and I didn't see another one in the garage last time because I found the hammer in the backyard. There's a big shed in the back, I suppose one could have been in there."

Harridan swore. He was starting to think Jace and LuAnn had joined forces against him. Maybe they were picking up the money together. He'd have Murdock's head if he was doing a double-cross. Either way he'd have to deliver the money tomorrow night until he knew for sure who was behind the blasted note.

"Stay there until he shows up. And see what kind of vehicle he's driving. Also, I need you to do a pick-up for me at the bank tomorrow. It should be ready by two o'clock." Bart had no intentions of telling Kastansa about the blackmail note; the less people who knew the better. One thing about his hired man, he usually did what he was told without question…usually.

It was almost midnight when his phone rang again.

"Bart, what the hell, you still up?"

Bart recognized Judge Ramous Porter's voice. "Of course, I don't have time to sleep."

Ramous laughed. "I hear you there. I'm calling to see if you want to hit some balls tomorrow morning. We could both use a break. How about it? Eight thirty good for you?"

Bart chewed his lower lip, thinking. "Would be better Tuesday afternoon." He'd rather have this whole business with the money taken care of before he concentrated on golf.

"Can't," Ramous said. "I'm heading for Las Vegas early Tuesday morning."

"I thought you went to Vegas last week."

"I did, lost my ass too. I need to recoup."

Bart had the urge to warn him about that kind of idiotic thinking, but Ramous was a smart man, he should be able to figure that out for himself. Well, what the hell, he thought why not play golf. It was better than sitting here and stewing. "Okay, let's do tomorrow. I need to be home no later than one thirty. We should be able to do eighteen holes by then."

After Bart hung up something nagged at him. If Judge Porter lost his ass in Las Vegas, maybe he was looking for some quick easy cash.

Shit. He was getting paranoid. Now he was suspecting one of his closest friends of blackmail. Time would tell. Twenty-four hours from now he'd know.

He'd already set his plan in motion. Today he'd scoped out the drop sight and discovered the trash barrel was backed up against some bushes and directly under a mercury vapor lamp that lit up the whole area. From his third floor attic window, he had an unobstructed view of the barrel. Tomorrow afternoon he'd set up his video camera. It would be worth ten grand to catch the bastard red-handed.

In a way he wished he'd researched that idea before he tried to get rid of LuAnn Barstow. He leaned back in his luxurious leather office chair and contemplated that idea. Even if he'd left LuAnn alone, he'd still have had to take care of Jace Murdock. Bart had thought he'd be satisfied getting him disbarred, but it wasn't enough. It still gored him that Marley Jacobs' killer had gone free and Jace Murdock was responsible. For some reason he hated Murdock even more than Marley's wife, Alexia. Granted Marley was a jerk to her, but she could have divorced him instead of killing him. And if Murdock hadn't submitted false evidence, she'd have gone to jail where she belonged. Bart didn't dare touch her. If it came out that Marley Jacobs was his son, it would come straight back to him. Huh, maybe Alexia had figured it out and was going after him for money.

He pulled out his bottle and poured a triple shot of Scotch.

* * * *

Chelsea yawned. It was way past her bedtime, but she didn't want to miss anything going on downstairs. Tomorrow when she went to the mall, she'd get the recorder. Then she wouldn't have to spend so much time in her room.

By the intensity of her father's fury after talking to Kastansa, it was safe to assume LuAnn Barstow had escaped. That thought brought a smile to her face. When she'd heard the phone receiver slam into its cradle, she figured the action was over. Listening to him make golf plans was boring. She might as well go to bed—tomorrow was going to be a busy day.

* * * *

The sun was barely cresting the eastern sky when Jace punched in Logan's number on his cell. Fortunately he had the same phone as Kayla, so he'd been able to charge it before he went to bed. Kayla had made coffee before she'd left for work, and he kept an eye on the gurgling pot while he waited for Logan to answer.

After the fourth ring he finally heard a click followed by Logan's grumpy voice. "Man, Jace, you need to get a life, or should I say wife."

"You're starting to sound like my mother," Jace said chuckling. "Sorry for the early call, but I need to pick your brain."

"It's kind of mush right now but go ahead. What are you looking for?"

"What, if anything, can you tell me about the current chief of police in Superior?"

Logan laughed. "I'm not even going to ask where that question is coming from, but it must be important or you wouldn't be calling at this hour. You're talking about Hank Jamison. He's in his late fifties. Used to be a beat cop here in Duluth before he got the chief position in Superior. Far as I know he's a decent man."

"Does he have any kids?"

"Two daughters. He had a son, but he was killed in a car accident a few years back."

This was getting more interesting by the minute, Jace thought. "How long ago?"

"Ah, I guess about ten, twelve years ago. You could check that out if you want an exact date. I think his name was Neil. Yeah, that's it Neil Jamison. He was just a kid, seventeen or eighteen. Star athlete. High school quarterback. Smart. Good looking, had everything going for him. Hank just about lost it when it happened. From what I hear, he still isn't over it. I don't suppose you want to tell me what this is all about?"

"All in good time, my friend. Thanks. I'll see you Saturday night when you tie the knot."

"You're welcome to bring a date you know."

"I might just surprise you." Jace hung up frowning at his own words. Was he actually considering asking LuAnn to go with him to Logan and Maggie's wedding? She didn't date. She'd told him that in a no-nonsense tone. Well, it didn't have to be a date. Did it? They'd enjoyed each other's company at Applebee's, besides he hated going to weddings alone.

He was filling his coffee cup when the woman in his thoughts walked into the room.

"I smell coffee," she said, smiling sleepily as she flipped a strand of wildly tousled hair out of her face. It fell right back in place. Her feet were bare, and she wore a pair of blue, Tinkerbelle pajamas he'd given Kayla last Christmas.

He definitely wasn't used to seeing a woman look that damn good at this hour, with no make-up, dressed in flannel yet.

Noticing her slight limp pulled him back to reality. Quickly giving himself a mental shake, he pulled a second cup out of the cupboard and filled it. "If you need coffee as desperately as I do in the morning, you better come and get it."

"Any chance you have cream and sugar?"

LuAnn sparked Jace's interest like no other woman had for a long time, maybe ever. He wondered if it was the similarity between her and his sister. Not in looks, not even in personality, but there was something he couldn't put his finger on.

"You might be in luck," he said. "I take it black, but Kayla uses that French Vanilla creamer stuff. It should be in the fridge." He set her cup beside the sink and took his seat back at the table. "Help yourself. I'm guessing there's sugar in one of those." He nodded toward a set of four canisters placed in a descending row against the back of the counter.

She must have noticed he was staring at her because she gave him a sheepish smile and using both hands, shoved the sides of her hair back. "Sorry, I must look a mess. I don't have a hair brush, and I could use a shower."

"You look…fine," Jace said, biting back the erotic word he wanted to use. "You had a rough night. Rest assured, Kayla told me before she left you should help yourself to anything you need. And if I know Kayla—and I certainly do—she means it whole-heartedly."

"I do appreciate that," LuAnn said, pouring French Creamer into her coffee. After returning it to the refrigerator, she took a spoon out of the first drawer she tried then went directly to the second canister and added two scoops of sugar.

Jace watched her move around the kitchen, surprised. "You and Kayla must think alike. How do you know where everything is?"

She shrugged, coming back to the table and taking a seat. "Most women arrange their kitchens in the same way.

Silverware is in the handiest drawer and sugar is always second to flour."

Huh, he didn't recall his ex-wife thinking like that. "How's the leg?"

"Seriously black and blue, but it doesn't hurt much anymore."

"You want to see a doctor?"

She laughed. "I saw one last night. You're sister's a sweetheart. You really are twins?" she asked.

"Yeah." He chuckled. "Hard to believe isn't it?"

"You don't look much alike. She's blond and blue-eyed. You have rust colored hair and green eyes."

He wanted to tell LuAnn that her dark brown eyes reminded him of rich chocolate, but this wasn't the time. "We're different in a lot of ways. I'm the reckless one. She's steady as a rock."

"I guessed that last night."

Jace gave her a sympathetic look. "Do you want to talk about last night?"

She visibly shuddered.

Chapter Thirteen

Last night was the last thing LuAnn wanted to talk about.

"No. I…I'm so confused. I don't know why this is happening to me all of a sudden. I suppose I have to go home, but I'm afraid to. Maybe…given a couple of days I'll feel different. I love my house. I just don't know what to do."

She blinked back tears feeling like a pathetic wimp.

"Those feelings are normal for someone whose home has been invaded. Plus, you were attacked, that doubles the fear. We need to figure out what's going on and why. If you're absolutely certain Bart Harridan's wife can't be your mother, then he told me a bald-assed lie. Being lied to doesn't sit well with me. He's after you for something, and until we find out what it is you're not going to be safe.

"I'm guessing you don't want police protection, so the only option I can see is you hang with me for the time being. If you don't like that idea, I can find a bodyguard for you."

She shook her head. "I can't afford a full time bodyguard. And who knows how long it will take."

"Whatever Harridan is up to should resolve itself soon. He was in a rush to locate you. I'm hoping if we keep brainstorming, we can find out what it is. The best way to do that is to stay together."

"Where will we go?"

"Today we can go fishing."

"Fishing?"

"Yeah, I have a big boat. Do you have a fishing license?"

"No. And I can't get one. I don't have my purse or my driver's license."

"Okay, forget the license. I'd rather not go back to your place to get it. Whoever has been following me could have your house staked out. How about your stomach? Do you get sick on the water?"

"Not that I know of. I've never been out on the lake, but I don't get sick on carnival rides, if that means anything."

"It might. I keep Dramamine on the boat so you can always take that if the water gets rough. Go take your shower and do whatever you women do in the bathroom, and I'll fix us some breakfast. By the way, Kayla always has a new toothbrush on hand in the medicine cabinet. Go ahead and take it. Bring it with you along with the extra clothes and PJs."

* * * *

At the marina LuAnn stepped out of Jace's pickup her eyes widening in awe. "Wow that's a big boat. I love the name, *Golden Dreams*. Did you do that?"

"I have joint ownership with a friend of mine—it had the name when we bought her three years ago. Why don't you go in and look around while I carry the supplies in. I'm going to go move the truck to the back of the parking lot." He didn't mention that Kastansa knew where he docked his boat and this might be one of the places he'd check if he couldn't find either him or LuAnn. Jace didn't intend to give him any leads he didn't have to.

Walking back to the boat, he did a mental checklist of things to do. He hadn't called Devon yet to tell him he was taking *Golden Dreams* out. That was first on his list after he got underway. Second was a call to Bart Harridan. He thought of a way to speed things up. Before he did, though, he wanted to run his idea past LuAnn.

"It has a darling little kitchenette with a microwave," LuAnn called out to him from below. "And a bedroom of sorts. Oh my gosh, there's a shower in here. What a great way to get away from the world."

As excited as she was, examining every nook and cranny, you'd think she was on the Good Ship Lollipop. He took pleasure in her enthusiasm.

"That's exactly what it's for," he said, ducking into the galley. She flinched when he put his hands on her waist to warn her he was passing her in the narrow space. "Sorry," he said, "I need to turn the fridge on."

"It's okay. You just surprised me. I guess I'm a little jumpy after last night."

"Understandable. I'll try to remember to warn you next time."

Her cheeks had a delightful hint of pink on them. "Do you want me to put some of this stuff away?" she asked.

"Sure, just stick it anywhere you find an open space. That'll keep it from rolling around when we take off. You can fill the refrigerator; it doesn't take long to cool down. And by the way, it's a galley not a kitchen."

"Huh, I guess that explains why it's so small."

"Coming through," he said, moving past her. "I'm going above to fire up the engines."

"No problem," she answered with a little giggle in her voice. "These are some cozy quarters aren't they?"

"Uh-huh, cozy," he mumbled, realizing he'd never taken the boat out alone with a female companion other than his sister. Karen hated fishing and didn't like the water.

Somewhere along the line he'd become very much aware of this particular female.

He could feel her eyes on his backside as he climbed the ladder to the bridge. Seconds later the twin diesels rumbled to life. He came back down and peeked in where she was busily filling cupboards.

"I'm going to cast off now."

She gave him a thumbs up, speaking in her best pirate voice. "Aye, aye, Capitan. All systems go."

He laughed at her antics as he jumped ashore to release the tether ropes. He then hopped aboard and scrambled back up the ladder where he took the helm and eased out of the slip.

He called down to her. "You can finish putting things away later. Right now you better come up here. You'll want to watch when we go under the lift bridge and through the channel. Can you make it with your leg?"

"I'm on my way," she said even as her head popped up. "Oh, this is nice up here too." She made it all the way up and took a seat beside him. "You have a beautiful boat, Jace. I love it. And best of all, nobody will know where we are."

As they moved under the lift bridge, she looked up and waved at the man sitting in a cage at the controls. When they entered the channel leading to Lake Superior, she stared in wonder at the mob of people calling from the shore. They lined the entire cement barrier.

"Are there always so many people here watching?" she asked.

"Pretty much. When it's raining, they still stand there, under their umbrellas. Haven't you ever come down here to watch the big ships come in?"

"No. I suppose that seems odd, since I grew up here, but without a mother I really didn't have a normal childhood."

He gave her a sympathetic glance only to find her staring out at the crowd. "What's wrong?" he asked.

"I think there's a man out there watching us with binoculars."

Jace peered into the crowd where she seemed to be looking. "I don't see him."

"He just left, disappeared into the crowd. You think he might have seen me watching him?"

"Was it Kastansa?"

She shook her head, shrugging. "I couldn't tell. A good share of his body was hidden behind the wall and other people. Then he wore a hooded sweatshirt and most of his face was covered with his hands and the binoculars."

"I guess I wouldn't worry about it. Lots of people use binoculars to check out the boats for one reason or other. We'll keep an eye out for him when we dock."

Once they left the crowded dock behind and moved past the lighthouse, out into the open water, LuAnn sat back surveying the wide expanse of water in awe. She'd grown up near the lake but had never actually been out on it. It was like sailing toward an ocean. You could see shoreline on three sides, but in the direction they were headed there was only water on the horizon. It didn't take her long to forget about Kastansa and all the problems she'd faced the last couple of days. At times like this the only piece of life she allowed herself to think about was permanently fixed in her heart.

Becca.

* * * *

When Chelsea got back from the mall, she ran straight to her room excited to set up her new *equipment*. She'd pushed Betty to get her home by one since she knew her father would still be golfing.

At the electronics shop she'd had a stroke of luck finding a recorder on sale with a voice activated microphone. It even had a cord attachment that extended the mouthpiece five feet—just like a real spy would use when they were secretly interviewing someone.

The first thing she did, after making sure everything worked, was move her dresser so the cord would be concealed when she slipped it down the vent. She then hid the recorder in the bottom drawer and covered it with neatly folded t-shirts. Even when the housemaid added clean clothes, she'd have no reason to disturb the ones that were already there.

Finished, she stood back to survey her handiwork. Unfortunately the cord was black and the vent and wall were white—too obvious. No way did she dare put the dresser in front of the vent, but if she got a screwdriver and removed the vent cover she could slide the cord behind it then maybe get some Wite-Out to paint the part of the cord that was still visible.

She headed for the garage to get a Phillips head screwdriver, priding herself in knowing what it was called.

Betty's father did woodworking in the shed behind his house, and the girls frequently had fun helping him. He even taught them how to paint the cute little birdhouses he made.

In the meantime, he gave them both tips on woodworking, along with Troy, Betty's dreamy fifteen-year-old brother. Betty had told her Troy was sweet on her. They laughed a lot at their house. Troy's mother always teased him by calling him by his baby nickname, Dweet. She'd said it had started out to be *sweet*heart.

Betty's nickname had been Little Booper. When asked what hers was, Chelsea was embarrassed to say she didn't have one, so she made one up. She said it was Peetzie because she liked the sound of it, and she'd heard some motorcycle dude call his wife that.

They were too stuffy in her family to do good-natured teasing or to do fun stuff like building birdhouses. Her father's only hobby was making money.

Deep in thought, Chelsea hurried through the kitchen, jerked the garage door open and literally ran into her mother.

"Holy cow, Chelsea, do you have to storm through the house like a hellion?"

"Sorry, Mother," Chelsea mumbled. "I was in a hurry."

"That's obvious. Is your room on fire or what?" Her mother groused, quickly secreting whatever she had in her hand behind her back.

"No, no. Everything's fine. Do we have any Wite-Out anywhere?" Chelsea asked, hoping to get her mother's mind off her manners.

"If we do, it's certainly not in the garage. Try your father's office. And quit running in the house," she added, strutting past like a peacock with its haughty nose in the air.

"Okay, thanks," Chelsea said, thinking at least she wasn't drunk today and thankful she didn't ask if Chelsea's room was clean since she'd left all her shopping bags scattered on the bed. She didn't even look around to see what *Gladys* was hiding behind her back since she suspected it was a bottle of wine she'd stashed in the garage.

She quickly found the screwdriver, hid it in her pocket and walked with measured steps back through the kitchen. Since she had a good excuse, she went into her father's sacred office, after knocking first even though she was sure he wasn't there.

The Wite-Out was in an immaculately organized tray on his desk.

Being in this room always made her uncomfortable, so she grabbed the little bottle and turned to leave, but a thought stopped her. She glanced at the door to make sure no one was there then looked up at the vent to make certain her tiny mike couldn't be seen and said loudly, "One, two, three, testing."

She then hurried to the door, but before she could pull it shut, her father's telephone message machine came on. A male voice spoke, "Mr. Harridan, it's Jace Murdock—"

Out of the corner of her eye, she saw her mother walk out of the den with a stemmed glass full of red liquid in her hand. Quickly, Chelsea pulled the office door shut behind her, smiled at her mother and held up the white container. "Found it." She then walked painfully slow up the five steps to her room. Inside she charged to the vent to listen to the rest of the message. "—you can send the balance of my fee to my home address. Good doing business with you."

Chelsea didn't swear very often, but right now she used several of the words she'd learned listening to her father starting with damn, damn, damn. Moving at the speed of light, she cleared the clutter off her bed and stuffed it in the back of her closet—just in case her mother thought she was acting strangely and came to check on her.

* * * *

Jace closed his cell phone, grinning. "What do you think?" he asked LuAnn.

She stared at him with her mouth hanging open. "I can't believe you said that to him."

"Not just to him, to his answering machine. I told you I was going to bring this thing to a head one way or another. It'll be more than a little interesting to hear his response. If he's pissed, he'll call to ream me a new one."

"What if his wife listens to it?"

Jace grinned. "And then the fun begins."

Her brows drew together in a thoughtful frown. "But he already knows where I live. Otherwise that guy, Kastansa, couldn't have broken in and attacked me."

Jace adjusted his fishing line and smiled. "Exactly, but if he admits that he knows where you live, he'll have to admit to having me followed. Plus if he calls to tell me he's not going to pay me, I'll have to inform him that all bets are off, discretion is no longer an option."

LuAnn took a deep breath and gave him a tremulous smile. "Sounds like you've thought this idea through."

"And getting the answering machine was a bonus. I don't know where in his house it's located, but wouldn't it be the cat's meow if his wife did listen to the message."

LuAnn's hand flew to her mouth. "But…what if he was telling the truth? What if his wife *is* looking for me?"

Jace cocked his head mischievously. "Then she'll be happy as a clam, and all will be well in the Harridan household."

"What about Kastansa? Why would he be trying to…to hurt me?"

He leaned forward in his chair, forearms braced on his knees. "I hate to tell you this, LuAnn, but there *is* an outside chance that Harridan is telling the truth and Kastansa was hired by someone else. Then…we have a whole new issue to deal with." He sighed. "Let's wait and see. Right now you're safe. Sit back and relax. You want to bring in the next fish?"

"Yes, but I don't have a license."

"We'll use Bart Harridan's money to pay the fine."

Chapter Fourteen

"They'll be taken care of for good this time."

Bart Harridan's hopes escalated. "You found them?"

Kastansa's cackling laugh grated on his nerves. "Sure did. I staked out the boat. And there they came, merry as can be, driving an old Chevy pickup, thinking they'd pulled one over on me. The last laugh will be on those two this time. I guaran-damn-tee it. They won't be able to scrape them up with a butter knife."

"Good. Great. Look, I'm out on the golf course. I'll call you when I get home. Don't forget to make the pickup at the bank."

"Consider it done."

Harridan hung up his cell and put on a forced smile for his companion. They'd finished the eighteenth hole early and stopped at the clubhouse for lunch and a drink. He didn't want to ask Kastansa too many questions; the less Ramous knew the better. The renowned Judge Porter had begun to push Bart's tolerance buttons.

* * * *

Chelsea checked the hall to make sure Gladys wasn't lurking about. Then, heart pounding, went back to the dresser and pulled the recorder out. She set it on the floor, pushed reverse until it stopped then hit play. Her voice came on. *One, two, three, testing* followed by:

Mr. Harridan, its Jace Murdock. I located LuAnn Randall, your wife's daughter. Her last name is Barstow now, and she lives in Superior at 1522 South Danube Street.

I believe that fulfills our agreement. You can send the balance of my fee to my home address. Good doing business with you.

Chelsea swallowed at the lump rising in her dry throat. *Your wife's daughter.* What in blazes did that mean? Gladys, Chelsea's supposed mother, had a daughter? She was the LuAnn they'd been talking about. The person her father had been trying to harm. What sense did that make? First he hires Jace Murdock to find her then he—what did he tell Kastansa? *Don't go in until dark* and *use the hammer.*

Was she dead? Chelsea felt sick. If she really was Gladys' daughter, why would he want to kill her? Of course, he wanted to run for some office. The Senate? Good grief she even heard him mention the White House. Would LuAnn Barstow be an embarrassment? Her father was even more of a monster than Chelsea suspected. Did that mean LuAnn was her sister? In an offhand sort of way?

* * * *

"Oh, my gosh," LuAnn squealed as one of the rods nearly bent in half. "Is that a bite?" Jace had brought in two fish, and he'd told her the next one was hers.

"Looks like it to me," Jace said. "You better grab it."

Excitement exploded in her veins. "I—I don't know what to do."

"Come here, I'll help you." He lifted the rod out of the downrigger, set the hook and thrust the thing in her hands. "Start reeling."

She had no choice but to take the heavy rod. Putting one hand ahead of the reel, she pushed the butt of it against her belly like she'd seen him do then started turning the crank. She was just starting to think it was easy when the fish gave a colossal tug that nearly pulled her overboard.

Instantly Jace was behind her. "Woman, either you're a wimp or you have a monster of a salmon on the line." He snaked his right arm around her waist, his long fingers splaying across her stomach, pulling her tight against him. His left hand went around her arm on the other side where he placed it ahead of hers on the rod. "Okay, start cranking again," he instructed. "I'm just here to guide you; you're going to do the work. And keep the rod up so he can get some play."

The very word *rod* was starting to give her vapors. With his full body hard against her, she could feel his heat, and she knew enough about men to know the bulge pressing her buttocks was not part of his clothing. With the crinkly hair on his forearm tickling her arm, he was literally wrapped around her, and suddenly the last thing she wanted to think about was fishing. But there was this insistent critter from the dark lagoon at the end of the line that was demanding her attention.

She turned the crank and said adamantly, "I'm not a wimp. I've just never done this before."

"What else of interest haven't you done before," he asked, his mouth in her hair so close to her ear she could feel the warmth of his breath.

This was going beyond flirting. Her own breath seemed to be coming in short pants, and she didn't think it was from exertion. She'd never been the kind of person who could come up with quirky little comebacks, so she said the first thing that came to mind, "Nothing you couldn't teach me, I'm sure." For some reason it didn't sound the way she meant it.

"Are you flirting with me?" he whispered. On the cusp of his words, the fish made a sudden mad dash for the bottom of the lake. His biceps tightened as did hers. "Don't stop reeling. You don't want to give him any slack. These salmon are very clever."

Both her arms were getting tired, but she continued to crank, determined not to be a *wimp*. "I don't flirt," she replied.

"Yes you do," came from behind her. "You've been doing it all day."

As the fish made another dive, she grunted, straining to hold the rod up and keep reeling at the same time. "I have not!"

"What do you call all that rubbing against me while you were making sandwiches?"

"It's a tiny kitchen—ah…galley. And you were in my way, you big lug. Why didn't you sit down?"

She could feel him shrug. "I liked it."

"You're disgusting," she said, thankful he couldn't see the absurd grin on her face.

His hand tightened on her belly pulling her tighter against his bulge. "This fishing is *hard* work, isn't it?"

"Yes it—" The line suddenly went limp, the reeling far too easy. "Oh, no, I think I lost him."

"No you didn't. He's coming at you, trying to get slack in the line and jerk free. Keep up with him. Rod up."

The rod was almost straight in the air as her hand flew in circles cranking. She barely got the slack out when the fish made another dive. "Oh," she squealed, "he's still there."

"Yup, and that was probably his last hurrah. Hang on tight. I'll get the net."

LuAnn instantly lamented the loss of his body snuggled at her backside, but she continued to crank, seeing an end in sight.

He took a long handled net off the wall on the side of the cabin and leaned over the railing to dip it in the water. "It's right here," he said, putting his hand on the line to maneuver the fish toward him. "And it's a whopper."

Excited now, she leaned over to watch him slip the net under the huge fish. Seconds later it was in the bottom of the boat.

LuAnn jumped up and down, clapping her hands, shrieking, "Oh, my gosh! Oh, my gosh! I did it! I caught a fish! Did you see that? I caught a fish! What kind is it?"

Jace laughed as he attached the scale to her catch. "It's a coho salmon. And it's a beauty." He strained to lift it free of the deck. "Take a look, see what it weighs."

"Holy cow. It's thirty-one pounds. That's big isn't it?"

Jace dropped the fish in the live well. "That is definitely big. The largest one I ever caught was thirty pounds."

"No wonder it was a bugger to pull in," LuAnn crowed gleefully.

"Most fun I ever had pulling in a fish," Jace said, washing his hands in a bucket of water set there for that purpose.

He had a decided smirk on his face that reminded her of the *fun* he was referring to. Then she did the most uncharacteristic thing she'd ever done in her life. She flew into him, threw her tired arms around his neck—and kissed him.

It took him less than a nanosecond to get into the act. One of his arms circled her waist, the other her ribcage as he lifted her off her feet snuggling his lower body against her. That familiar bulge was much more pleasurable front to front she decided, putting a little wiggle in her hips. He made a groan deep down in his throat as he responded to her lips, allowing her full control.

LuAnn could feel moisture pooling in her danger zone. She should pull back, run for her life, but…

When she finally came up for air, she was gasping. She didn't move her arms and neither did he. Instead he buried his face in her hair and kissed her neck.

"LuAnn," he said huskily. "You're flirting again."

She threw her head back and laughed. She knew it was a soft, wanton, sexy laugh, an answer to the way her body was feeling. "You started it," she managed to say in a breathless whisper.

One of his hands slipped between them to cup her breast. "Do you want me to finish it?" He asked trailing kisses past her ear.

A shudder ran through her the likes of which she'd never experienced. In the back of her mind the words *turned on* surfaced. Yes, she was definitely *turned on,* and she didn't want to be turned off anytime soon.

"Define finish," she breathed, scarcely recognizing her own words.

He moaned deep and long. Or was it her moaning. She'd lost track.

"Take you down to the bed, strip you naked and give you a nice little surprise."

"*Little,*" she quipped, "only if that's a ten pound salmon you have pressed against me."

He chuckled wickedly. "Well, maybe not so little," he murmured, moving his other hand to the side of her face, kissing her so thoroughly her knees weakened. Any minute she'd collapse to the bottom of the boat as played-out as the salmon had been.

He set her on her feet and pulled back after a moment, looking down at her with intense green eyes. A frown creased his dark brows. "I want you, LuAnn, but this is all happening a little soon. I can't follow through unless you convince me I'm not taking advantage of you."

"You're not," she said, wishing he'd stop talking and get back to kissing.

"Listen to me, LuAnn. You told me you don't even date."

"This isn't a date."

"That argument doesn't cut it," he said, blowing out a frustrated sigh. "I won't take you unless you prove to me you're ready for this step."

Her body was on fire, and he wanted to quibble about taking advantage of her. She wasn't fifteen anymore, she was a grown woman. "How do I do that?" she asked, hoping it wasn't going to be a written test.

"Take my hand and lead me down the steps to the bed."

That was easy, she thought. Reaching between them she pulled his hand from her breast then held it while she descended the four steps to the galley toward the minuscule bedroom—or whatever it was called on a ship.

Then he was kissing her again. She wasn't sure how he managed it, but other than slipping her t-shirt over her head, he undressed both of them without breaking his hold on her mouth.

Seconds later they were on the bed in a tangle of arms and legs. He touched and caressed every inch of her body, making it sing like a fine-tuned violin. An amused thought struck her momentarily—he was a lot more skilled at playing her than his sister's piano.

When she couldn't stand it any longer, she begged him to do it. He refused, until she verbalized exactly what she wanted him to do.

She was horrified, but he laughed when she actually blurted out the f-word followed by, "Jace Murdock, you are an exasperating lover."

"Honey, it excites me beyond erotic when you talk dirty," he crooned in her ear as he entered her. She cried out with pleasure so intense it shocked her. Never had she thought sex could be like this. He was larger than she'd imagined, and he filled her with an exhilarating thrusting force. Not a quiet partner, he continually spoke of his desire for her, telling her what he wanted to do to her…and then he did it.

Over her mounting gasps she clung to him, shrieking when her release came, "Oh, my gosh. Oh, my gosh."

Jace's entire body shuddered before he collapsed on top of her. She could feel his heart hammer, keeping time with her own throbbing pulse.

"That's exactly what you said when you landed that fish," he managed to say as he rolled off her breathing heavily. "I hope that shower's working." He barely had the words out when a shrill blast split the air.

Chapter Fifteen

"Oh shit!"

Jace was on his feet charging for the stairs at the speed of light. The echo of LuAnn's screams blended into the sound of the second blast. Buck-naked, he mounted the ladder two rungs at a time. It took a fraction of a second for him to assess the situation and react.

He slammed the boat in reverse and shifted the thrusters to full speed three seconds before a Japanese freighter moving like a lumbering mountain blocked out the sun in front of him. A line of oriental sailors stood at the railing hooting in a foreign language, laughing and making obscene gestures. He noticed they weren't looking at him.

Whirling around, he saw LuAnn on the deck, wearing nothing but skin. She'd obviously been right behind him coming up the steps then got caught off guard when he'd opened the thrusters because she was now sprawled on her back with her beautiful long legs in the air, giving the sailors a show that likely made their long trip from the orient worthwhile. The fact that he too was naked added fuel to their revelry.

He had to stop the reverse motion and set it to idle before he could go down to her. She'd made it halfway to her feet when he took her hand and brought her up against his chest. That motion brought another volley of cheers from the freighter where the sailors had moved to the rear of the ship to enjoy the last of the show.

LuAnn trembled like a tissue in the wind. The color of her face resembled an overripe tomato.

"Are you hurt?" he asked.

She shook her head, burying her red face in his chest.

"Then do me a favor," he said. "Turn around and wave."

"Are you nuts!" she shrieked.

"Nope." To show her how serious he was he kept one arm around her, faced the receding ship and swung his free arm, grinning like a jack-o-lantern.

She apparently appraised the situation then must have decided the freighter was far enough away, and she too faced it and waved. He hoped she wouldn't notice that several of them had binoculars.

Laughing, he pulled her against him, circling her with his arms. "Honey, you just made those poor lonely sailors' day."

She slapped him on the arm. "That scared the daylights out of me. I thought the boat blew up. Did we just about hit them?" she asked as an afterthought.

"Uh-huh."

Her eyes widened as the enormity of what almost happened struck her. "Oh my God."

"You can say that again," he muttered. "I can't believe I went below and left the helm unattended going in trolling speed. And I can't even put the blame on our friend Kastansa."

She held her hand out to show him how it was shaking.

"Some climax, huh?"

"Cripe sakes alive," she mumbled, a laugh caught in her throat. "I'm going to go below, take a shower and get dressed. You think you can manage to keep us from hitting anything while I do that?"

He tilted her chin up and placed a long slow kiss on her lips. "Yup, but you'll have to take over the helm while I shower."

"You keep this up," she murmured. "And we're going to end up back in that bed."

"I'm ready if you are." He pressed proof of his declaration against her.

She rolled her eyes laughing and headed below to the shower.

A moment later, her head popped back up. She threw him his jeans. "Here, your cell phone is ringing."

"Probably one of the sailors," he said, chuckling. She held up her middle finger over her head as she descended the steps swinging her delectable derriere.

He plucked the cell from his pocket and snapped it open, his mood in high spirits.

"Jace? It's Devon."

"Yeah buddy, what's up?"

"I have a front-page scoop for you."

Jace laughed. Devon always went into dramatics when he was excited about something. He could have given Devon his own front-page scoop right now. "Go ahead. Lay it on me."

"I just came off the golf course, and who do you think was having lunch at the clubhouse?"

"Gee, I don't know. The president and first lady."

Devon chuckled. "Better than that, baby. Judge Ramous Porter and Bart Harridan."

That got Jace's attention. He hadn't told Devon that Harridan was his mystery client, but he was extremely interested in anything concerning the two of them—especially together.

"Any idea what they were talking about?" he asked.

"Oh yeah, they were sitting at a table back in the corner near the restroom. I stood out of sight, pulled out my cell phone, and leaned against the wall, moving my lips like I was talking. It seems the Judge is headed for Las Vegas tomorrow. He hit Harridan up for money, said he'd lost a bundle a couple of weeks ago and needed to recoup. Sounds like the man has a serious gambling problem."

"Did Harridan give him money?"

"I don't know. The first thing he did was give the Judge a lecture on gambling. That's when Porter lowered his voice. I couldn't hear what he was saying, but if I had to make a guess, I'd say he was threatening Harridan. The rest of their conversation was in heated whispers. One thing was clear, they both had steam coming out of their ears when they left."

* * * *

When Bart Harridan returned from his golf outing, he was in a sour mood. He'd had a mega fight with his long time friend Ramous Porter, and they'd ended up storming away from each other. The man, powerful and educated as he was, was an idiot. Ruining his life and threatening his brilliant career because he refused to control his gambling habit. What pissed Harridan off was, he'd counted on Porter to stand behind him when he made a bid for the Senate nomination next year.

Shit.

A simple glance in the den told him Gladys was asleep on the settee. He was going to have to do something about her, too. Maybe he could poison her wine.

Chelsea was about the only person in his life who would be an asset in his hopes for a political office. She was an exemplary child. Kept her grades up, never made a scene, could be trusted to behave in public and best of all she stayed out of his way. He'd done a great job of raising her. The only problem where she was concerned began thirteen years ago and never seemed to go away. That might, however, be taken care of if Kastansa accomplished what he'd promised this morning. If he was rid of LuAnn and the money wasn't picked up, that issue would be resolved.

He glanced at his watch. Kastansa would have picked up the money by now, should be there in half an hour or less. He could set up his camera, get the drop taken care of and maybe go visit Olivia Jacobs in the hour he had to be gone. If he got rid of Gladys, he mused; maybe he could marry Olivia, or better yet just hire her as a housekeeper—then she could service his needs anytime he had the urge. She was strapped for cash since Marley died. Their son, asshole that he was, helped provide for her.

He sat behind his desk and thought about pulling out his bottle when he noticed the answering machine blinking. Hell, now what? Maybe it was Porter calling to apologize for his behavior at lunch.

He pressed the play button and practically wet his pants.

* * * *

LuAnn gave a heavy sigh, sorry to see the day ending.

"Did you have a good time?" Jace asked her as they slowly made their way back to the channel.

She sat beside him, collapsed wearily in the chair. "Wonderful. I'm exhausted, but I'd repeat this day any time."

"What was the highlight?" he asked, winking.

She thought for a moment then with a mischievous smirk said, "Catching the fish."

He pretended to be crestfallen. "Ouch, that's a pot-shot at my male ego."

LuAnn laughed. "You already have more of that than you need."

"You think so?" He grinned.

"Of course, there was also that experience of streaking in front of an entire crew of sailors. That's right up there on the list of highlights."

"I hope you're not putting that ahead of me."

"Reflecting on that issue, I did only get one fish."

He chuckled. "Oh, yeah, you got me twice. By the way, I'm assuming you're on some form of birth-control."

"Nope."

"Nothing?" he asked incredulously.

"It's okay," she said softly. "I'd love to be pregnant."

"You're pulling my leg, right?"

"No. You already have a son. I'm twenty-eight. My biological clock is ticking. I wouldn't worry about it if I were you. The chances are slim to none."

"Why is that?"

LuAnn took a sip of her iced tea. She didn't like talking about her disastrous marriage, but he deserved an answer. "I was married for six months and never used birth control." What she chose not to tell him was, other than the first two months, they rarely had sex. "Roger didn't want children, but he failed to mention that until after we were married."

Jace gave her a long look then stared out at the water. "Dustin isn't my biological son," he said finally.

"He's adopted?"

"I wish. No, he was two-years-old when I married his mother. I wasn't able to adopt him because his father wouldn't allow it. I love that kid, but I have no rights whatsoever to him. I'm at Karen's mercy—that's my ex. She decides when I can see him. That's why I brought him along to Applebee's. She asked me to take him that day, and since I rarely get him, I picked him up, even though I knew I might have to take him with me to meet you."

"That's an awful situation for you…and him."

"Yeah. But there's even a more depressing thought. If anything happens to Karen, Dustin will go to his biological father, and I may never get to see him."

"Sometimes life sucks," she muttered, thinking of Becca. "Especially when it comes to innocent kids."

"Yeah."

"I wish we didn't have to go back."

He adjusted the speed and controls to let a smaller boat go by. "It's too dangerous to stay out overnight. I left the helm for twenty minutes today, and you saw what almost happened. That was sloppy on my part. But damn, I'd do it all over again."

She snickered saluting him with her tea. "You did. Well, not the play-chicken-with-the-freighter part."

He reached over, picked up her hand and kissed it. "LuAnn, I enjoyed being with you today, and I don't just mean the making love. Most women probably want to hear words of commitment after sex, but I hope you understand I'm not ready for that conversation. We jumped into this a little early in this relationship, if you can even call it that after a day and a half. Are you satisfied spending a little more time together before we get into any serious discussions?"

"I'm very satisfied," she said, smiling. "Kayla and I talked about that last night. We agreed men just complicate your life."

Jace snorted at that. "Is that why she can't stand it that I don't fall all over all her Jace-hopefuls. Trust me—don't take any advice from my sister—or my mother."

"You have parents?"

"Uh-huh, and an older sister, a younger brother in Iraq, plus a niece and a nephew."

"Oh, that's so fun. Tell me about them."

* * * *

At seven thirty Jace guided *Golden Dreams* into its slip at the marina with the skill of having done it for the past three years. He cut the engines and hopped out to secure the lines while LuAnn was below gathering their things together.

He paused to scan the immediate area looking for anything suspicious. Satisfied, he called down to LuAnn, "I'm going to go get the truck so we can load the fish."

She came up the steps carrying a bag. "I'll go with you. I'm done here."

He took the bag from her and gave her a hand stepping out of the boat, looking down at her leg. "You seem to be moving around pretty good. Leg's okay?"

"Real good. I wish I knew what he threw at me. It was too heavy to be a knife. Are we going back to Kayla's?" she asked.

"No. I don't want to put her in jeopardy. Just in case that guy you saw with the binoculars was Kastansa. I have another idea."

He opened the pickup door to let her in then stowed the bag in the back, next to the big cooler he planned to put the fish in. As he started to get in behind the wheel, he caught sight of Calvin, the kid who stood guard over the marina in the evenings, coming toward him. Seeing Calvin was a rarity since he spent most of his time behind the counter, his nose buried in a mystery book. Jace waited for him, an uneasy feeling crawling up his spine.

Jace acknowledged him with a nod. "Hey Calvin, what's up."

"Just a curious. Did you send a fella in here to work on your Silverado today?"

Jace froze. "No. What are you talking about?"

"There was a guy here looking at your truck. He was fiddling with something underneath. I questioned what he was doing, and he said you were having a problem and asked him to check it out. I figured you would have told me if—"

"LuAnn get out, now!" Jace yelled as he ran around the truck to open her door.

She looked at him as if he'd lost his mind but obeyed quickly.

"What's—"

"Get away from the truck! You too, Calvin! Get over behind that trailer." He pointed to a semitrailer about thirty feet away.

When they were safely out of the way, Jace stooped down, lay on the ground and pulled himself underneath. What he saw made his blood run cold. Four sticks of dynamite were wired to the tailpipe.

He slid out from beneath the truck and called Calvin over. When LuAnn made a move to follow, he ordered her to stay put.

"What did that guy look like?" he asked Calvin.

"Big man, hairy, resembled an ape. He had dirty hands, looked like a mechanic. What's going on?"

Jace swore. "He wired dynamite to the tail pipe. I need wire snips."

Calvin's eyes widened. "Good God. Are you serious?"

"Very."

"Should I call the authorities?"

"No, I'll handle it. Get the snippers."

Calvin nodded numbly and hurried back to his workshop. Jace walked over to LuAnn. She was shaking. Obviously she'd heard what he said to Calvin. He took her in his arms and held her. "Don't worry, honey. I'm taking care of it."

"It…it was him…wa…wasn't it? What did he do?"

He rubbed her shivering arms as he saw Calvin returning. "Give me a minute. Right now stay here until I tell you it's safe."

"Be…be careful," she called after him, her voice trembling.

He strode over to the truck, pulled the snippers out of Calvin's stiff hand and told him to get back with LuAnn. Calvin obeyed with the speed of lightening.

Jace crawled under the truck, carefully snipped the wires and let the dynamite drop in his hand. He quickly surveyed the rest of the undercarriage then wiggled back out.

Once he was back on his feet, he pulled out his cell phone and called Logan.

"Sorry to bother you, pal, but I have a handful of dynamite here I don't know what to do with." Jace gave him a brief summary and told him where he was.

"Hang tight," Logan said. "I'll be right there."

Jace walked about twenty feet away and placed his precarious package on the ground. He then went back to his truck, took a blanket out of the back and carried it to LuAnn. She was pale as a ghost and shaking so hard he thought she might faint as she had once before. She gripped the edge of the blanket and seemed to draw herself inward.

"Can you get her a chair?" he asked Calvin. Calvin nodded and hurried away.

Jace wrapped the blanket around LuAnn and pulled her in his arms. "You're okay, sweetheart. We both are. I promised we'll get to the bottom of this."

She made a sound indicating she was listening but didn't speak. Calvin came back with two folding chairs. He opened them up, and Jace sat LuAnn into one. He stood up and gripped Calvin by the shoulders. "Young man, I don't have words to thank you. You saved both of our lives tonight and possibly more. Who knows how long it might have taken before that shit blew."

"Shouldn't we call the police?" he asked.

"I already did. They'll be here shortly." Jace pulled the second chair up in front of LuAnn and sat down. "Don't worry. Everything's going to be okay. I called my friend Logan, he works with the Duluth precinct…no connection with Superior," he added.

"Two days ago," she said softly as though speaking to herself. "I was a first-grade schoolteacher. My days consisted of teaching children how to cope in the world we live in. My evenings were spent preparing lessons, correcting papers, tending my plants and entertaining Max. Sometimes I watched TV, read or listened to music. The most dangerous thing I had to live with was a spread-legged chair that I continuously stubbed my toe on."

With sirens screaming in the distance, Jace took a deep shuddering breath. Both his sisters had told him numerous times he was an insensitive clod when it came to women. Reaching deep in his soul, he searched for the words she needed to hear.

He gave her a gentle shake so she'd look at him. "LuAnn, honey, listen to me. I could tell the way you were with Dustin that you are a wonderful teacher. And you'd also make a terrific mother. I promise you, we'll get to the bottom of this, and you'll get your life back."

A single tear traced a path down her pale cheek. "Maybe I don't want it back."

Chapter Sixteen

Bart placed the ten stacks of hundred-dollar bills in a bag, scowling at the small bundle it made. It was like pocket change to a man like him. Why the hell would somebody bother blackmailing him for such a paltry amount? If he were in a humorous mood, he'd call it an insult.

But he was *not* in a humorous mood. First he had a lousy round of golf, then Porter hits him up for a gambling stake and top that off with Murdock's phone message. It was enough to put a saint in a rotten mood. He couldn't believe Murdock's nerve. What a jackass. What if Gladys had heard that message? And now he expected Bart to send the balance of his fee. Was it possible the man was so dense he didn't know that Bart already knew everything? Or was he playing games. Even if he was, if Bart didn't send the money, Murdock would be under no obligation to honor the discretion part of their deal. Who knows who he'd talk to. God Almighty—the press?

And to top the day off, now he had to go out to the park and throw money in a *garbage can.* Couldn't he or she have been a little more creative?

At eight thirty Bart went up to the attic to activate the video camera. The house was quiet except for soft music coming from Chelsea's room. Thank God it wasn't blaring, he already had a headache. He'd peeked in at Gladys and found her either sleeping or passed-out in her little den hideaway. Interestingly enough, the door was open. It hadn't been open when he'd looked in on her earlier.

Bart didn't know the status of LuAnn and Murdock. He hadn't heard from Kastansa since the whiner dropped the money off, complaining that he hadn't been to bed in three days, so he was probably home sleeping. Just as well, he didn't want Kastansa knowing about the blackmail fiasco. *Hell,* Bart thought grumpily, *maybe it was him.*

By the time he got back downstairs it was eight forty. He grabbed the brown paper bag and walked out the back door. It wasn't dark yet, so he didn't need a flashlight to find his way. The can was exactly as it had been yesterday when he'd checked it out. He looked around to make sure nobody was watching—or to see if someone *was* watching— then dropped the bag inside. As he slipped it through the swinging top, he noted something he hadn't noticed the day before. The top looked quite heavy. It could take a minute or so for somebody to pull it off, reach down in the near-empty can for the bag, and put the cover back on—providing they did put it back on. Either way, he hoped it would be long enough to identify the person. For sure he'd get the size and stature, maybe hair length and color if they weren't wearing a disguise.

Back at the house, he grabbed the keys to his Mercedes and headed for the garage. A sharp voice from the den stopped him.

"Where the hell are you going?" It was Gladys. She stood in the doorway of the den and didn't appear to be drunk at all. *Just a matter of time,* he thought. She must have slept it off.

"For a drive," he announced, barely sparing her a glance.

"Going to see that Jacobs bitch, I suppose."

That stopped him short. How the hell did she know about Olivia? Was she having him followed? If she was fishing, he wasn't going to take the bait.

"I'm going to have something to eat. It's Juanita's day off in case you haven't noticed. Unless you want to cook?" he asked snidely.

Gladys snorted. "Go fuck yourself—or whoever else you want to." She whirled around and slammed the door behind her.

Bart hopped in his car, backed out and took off. It was 9:05.

* * * *

Jace drove past the farm a mile then doubled back, checking for a tag-along. LuAnn had fallen asleep with her head on his lap. He had his fingers in her hair enjoying the silky feel. Her statement about not wanting her life back had thrown him for a loop. He wasn't exactly sure where that was coming from, and with Logan showing up moments later, he didn't have time to question her.

Logan had arrived at the marina with a bomb squad. He chastised Jace for removing the dynamite himself. Well, yeah, he admitted that may not have been the smartest thing to do, but he wanted it off his truck.

After Calvin identified the picture of Kastansa, he was delighted when Logan asked if he could pick him out of a lineup. You'd have thought the kid was asked to star in a mystery movie.

LuAnn sparked Logan's curiosity just by being there. She spoke only when spoken to, saying as little as possible, clutching the blanket around her like a shield of armor. All the while she continued to shake. When Jace asked her if she wanted to see a doctor, she adamantly declined, said she just wanted to go to the truck…if it was safe.

When he joined her half an hour later, she'd managed a smile for him then lay down with her head on his thigh.

Jace pulled in and parked behind the cabin to hide the truck from the main road, even though it was a mile away. He gave his snoozing passenger a gentle shake. "LuAnn, we're home."

She sat up with a start, fear in her wide eyes. "Where…are we? Why is it so dark?"

"We're at my father's cabin in the woods. We're safe here." He sure as hell hoped he wasn't lying to her. "How are you doing?" he asked.

"I'm hungry," she said with a little smile.

"Me too. We have the bag of groceries in the back from the boat. There are always some non-perishables left here in the pantry too. We can fix a snack using whatever we have, then light a fire. How does that sound?"

She nodded eagerly.

He got out, went to the back and retrieved the bag, while she followed, still clutching the blanket around her.

"It smells earthy, like a forest. I can't believe how dark it is. It doesn't seem like it should be that late."

"It isn't. There's a heavy cloud cover. Probably more rain coming. Plus we *are* in the woods." Balancing the bag, he reached down into a clay pot and pulled out a key.

"Wonderful security," she said dryly.

Jace laughed, happy to see her back in good spirits. "There's not much here to steal. No television, no computer or electronics. Dad keeps a couple of shotguns and a twenty-two pistol to shoot varmints, but they're well hidden. He and I used to come out here hunting when I was a kid."

"You don't anymore?" she asked as he pushed the door open, flicked a light on and stood back waiting for her to enter.

"He has a bad hip, took a tumble from a ladder. We still come out every fall, but he does his hunting with a camera."

She stopped inside the door turning in a circle, a look of awe on her face. Surveying the room through her eyes, he imagined it was quite impressive. Built of pine logs, it was one huge room with a five-foot wide-open stairway to a loft that made up the only bedroom. Below the stairs was a half bath and pantry.

"My dad built this cabin thirty years ago, all the bookshelves, the log furniture, the cupboards, everything. He really is quite a handyman—and a photographer. He took most of the pictures on the walls."

"This is not the work of an ordinary handyman."

Logan laughed. "You're right. He spent forty years building houses for a living."

"I love this place," she whispered, a note of reverence in her voice.

"It is nice," Jace admitted, setting his bag on the counter. Grabbing a couple of logs from the wood box, he laid them in the fireplace then knelt down to strike a match to the kindling beneath.

She walked over to study a framed photo of a boy about three years old holding grass out to a deer. "Did your father take this one?" she asked.

"Ah…no…that's actually one of mine."

She turned to give him a surprised look. "You take photos too."

He stood up wiping his hands on the back of his jeans. "Yeah, of sorts. He taught me that too. That's Dustin just a few months after he came into my life."

She smiled at him. "You love that boy, don't you?"

"As much as if he were my own."

"I learned something about you here in this cabin."

"Yeah? What?

"You're a better photographer than you are a musician."

"What? You don't like my music?"

"Music?" she asked, lips twitching.

"Ouch. Come and help me with this food. I don't cook any better than I play piano."

"What did you do about the salmon?" she asked, picking her pajamas and toothbrush out of the bag.

"Gave them to Calvin." At her crestfallen look, he added, "He said he'd take a snapshot of the big one with his cell phone, besides we can go out again sometime."

"I had fun today," LuAnn said. "Except for the part about almost blowing up."

"If you're really hungry for salmon, there's some in the freezer. It's the one thing I do know how to cook."

She shook her head making her hair swing. "No, that's okay. Maybe another time." The sadness in her downcast eyes was palpable, the tone of her voice flat.

Jace took a bottle of red wine out of the refrigerator along with two glasses from the cupboard. "If it's any comfort, Logan said the makeshift bomb probably wouldn't have gone off. It needed a detonator. He said either that yahoo didn't know anything about explosives or he was interrupted before he finished. Usually a car bomb is connected to the battery."

"Usually?" she repeated grimly. "Does this sort of thing happen often?"

Jace filled the two glasses with wine and handed one to her. "First time for me, scared the shit out of me too. Whether it was loaded to go off or not, I didn't want to be driving around with that package tied to my tail pipe."

"So it could have gone off?"

"Practically speaking, no, but according to Logan, dynamite is volatile and when it gets hot you can't be real sure what it will do."

LuAnn blinked rapidly. "He's not going to give up is he?"

Jace saw the fear come back in her beautiful brown eyes. He hated that look, and he hated Bart Harridan for putting it there.

"Logan was going to put an APB out for him. Calvin identified him off the picture I had. No doubt about it. It was Kastansa. With any luck he'll get picked up in the next day or two."

She didn't look convinced, so he bent across the counter and did the only thing he could think of right now to get her mind off Kastansa. He kissed her.

He'd meant it to be a peck on the lips, but she reached around his neck and held on, putting her own energy into the kiss. His body responded like putting a flame to gasoline. He was about to come around the counter and get serious when she released him.

Her lips were puffy and wet—they turned up into a tremulous smile. "Thanks, I needed that."

He wanted to tell her he needed a hell of a lot more than a kiss but suspected she wasn't ready for that so soon after Kastansa's little dynamite trick. Inwardly sighing he lifted his glass to her. "Here's to a phenomenal day."

She clinked her glass against his. "I'll second that. Now, before we do anything else, show me where you hide those shotguns."

* * * *

Bart was in a far better mood when he returned home at ten thirty than he had been when he left. Not because he'd seen Olivia—the gallivanting broad wasn't home—but because he'd stopped at Clancy's. He'd found a cute little divorcee who was looking to spread her wings and her legs. When she got a look at his Mercedes, she was more than willing to go for a ride in it. Since she only lived a couple of blocks away, he was able to do her and still be home at a decent hour to check the barrel.

That was the other thing that lightened his mood. Ten thousand dollars was a cheap price to pay to find out who was trying to jerk him off with a blackmail threat. When he found out who it was, he'd have Kastansa take care of it.

First thing he had to do was verify the money pickup. He didn't want to remove the camera until he confirmed that. Without going through the house, he grabbed a flashlight from the car and made his way through the trees to the park.

The can was there with the cover on. So far so good. Glancing around to ascertain he wasn't being seen, he lifted the heavy cover off and shined his light inside. The can was still about an eighth full as it had been before.

The brown paper bag was gone.

Bart Harridan resisted the urge to whistle as he hurried back to the house. All was quiet on the home front. The wino queen must have finally drunk herself into a stupor, and there was no light under Chelsea's door.

He went straight to the attic, retrieved the camera and carried it down to his office. There he connected it to his TV and hit play. He poured himself some Scotch and sat down in his favorite reclining chair to enjoy a great show.

* * * *

LuAnn stared at the flames dancing in the fireplace while Jace worked the poker to reposition the burning logs. They'd finished the ham and cheese sandwiches she'd made, and the wine had relaxed her. With growing interest she watched his backside as he bent to pick up more wood. He had a terrific body.

It wasn't the first terrific male body she'd seen, and she wondered why his was the first one she'd wanted in a very, very long time. Roger had looked good, but she never felt a quiver of excitement looking at him. Also he had a flat butt. In comparison Jace's tight back-end looked so damn good in jeans, she had a strange desire to slip her hands in the back pockets and yank him against her. Then she had to wonder where that ludicrous thought came from.

What was it about Jace Murdock, especially since he was the person who'd introduced her to the element of danger she was suddenly living under? She noted his time weathered hands and rugged features and recalled the touch of those long fingers, tender not only when they'd made love but when he was protecting her, looking out for her. Having a man look out for her was a new experience in her life, and she rather enjoyed it.

Finished with the fire, Jace sat down beside her and slipped an arm around the back of the sofa. Immediately she snuggled up against him. He kissed the top of her head murmuring something she couldn't hear, but the mere vibrations of his husky voice turned her insides to jelly. His hand rubbed her shoulder in a way that sent shivers through her system and had nothing to do with the temperature of the room.

All was well, but she needed to set something straight.

"Jace?"

"Hmmm?" he made a sound that acknowledged the question in her voice, all the while his tongue doing magic to her ear.

"Oh, now if you do that, I won't be able to talk," she managed to say through breathy gasps.

"Then don't talk."

She wanted nothing more than to tear her clothes off and leap on top of him, but she had to clarify something first. "Sorry. But it's necessary. Just give me a minute's attention."

"Honey, you have all my attention for as long as you want it."

She laughed softly and wriggled away from him. "If I don't say this now, I'll never get it said."

He stayed where he was, allowing her the space she wanted. "Go ahead," he said. "Talk."

The only light in the room came from the crackling fireplace. The soft glow helped give her courage. "I…ah…sort of jumped into this thing a little sooner than I maybe should have. I'm concerned you might get the idea that I'm…you know…in the habit of practicing casual sex. It may sound cliché, but I don't normally do this—"

"Do you think that I do?"

She lifted her shoulders uncertainly. "Well, you're a man—"

"What does that have to do with it?"

"Aren't men always wanting to have sex, anytime?"

"Maybe want to, yes, but do it, no."

"I've been divorced eight months, and I haven't even dated."

"Yeah, I got that picture."

"Then you understand that it's been that long since I've done what I did today—twice."

"I have news for you, you didn't do it alone."

She felt her face heat up, but she smiled.

Jace picked up her hand. "Let me ask you something, if I was the kind of man you seem to think every man is, don't you think I'd be carrying condoms?"

"Well, I…" She found it hard to concentrate when he played with her fingers. "I never thought about it."

"While you're mulling that over, I'll give you something to chew on. I've been divorced well over a year, and today was the first time I've had sex since my wife."

"But…I understood Kayla set you up numerous times."

"True, at least in the beginning, but going out on a date doesn't necessarily mean having sex. I'm very choosy about who I hop in the sack with."

"You mean you…today…when we…"

He laughed. "I'd say we broke our fast together."

She gave him a sideways look. "That's not just a line is it?"

He lifted her hand to his lips and kissed the palm. "Not even I am that creative. Besides why would I need to give you a line, you're a sure thing."

She grabbed a sofa pillow and hit him over the head with it.

"Ow. Hey that hurt." He tossed the pillow aside, wrapped his arms around her and wrestled her to the floor. When she tried to wriggle free, he climbed on top of her, held her down and lowered his mouth to hers. She melted instantly, and the kiss went from fun and laugher to raw passion with the velocity of exploding fireworks.

He picked her up and carried her up the stairs to the loft. They slowly undressed each other, and LuAnn discovered she'd never wanted anything as badly as she wanted the heat of Jace's body against hers. In his own eagerness his tongue circled her mouth, and his big hands stroked her from shoulders to hips to back as he rocked his pelvis against hers, reducing her to liquid silk.

Responding without hesitation, she matched him thrust for thrust, hungrily, greedily trying to devour him. Without taking his mouth from hers, he laid her on the bed and came down on top of her.

She sensed he was holding himself back. Feeling sexy, hot and reckless, she wrapped her arms and legs around his firm smooth back, pulling him closer, until he buried himself inside her.

Her body on fire with satin heat, she screamed out as her hands continued to explore, enjoying the different textures of his masculinity. His mouth went from her lips to her neck, to her ear, first on one side then the other, all the while his hips moved rocking slowly between her legs into her fluid heat.

With every motion he made, the sensations escalated until she gasped for air.

"Honey," he asked, stopping long enough to breathe himself. "Are you okay?"

"Yes," she panted. "Don't stop."

He reached down between them and plucked her sensitive bud. Her body tightened around his engorged erection, and she knew instant release. Moments later he made his own soft wailing sound and collapsed on top of her.

In her mind she shouted words of jubilation, but she had no energy left to force them from her lips.

He rolled to his side, pulling her with him, refusing to break the connection. For a long time he simply held her while their collective breathing subsided.

"What just happened?" she asked when she could find her voice.

"I'm not sure," Jace rasped. "But I think we need a fire extinguisher."

She managed an impetuous laugh. "Never in my wildest fantasies did I imagine it could be like this."

"I guess that means we're on the same page," he said huskily.

Chapter Seventeen

Staring at the television screen as the video ended and automatically rewound, Bart Harridan could feel the blood all but boiling in his veins. His head throbbed, and his chest felt like a truck had parked on it. He hadn't moved other than to blink for an hour and a half.

The first fifteen minutes of the tape had shown nothing but him dropping the money in the trash container. Then two young boys came by on bicycles. They sat at a bench near the barrel and ate from a McDonald's bag. When they finished, they dumped the bag in the trashcan and left.

Twenty minutes later an older man wearing baggy sweatpants and a scrubby jacket came to sit on the bench. He eyed the barrel for a moment then got up and pushed the revolving cover back, peered inside then reached way down the full length of his arm. Bart about had an apoplectic fit. If the homeless guy found the money, he'd sure as hell make off with it. However, instead of a brown paper bag, he retrieved the McDonald's bag the boys had discarded. He sat back on the bench and feasted on half a hamburger and some leftover fries. Then he lay down on the bench and closed his eyes.

Bart had kept his eye on the can, but nothing happened. Sometime later the sleeping bum got up from his nap and left. Bart breathed a sigh of relief and waited and waited.

The next thing he saw was himself walking up to check if the bag was gone.

That's when he started swearing. Hell and damnation. Somebody must have grabbed it from behind. Even if they did, the cover should have swung open forward. He must have missed it. The homeless man had used a bit of exertion to reach in but had managed to snag the McD's bag. Anyone else would have had to go through the same procedure. How had he missed it?

The machine made a clicking sound and started to replay. Bart got up and pulled his chair closer. An hour and forty-five minutes later, his eyes burned and the pain in his head had escalated to colossal proportions.

Charging to his feet, he grabbed his flashlight, stormed out of the house and stalked into the park. Once he got to the can, he didn't need the flashlight as the overhead vapor light lit up the whole area.

Swearing profusely, Bart yanked the cover off and upended the can. Trash scattered around his feet. He kicked at it, furiously looking for that damn brown bag. Then he found it crumpled in a tight little ball—empty. He stared at it, his breath coming in short gasps trying to wrap his brain around what he was seeing.

Then he saw the answer out of the corner of his eye. A small, approximate three-inch square, hole had been cut into the backside of the barrel near the bottom. Bart's anger was so intense he nearly vomited. Leaving the mess he'd made behind, he stomped back to the house wondering who he could kill to pacify his rage. His big hand squeezed down on the ball that had held his money and wished it was somebody's throat between his fingers. He just didn't know whose throat it should be.

* * * *

When LuAnn awoke, she rolled over to press her body against Jace as she'd done at least twice during the night. Her body met with empty space. Slightly disappointed she figured he must be an early riser. It had been a long time since she felt the desire to have a man next to her when she woke up. Maybe she never had. When she was married to

Roger, she'd always been relieved to find him gone in the morning.

Stretching like a content cat, she opened her eyes to sunlight overhead. She hadn't realized the night before that there were two skylights in the loft. Mixed with the blue of the sky were different shades of green from the trees. There must be some big old trees on this lot to be tall enough to tower over the cabin.

She was anxious to get a look at the area surrounding the cabin in the daylight, but since the roof of the loft extended to the floor on either side, there were no windows other than the skylights.

She knew, however, there was one in the bathroom on the back wall. When she got up, she realized she'd slept naked; another first among many since she'd met Jace two days ago. Wishing she had her robe, she quickly grabbed her clothes which were neatly lying over a chair. She knew for a fact they hadn't been left there in the frenzy last night. Of course, Jace had thoughtfully gathered them up and put them on the chair.

She hurried to the little bathroom, took care of urgent business then glanced out the window. Jace's pickup was right outside, and she saw a small, red, hip-roofed barn about a hundred feet away.

As he'd mentioned last night the cabin was nestled in the middle of a heavily wooded forest. Except for a small pond and the barn, all she saw was trees: tall pine trees, impressive oaks, maples, birch, it was spectacular—and she only had a view from one window. A movement in the woods to her left caused her heart to quicken and recall the reason they'd come here.

When the moving figure came closer, she recognized Jace on the back of a chestnut horse, picking its way on what she could now see was a path through the pines. She released a rush of air, not aware that she'd been holding her breath.

Would her life ever get back to normal?

When he looked up at the window, she quickly backed away since she stood there with no clothes on. She managed to laugh at herself when she thought about baring her nude body to half the population of Japan just yesterday. Now there was a first!

Expecting Jace to come back in the cabin any minute, she showered quickly, dried off and donned the same faded Capri jeans she'd put on two nights ago before she went to the basement to find her birth certificate—a lifetime ago.

She really had to either go home and get some clothes or go shopping.

Digging through the drawers in the vanity, she located a brush that likely belonged to Jace's mother. Didn't matter—she was desperate. Anyway it was better than imagining it had belonged to one of his old girlfriends. Pulling the brush through her long hair, she remembered him saying he hadn't had sex since his divorce over a year ago. Hard to believe but…maybe she did have a lot to learn about men, Jace Murdock in particular. He didn't seem to fit the mold for most men in her world.

She tied her hair back at the nape of her neck with a ribbon she'd found in the drawer with the brush, made the tousled bed and headed for the kitchen with food on her mind.

She was halfway down the stairs when Jace came in. He stopped with the door in his hand and gazed up at her, a look of appreciation on his face. His vivid green eyes sparkled with humor and something else. It made her feel warm and sexy. Smiling, she sashayed down the wide staircase feeling like Scarlet O'Hara, in jeans that could probably stand up in the corner by themselves, no less.

His gaze flicked over her from top to bottom, zeroing in on her torso. "You look good enough to eat," he remarked.

LuAnn had a hard time keeping a stupid grin off her face. She had no experience with male/female banter, but she gave it a shot. "Does that mean you don't want any breakfast?"

He closed the door and locked it. "What are you offering?"

Drawing on her paltry flirting skills, she put her hands on her hips and walked up to him, going so close their bodies touched. "What's your pleasure," she whispered throatily.

His brows rose, then he tipped her head up and pressed a firm kiss on her lips. That's when she did something she'd been thinking about since last night. She put her arms around him and slipped her hands into his back pockets. Then standing on her tiptoes, she jerked him roughly against her groin. "This," she said, aware that her face was heating up from her unaccustomed wild behavior. She could feel him growing hard. It sent a tingle through her entire body. Her excitement increased when he slipped his hands around her grabbing her buttocks. Something thumped the back of her leg; she realized he held a bag in one hand.

"What do you have there?" she asked.

He pressed his erection toward her. "You mean this?"

"No, I mean that silly plastic bag you're carrying."

He brought his hand out to produce the bag, the handles wrapped around his wrist. "You mean this one?"

She glanced at the mysterious bag, frowning. It held something long and narrow. Her curiosity got the best of her. "Yes, that one. What's in it?"

"Fresh eggs, from the farmer up the road. He has chickens."

Her eyes widened. She pulled her hands out of his pockets and stepped back. "Hand them over."

"You're throwing me over for eggs?"

"Not any old eggs. Fresh eggs. We have leftover cheese and ham. I'll make omelets. You make the coffee. You *can* make coffee can't you?"

He threw his head back and laughed. "LuAnn Barstow, you are one crazy woman."

* * * *

Bart paced his office willing Armon Kastansa to call him. He'd tried calling his cell, but the phone was either off or out of the service area. Heaven forbid the man would accept a roaming call. Where the hell was he anyway?

And where were LuAnn and Murdock? Were they still alive, or had Kastansa taken care of them as he'd bragged about? Bart ground his teeth together in frustration.

Who in bloody blazes had picked up that money? He guessed the person had been hiding in the bushes and made the pickup minutes after he'd thrown it in the can. The tape was worthless, and now all he could do was start killing people off hoping eventually he'd get the right person. Of course, that was an insane idea. Maybe he was losing his mind.

For all he knew it could be the neighbor across the street. Huh, now there was a thought. The man had lost his job a month ago. He lived in a big house, and all he had for income was selling silly-assed birdhouses he made. Who the hell wanted a birdhouse anyway? All birds were good for was shitting on your car.

Damn he wanted a drink, but he hadn't eaten yet. He needed to keep a clear head. Make a list of suspects. He hadn't slept all night, had been too wound up since watching that tape for the second time. He took a deep breath and collapsed in his chair.

Shit and damn! He was getting light-headed; if he didn't eat something, he was going to work himself into a heart attack. Picking up the phone, he called the housekeeper and gave her an order for eggs and toast and coffee—immediately if not sooner. His patience was wearing thin.

That finished, he sat back and willed himself to calm down, think rational thoughts. Reason out his options. Best-case scenario, he'd never hear from the blackmailer again.

Hah! Fat chance. So the other alternative was he'd get another note asking for more money. At that point he could make a new, better plan to catch the culprit. A bomb, that's it. He could stick a bomb in with the money; let it blow them to smithereens. Then he could just wait and find out who in his miserable life was missing.

* * * *

After breakfast Jace took LuAnn outside to show her around. She was ecstatic when she saw the horse tied to an old-western hitching post behind the house.

"Dad built it," he told her.

She walked tentatively up to the horse and ran her hand over his velvety nose. "What a beautiful animal."

"Do you ride?" Jace asked.

She shook her head reaching up to rub the horse's ears. "No, I've never even been on one. What's his name?"

"*Her* name is Sandy. Kayla gave it to her. It's the one she usually rides when she comes out. I brought her up here because I thought you might like to get on her—if you're not too sore that is."

LuAnn flushed when he winked at her.

"My leg is fine," she said quickly.

"I wasn't referring to your—"

"Don't worry, that part of me is fine too."

"That's good to know, because I have plans for this afternoon."

This time she laughed. "You are insatiable, aren't you?"

His eyes got a far-away smoky look. "Yeah and I don't understand it. I've never been this way before. I think it's you. I look at you, and I can't wait to get your clothes off."

She didn't want to tell him that she felt the same way. Just the sound of his husky voice had her wanting to fling herself into his arms like she had on the boat. She wanted to press against him, wanted to… "If I get on, will you lead her?"

His smile told her he read her thoughts. "Sure, come here." He walked around to the side, and she followed him. He instructed her to put her foot in the stirrup and one hand on the horn. A second later his strong hands had lifted her into the saddle, and she was looking down at him wide-eyed.

He took the reins in his hand and headed for the path in the woods.

"Did you know," she said from her perch, "that your hair is the exact same color as Sandy's?"

"Yeah," he muttered. "Kayla's mentioned that a few times."

"The two of you are really close aren't you?"

"Uh-huh. My other sister is seven years older than we are, and my brother is five years younger so we pretty much grew up together."

"That's so neat to be close to someone. I…I never had that in my life."

"Never?" he asked, glancing up at her.

"No, there was my mother, but I barely remember her. I'm not even sure I do."

"What about your grandmother?"

LuAnn made a rude sound. "You met her. What do you think?"

"I don't know. Her friend Nelly made some derogatory remarks, and Emma, your grandmother, jumped all over her. I got the feeling she was defending you."

"She doesn't even like me. At least not since…since I was a teenager."

"What happened when you were a teenager?"

His question was matter-of-fact, but LuAnn knew he'd heard the word *tramp* from Nelly. Gram wasn't being defensive; she was humiliated. LuAnn had to end this conversation, it was bordering on uncomfortable.

"You know, just ordinary teenage stuff," she said evasively.

"Like what?"

"Like I didn't have a mother, and my dad didn't care a whit about where I went or when I came home—or even *if* I came home."

"Is that when you got into trouble with the police?"

"You might say that." She leaned forward and patted Sandy's neck. "I think I could get into this riding business. Maybe you can give me some lessons."

The smile he gave her told her she didn't fool him one bit. He knew she was hiding something, and she knew it would keep coming up until he found out what it was.

Becca was a private thing in her life, and she wasn't ready to share it with anyone.

* * * *

"Mr. Harridan, it's Armon."

"Where the hell have you been?"

Armon Kastansa was seriously starting to dislike his employer. "I told you I had to get some sleep. I just now woke up."

"What happened with LuAnn and Murdock—are they dead?"

Kastansa took a long pull from his coffee cup. He was not anxious to share his news on that subject. "Not exactly."

"Dammit, quit beating around the bush and tell me," Harridan demanded.

"Well, here's what happened: I planted some dynamite under his truck, and the bastard must have found it because it didn't blow." He didn't mention that he hadn't put a bug on the Silverado because he'd expected it to pulverize.

Harridan blew a deep audible sigh into the phone. "Where are they?"

"Like I said, I had to get some sleep, so I don't know. But I have GPS tracers on both their cars. Neither one has moved for a couple of days, but as soon as one does I'll be on it like dog shit on your shoe."

He heard Harridan mumble something unintelligible, and he could tell by the tone that it was aimed at him. He was beginning to wonder how bad he needed this job, but looking at the other side, that SOB Murdock was pissing him off something fierce. If he was going to kill the man, he might as well get paid for it.

"Don't worry Mr. Harridan. I'll take care of them one way or another."

* * * *

LuAnn left Jace in the barn to take care of his horses while she walked up to the cabin to make some lunch and use his phone to call the neighbor who'd check on her house. Her own cell had died some time ago, so he'd suggested she use his.

It was sitting on the counter with his truck keys.

She went to the bathroom, washed her hands and going back to the kitchen thinking about lunch, punched in the number.

"Hello."

"Hello, Tom, its LuAnn checking back with you. Sorry it took so long I've been…involved in things. What did you find over there? A broken window?"

"Nope. No broken window," Tom said. "The back patio door was unlocked though."

"Oh dear, I must have left it open when I let Max in. Well, at least I don't have to fix a window."

"There was a vase on the coffee table that was smashed to smithereens though, so if you heard glass breaking that was probably it. I did close the basement window. Are you going to tell me what went on over there?"

"Sorry, I don't have time right now. I'll explain everything when I get home."

"When will that be? Max has been over at your door every night."

LuAnn smiled hearing about her faithful friend. "I'm hoping not long. Thanks, Tom."

She started to hang up when he said, "Oh wait, there was something else. I found a hammer by the open window in the basement—" LuAnn's heart did a double take. So that was what Kastansa had thrown at her— "I didn't think it was yours because it had a name etched into the wooden handle. Anyway I left it on your table."

"A name?" she repeated, holding her breath.

"Yeah, it was quite clear—Murdock. Is that someone you know?"

LuAnn dropped the phone on the counter. Breathing heavily, she quickly picked it up and said in a constricted voice, "I'm afraid so."

"LuAnn, if that's Jace Murdock be careful. He's a slick ambulance chasing lawyer, or at least he was."

The tone of Tom's voice was scaring her. "What do you mean, *was*?" she asked.

"The guys at work were talking about him a few days ago. I don't know all the details, but he was defending this woman who murdered her husband, and he entered some false evidence and got her off. Scuttlebutt is he was having an affair with her." LuAnn swallowed a lump building in her throat as Tom kept talking. "A few weeks earlier he got a drunk driver freed who put an old lady in the hospital. The good news is the shyster got disbarred for the false evidence trick, and he's not practicing anymore. All I'm saying is, if you're dealing with him in any way, be careful, he's slick."

LuAnn managed to thank him and hung up.

Murdock!

A slick, disbarred lawyer.

False evidence.

A hammer with his name on it.

Collapsing on a stool, she tried to think. Her brain was mush. Murdock. Was that how he'd found her so quickly in the pouring rain that night, why he'd held her mouth shut so she couldn't scream? It wasn't possible. Was it?

Why would Jace want to kill her? Did she inadvertently have something to do with those cases? What did he really want from her? And why had he never mentioned he'd been a lawyer? She was quite certain she would have remembered something that significant.

Was the story about Bart Harridan's wife looking for her all a made up lie? Did it all have to do with Becca? It seemed every time the subject of thirteen years ago came up, he got very interested. She had to think, but to do that she had to get away from him.

She grabbed his truck keys and ran.

* * * *

Bart was coming out of his office when he saw Chelsea bounding down the steps from her room. When she saw him, she slowed to a walk looking at him like a deer in headlights.

"Chelsea, are you afraid of me?" he asked.

"No…no, sir. It's just that…that Mom gets upset when I run in the house."

"So, where are you off to in such a rush?" Bart gave her his best politician's smile. He knew he was being uncharacteristically friendly, but he didn't want her telling people he was an ogre.

She shrugged. "Just across the street to Betty's house. Her father made this neat little three-story birdhouse she wants me to help her paint. You wanna come see it?" she asked brightly.

Like he'd actually want to see a ridiculous bird condo. "Sorry, I don't have time now. But tell me, Betty's father, didn't he lose his job?"

Her face saddened. "Yeah, he worked in the paint department at Menards, but they laid him off."

"So how does he make his house payments?"

Chelsea flashed him a proud smile. "His wife, Debbie, is a vice-president at some big corporation, and he sells his birdhouses in a boutique downtown."

Oh, wow, Bart thought sarcastically, that must bring in a bundle. "All right then, go have fun."

She gave him a little wiggle finger wave. "Okay, bye."

She'd taken three measured steps when the doorbell rang. Looking back at him, she asked, "You want me to get that."

"Sure go ahead." He waited at his office door to see who it was.

She opened it to none other than Judge Ramous Porter. Porter gave his daughter a smile as she gave him a quick greeting and brushed past him.

"Hello, Bart," Porter said. "I thought we might need to talk."

Bart motioned him into his office then closed the door firmly behind them.

"I thought you left for Las Vegas this morning," Bart said, indicating Porter to sit down while he took his place behind his desk.

Porter took a seat in a cushy side chair. "I was, but I got to thinking about what you said and decided you were probably right. If news got out that I had a gambling problem, things could get sticky."

Bart raised his dark brows. "You're giving up gambling?"

"Well, no, but I'll stick to private games. Much safer that way."

Bart grunted. "I guess. So to what do I attribute the honor of this visit?"

Porter shuffled in his seat. "Well, I still need that stake. I swear I'll pay you back in three days. You can trust me just like I trusted you to pay me when you asked me to fix it so Jace Murdock got disbarred. I put myself on the line for that you know. I had to call in a lot of markers. What he did wasn't all that unheard of, and it wasn't grounds for disbarment."

"That son-of-a-bitch got Alexia Jacobs off for murdering my son," Bart sputtered angrily. "And those damn women advocates were prepared to give him a fucking medal."

"Yeah, well, I can assure you I didn't make any friends by getting him expelled—a lot of men felt the same way. Maybe you should look at the big picture. If you want to run for a political office, Marley Jacobs would have been a burr in your saddle."

Bart wanted to argue that but he couldn't. Unfortunately the Judge was right.

Bart opened a drawer, pulled out the Scotch, two glasses and his checkbook.

Chapter Eighteen

From the trees Jace saw the dust kicked up by his truck as it raced up the gravel road toward the main highway. He couldn't believe what he was seeing. Twenty minutes ago she'd kissed him firmly on the lips then put on a display of wiggling her fanny as she left the barn. They'd spent two hours riding, and she'd appeared to be having the time of her life.

Now she'd stolen his truck and was gone. What could possibly have happened in the last few minutes that would make her want to run away from him—if that's what she was doing. His mind vacillated from anger to cold fear. With the topper on the truck, he couldn't see how many people were in it.

Was there a chance Kastansa had abducted her? For it to have happened that quickly, he'd have had to been in the truck waiting for her. But then, where was Kastansa's vehicle.

Then he remembered—she'd asked to use his phone. Pressed by apprehension and something he couldn't name, he charged into the cabin. There he spotted his phone still on the counter where he'd left it, minus the keys he'd also left there.

Before he could reach the phone, it rang. In his haste he flipped it open without checking caller ID. His worst fear was that Kastansa would be on the other end offering some sort of ultimatum. With that thought in mind, he put the phone to his ear but didn't speak. It took everything he had in him not to shout out LuAnn's name even though logic warned him it couldn't be her—she'd only left five minutes ago, and she didn't have a working phone.

"Jace? Are you there?" He recognized Kayla's voice. It had a hint of anxiety in it, and again his mind worked overtime as he imagined Kastansa harming his sister. The mental exertion had him breathless.

"Kayla, what's going on? Are you all right?"

He heard a little sob that tore at his gut. "I'm fine. It's Mom. She's in the hospital. They think she had a heart attack."

It was so not what he expected to hear; it took him a second to comprehend. "Mom?"

"Yes, Dad called. They took her by...by ambulance." She let out another bout of weeping.

"Where! Where did they take her?"

"St. M-Mary's. I'm on my way there now. Please hurry."

"I'll be right there."

He hung up the phone and reached for his keys.

Oh shit.

He had to breathe, had to think. He couldn't ask Kayla to come and get him, not in her distraught state. The only neighbor within five miles was the one who'd given him the eggs. He and his wife car-pooled, and they'd have left for work long ago. But the girls, Jessie and Mikaela, would be home. School was out for the summer, and both of them were old enough to drive.

He ran down to the barn, grabbed Sandy and mounted her bareback. Using the halter to guide her, he made it the half mile to the edge of the fence which was only thirty yards from the Johnson's farmhouse. Relieved to see both girls out in the yard, he jumped off the horse and released her.

Twenty-five minutes later Jessie dropped him off at St. Mary's. He'd called ahead to Kayla, and she was waiting for him.

"How is she?" he asked as he gave her a hug.

Tears welled up in her eyes. "They're doing some tests. Sounds like she has a blocked artery. She might need surgery."

"Can we see her?"

Kayla dried her eyes with a soggy looking tissue. "No, but you better go see Dad. He's beside himself. He told me she had some chest pains last week, and he wanted her to go to the doctor, but you know how stubborn she is." She snuffled and looked up at him. "Where's your truck?"

* * * *

LuAnn parked the Silverado at the Holiday Station down the street from her house. From there she walked, or rather ran, home. Her thighs were sore from riding, but it was nothing compared to the ache in her heart. But she couldn't think about that now. If she did, she would break into gut-wrenching tears. Somehow she'd managed to drive the thirty-five miles to her house by staying focused, trying to understand how this mess had all started. She let herself in with a key hidden in a crack in the front steps.

Everything looked the same as she'd left it with the exception of the shattered vase she'd received from Barb for Christmas last year. When her gaze fell on the hammer Tom had left on the table, she nearly lost it. Blinking rapidly she picked it up and turned it over in her hands. The etching was burned right into the wood and look like it might have been there a long time. Even worn, there was no mistaking the letters. M-u-r-d-o-c-k.

She had to hurry. At the least she had half an hour before Jace could get a ride to his house, get his car and show up here. Grabbing a small overnight bag, she zipped it open and began throwing things into it. Clothes and toiletries, underwear and running shoes, plus anything else she might need including her passport—and as an afterthought—the hammer.

She set the loaded suitcase by the door leading to the garage along with her purse, where she'd thrown the can of mace she kept in her nightstand drawer. As she raced through the house again looking for anything she might have missed, a sound from the patio door made her freeze.

Sneaking a look, she saw Max there calling for her to let him in.

She opened the door, grabbed Max and fell into a chair, pressing her face into his furry coat. The cat must have sensed her distress because he rubbed his face along her cheek, his internal motor running in a soft rumble.

Breathing deeply, swallowing hard, LuAnn refused to cry. She didn't have time for tears. Putting Max down she gave him his treat, stood there while he ate then picked him, kissed him goodbye and apologized for putting him outside. She then forced herself to close the door on his sad, confused look. As she turned to leave, a blinking light caught her attention. The phone…it must be the call she'd heard when she was downstairs looking through her father's files.

With an eerie feeling, she pressed the play button. *LuAnn, be careful I think someone is trying to harm you.* LuAnn's heart skipped a beat. It was a female voice LuAnn didn't recognize, but it sounded like the person had marbles or something in her mouth, like she was deliberately trying to disguise her voice. The caller ID said it was a *blocked call.* She didn't have time to ponder over it, besides it was a moot point now. What it told her was that someone in the world out there knew what was going on.

Before she left she debated watering her plants. There were so many it would take a good twenty minutes. She didn't have that kind of time.

A minute later she plugged her cell phone into the car charger then backed out of her garage and headed for the high bridge. She'd have to cross over into Duluth to head for the north shore. Jace had talked about his friend Logan, the Duluth detective, who lived near his grandmother. She owned a B&B somewhere up there. LuAnn didn't remember the name of it but was certain she would recognize it if she saw it. Surely there'd be billboards along the way to direct her.

She had absolutely no one to turn to and going to Logan was the only plan she could come up with. Her one hope was that Logan was an honest cop and he could shed some light on why Jace would attack her.

Had he wired the dynamite under his own truck when he parked that day before coming to the boat? That would explain why he had no concern about removing it himself.

Another idea struck her. Maybe Kastansa didn't even exist. Jace could have made him up. She'd gone to the truck when he claimed to have shown the photo to Calvin.

That's it. She could stop and question Calvin. Of course, what would that prove? So he showed a photo to Calvin and Logan? He might have cut it out of a magazine for all they knew. Or, she shuddered, maybe he pinpointed the lone diner at Applebee's in a flash of insight, a flesh and blood person she could identify with. In addition, his refusing to tell her who the intruder was until she mentioned she hadn't seen the man's face supported that theory. If that was true, she had no one to fear but Jace Murdock.

Leaving the city lights behind, she turned northeast to follow the shore of Lake Superior. A short while later she checked her cell phone to see if it had charged up enough to make a call. It looked like it had.

Pulling to the side at a scenic overlook, she took her phone and the fast-food bag she'd picked up on the way out of town and got out of the car. For a short time she stood watching and listening to the roar of the waves crashing into the rocks about thirty feet below. With each wave a misty spray shot into the air. There was something melancholy about watching crashing waves. Normally she loved the sight and sound, but tonight, a deep sense of sadness engulfed her.

Had she foolishly fallen in love with a devil in disguise? A man who was so good at acting he had made her feel, for the first time in her life, like she was special?

She remembered questioning him that first night as to how he'd found her so easily. When she'd seen the marks on his face, she'd actual suspected he'd been the man who'd attacked her in the basement. His reaction had been one of humor. That, strangely, was what had reassured her.

What about Kayla? Did she know what he was up to? LuAnn gave a mirthless laugh at that thought. She'd spent three days with him, a good share of it skin to skin, and *she* didn't have a clue what he was after. Besides, Kayla was his twin; she'd love him no matter what he did.

LuAnn opened her phone and flipped though the stored numbers. Then she realized she had nobody to call. Nobody cared where she was or what she was doing. Even her friend Barb, who constantly tried to get LuAnn to join her in doing things, was not that close of a friend—because LuAnn made no effort to cultivate the relationship.

But…maybe there was someone she could call. *Call me anytime even if it's just to talk.* Kayla had said those words when she tucked a piece of paper in LuAnn's pocket. Was it possible she was the mystery person calling to warn her that night she was in the basement? LuAnn searched her pockets, found the number and punched it in before she could change her mind. A message service came on. After the beep she opened her mouth to talk, but what could she say? A tear slid down her cheek as she hung up.

Looking out at the afternoon sun glistening over the water, she made a promise to herself. When this was over, she'd work at getting a life. Maybe she'd call that teacher Ron Bennet and go out with him. Sighing wistfully, she sat down on a stone bench and took the fast-food hamburger she'd bought out of its wrapper. Of course it was cold, but she was hungry, and it was better than nothing.

While she chewed the tasteless food, she wondered where Jace was. Was he worried or just concerned about his old pickup? He'd probably called one of his many relatives or friends to come and get him.

Life wasn't fair she told herself.

Yeah, well, nothing new there. You've known that since you were five.

* * * *

"She stole your pickup!" Kayla shrieked.

"I didn't say she stole it, I said she took it."

"What did you do to her?"

Jace gave his sister an exasperated frown. "I forced her to have sex then slapped her around."

"Be serious. What did you do?"

He glanced at the waiting room door wishing the doctor would come in and tell them something. "I didn't do anything. We went for a ride then she went in to make a phone call and fix lunch. I came up to the house in time to see the tailgate of the truck speeding up the road."

"Huh, I don't get it."

"Frankly, I don't either."

"Did you have sex with her?"

"What the hell does that have to do with anything?"

"Ah-ha. So you did have sex. How was that for her?"

Jace charged to his feet. "Kayla, you are way off base!"

She sucked her lower lip into her mouth and shrugged. "I'm just trying to help you out here. Women can be fickle about sex."

"She's not fickle! The sex was good! She climaxed three times! Satisfied!"

"Oops. Well, okay, then, sorry. I didn't realize you were in love with her. You've only known her—"

"I didn't say I was in love with her!"

"Maybe that's the problem?"

"Oh, for—" Jace stomped over to the window and stared out. "What is taking them so long?"

"Want me to go ask?"

His cell phone chimed, and Kayla raised her brows at the speed in which he answered it.

"Hello, LuAnn?"

"No, this is Stan Bender at the Holiday Station over on South Danube." That was LuAnn's street. Jace's heart rate kicked into drag racing speed. "One of the guys found a note with this phone number on a Chevy Silverado out back. It said to call you."

"Do you know who left the note?" Jace asked.

"Nope, but my man said he saw a woman drive it in."

"Was she alone?"

Stan held the phone to the side and hollered at somebody in the background. Jace heard a muffled voice then Stan came back on the line. "Yup, Rickie said she was alone, and he said the keys are in it."

"Thanks. I appreciate the call. I'll be there to pick it up as soon as I can."

"No problem. It's not in the way."

Jace closed the phone and looked at Kayla who'd come to her feet to stand beside him.

"They found her?"

"No, she abandoned the truck at a service station near her house."

"That's just plain weird," she said. Suddenly her eyes widened as though she had a bright idea. "Didn't you say she went into the cabin to make a phone call? Did you try redialing that number?"

"Yes."

When he didn't continue, Kayla spread her hands out in front of her. "And?"

Jace huffed out a breath of air. "She told me she was calling, Tom, her next door neighbor who'd checked on her house. I redialed the number and when he answered, the first thing he did was ask who I was. When I told him, he ordered me to leave her alone. Said she was a nice lady and didn't need a slime ball like me in her life."

Kayla stared at him with her mouth hanging open. "What in the world did she tell him about you?"

"It's not what she told him—it's what he told her that made her run." He thrust a frustrated hand through his hair. "At least the kid who called about the pickup said she was alone. That tells me no one else was involved."

Before she could ask what he meant by that, the doctor walked into the room.

He was smiling.

* * * *

"I got her," Armon Kastansa said with a cackling chuckle.

Damn, Bart hated that despicable laugh. "What do you mean you have her?"

"She's in her car driving up the north shore. I'm head'n out right now tryin' to catch up with her."

Bart needed a moment to think. It was too late to find out if LuAnn Barstow had written the note, and if Kastansa killed her, he'd never know. And, dammit, even if it forced him to pay another ten grand—even twenty, he wanted to know who it was. Then he wanted to kill the culprit himself—with his bare hands—if he could be guaranteed he'd get away with it.

He couldn't tell any of that to Kastansa without explaining about the blackmail.

"Just find out where she's going, but don't touch her."

"I thought you wanted her dead," Kastansa grumbled, clearly disappointed, his tone bordering on a whine.

"Things have changed. Just follow her and see if she starts throwing money around."

Kastansa harrumphed, "What about Murdock?"

"He's all yours. But you have plenty of time to do that. Right now stay on LuAnn's ass. Oh, and good job with the GPS tail."

Bart hung up disgusted with himself for complimenting the a-hole, but even stroking a-holes could pay off down the road.

* * * *

Relieved that his mother was improving, Jace asked Kayla to drive him to his truck.

He hated that his mind was elsewhere while she chatted happily about the stint they were going to put in their mother. Granted, he was concerned too, but LuAnn's situation was more urgent right now.

Kayla must have understood because when she dropped him off, she leaned over and kissed him on the cheek. "Keep me posted. And it's okay to fall in love."

Jace had snorted at her remark, but when he drove straight to LuAnn's house and found it buttoned up with no car in the garage, the tightness he felt in his chest had him wondering. Could you love someone you'd only known a few days? He didn't want to think about that right now. He just wanted to find her.

The only sign of life he found was a gray and white cat at the back patio door. Max, he supposed, the neighbor's pet. He bent down, stroked the cat and asked him if he knew where LuAnn was. Max's answer was to rub up against his leg and purr.

What if he picked up the cat and brought him back to the neighbor. Would the man give him the time of day? Jace didn't have to be a genius to know the answer to that.

Everything, he'd come to believe, concerning this whole damn fiasco seemed to stem from something that happened thirteen years ago. He could think of only one man who might be able to share some insight. With that notion in mind, he got back in his pickup and programmed his GPS for the Superior, Douglas County Police Station.

Chapter Nineteen

Surprised at how close it was, Jace drove up to a newer four-story building. He parked his car, walked inside and approached the receptionist's desk. A bright-eyed young woman looked up at him inquiringly.

He gave her a friendly smile which she reciprocated. "Hank Jamison here?" he asked.

"Sure," she nodded toward an open door directly to her left. She glanced at her switchboard, apparently to see if he was on the phone then called out, "Hank, someone's here to see you."

Hank appeared at his door, eyed Jace up and down then gestured him into his office. "Come on in."

Hank, a bit on the round side, dressed in full uniform, had a badge identifying him as Chief of Police. He was pleasant looking, but not smiling. Jace judged him to be around sixty.

He held out his hand. "Hank Jamison. What can I do for you today?"

Jace took the hand, gave it a firm shake and identified himself, "Jace Murdock."

Only a slight lifting of Jamison's brow told Jace he recognized the name.

Oh shit. That could be good or bad. There was no clue in the chief's stoic face.

Jamison took a seat behind his desk and with a wave of his hand invited Jace to sit. That, at least, was a good sign.

"What's on your mind?" he asked.

"Information."

"Go on," Jamison said cautiously.

Jace took a deep breath and cleared his throat. "I realize this is a delicate subject for you, but I have to ask a couple of questions about your son, Neil."

A flicker of pain crossed Jamison's face. He got up, came around his desk and closed the door. When he returned to his seat, moisture had pooled in his eyes. "It's been a long time," he said gruffly. "What could you possible want to know?"

There was no gentle way to approach this. Jace had to dive right in. "It concerns a young girl Neil dated thirteen years ago, LuAnn Randall."

Other than his eyes, Jamison's face froze. Those dark eyes spewed anger. "That's all in the past," he said through clenched teeth. "Twelve years, five months and eighteen days."

"I'm sorry," Jace said, realizing the extent of the man's misery. "What happened between them? Why is she afraid of you?"

"She has no reason to be afraid of me."

"Maybe I misunderstood, but she recently had a break-in and refused to let me call the police because you were here."

Jamison gave a disgusted snort. "That's nonsense."

"Maybe so, but I'd certainly appreciate it if you'd explain what went on to make her feel that way."

Jamison was silent for a long time, obviously debating with himself. "The night before Neil died he told me LuAnn was pregnant. He wanted to quit school and marry her. The kid was captain of the football team, pulled straight A's. He was good-looking, smart and athletic. He had his whole future ahead of him. And he wanted to throw it all away to marry a fifteen-year-old girl. I blew up."

Jace struggled to keep his face impassive at the news that LuAnn had been pregnant. He remained silent waiting for him to go on.

Jamison leaned forward, put his elbows on his desk and dropped his head in his hands. "We exchanged a lot of angry words that night. When he stormed out of the house, I never saw him again—at least not alive. He wrapped his car around a tree, driving too fast with a good amount of alcohol in his blood."

The man's pain was so palpable Jace didn't know what to say…but he had to know the rest of it. "What about LuAnn? The baby?"

Jamison raised his head, his anguish replaced by anger. "If you're thinking I blamed it all on LuAnn, you're wrong. Neil was a smart kid, and he was older than she was. He should have known enough to use birth control. I waited until I knew the baby would be born. I thought maybe I could get some peace if I could hold my grandchild in my arms. I hadn't seen her in those months, and when I went over there, Jack Randall came to the door. He wouldn't let me see her. He said she'd had an abortion. It was like losing my son all over again. That's when I started hating her."

"I understand, but I suspect she was pressured into that abortion by her father who wasn't any happier about the pregnancy than you were."

Jamison nodded. "You're probably right. Jack Randall wasn't an easy man. But he couldn't have forced her to do it." He hesitated then added, "If you see her, you can tell her she has no reason to avoid calling the Superior police because I'm here. I'm not the enemy."

"I'll give her that message next time I see her."

And I damn well hope that'll be sooner than later.

"One more thing," Jace said, standing up to leave. "This may not be a comfort to you, but when I was a teenager, if I had wrapped my car around a tree every time my father blew up at me, with good reason I might add, there wouldn't have been enough trees in Minnesota to accommodate me."

Jamison smiled, and this time it reached his eyes. "Thanks, I appreciate that."

Jace sat in his truck trying to put it all together. He'd found out what he came here to learn—thirteen years ago LuAnn had had an abortion. He could understand why she was reluctant to talk about it. The problem was what could that possibly have to do with Bart Harridan? The Jamison family yes, but Harridan? It just didn't make sense.

While he sat there, he realized his phone was beeping. There was a message from Kayla.

"I don't know where you are, but you better stop over. I have something for you to hear. Oh, and Dad called. Mom's having surgery day after tomorrow. He wants us to be there with him. Wanda's still on vacation."

He hit redial and told her he'd be there in twenty minutes depending on traffic.

Halfway to Kayla's house his gut tightened. LuAnn had said she'd given up her imaginary friend when she was fifteen. Had she named her aborted baby Becca?

Damn, where was she, and why was she hiding from him?

He slammed his fist into the dash and grimaced in pain for the reckless impulse. It was still smarting when he pulled up into Kayla's drive. She was waiting for him at the front door.

"You look like hell," she said by way of greeting. "When's the last time you shaved?"

He stepped past her into the house rubbing his hand over the two-day stubble on his chin. "Not since you saw me two hours ago. What do you have for me?"

"A call. I think it could be from LuAnn."

That statement gave Jace's drooping spirit a jump-start. "Did she say where she was?"

"No"

"What *did* she say?" he asked anxiously.

"Nothing."

He gave her a look that suggested she'd best quit toying with him.

Kayla returned the look with equal hostility. "Don't you have her phone number?"

"Hell no, I spent two days with her, and she never told me what it was. And she didn't make any calls on her cell phone because she said it was dead."

Kayla held up her phone smiling. "Okay listen to this." She put the phone on speaker and punched some numbers.

All he heard was static. "You called me here for that?" he bellowed absently flexing his fingers. "What makes you think it's her?"

"What's wrong with your hand?"

"I smashed it…never mind. How do you know it's her?"

"Female intuition, and if it is her, the call recorded the phone number."

That woke him up. "Man, I must be tired. I should have caught that. What is it? I'll call her back."

He grabbed for the phone, but she held it out of his reach. "Wait, let's talk about this first."

"What's to talk about? Give me the damn number."

"If she wanted to talk to you, she'd have called you."

He closed his eyes and pinched the bridge of his nose. Gritting his teeth he said, "Fine! You call her. I just want to know if she's all right."

"I already tried. She didn't answer."

Jace blew out a huff of air. "How did she get *your* number?"

Kayla smiled mischievously. "I gave it to her when she was here. I told her to call me anytime even if it was just to talk—you know, woman to woman, which is why I can't give you the number. I'm hoping she'll call again, but I doubt she would if she discovered I'd shared the number with you. I suspect, fear of that, is what made her hang up."

Frustrated, Jace thrust a hand threw his hair. "I hate admitting this, but you're actually making sense. Damn, this not knowing where she is does a number on my nerves." He sank down into a chair at the kitchen table.

He must have looked as bad as he felt because Kayla took a seat across from him and gave him a sympathetic smile "You're hooked on her aren't you?"

He gave her a long level look. "I honestly don't know. What I do know is that I'm worried out of my mind. Why the hell did she take off like that? It had to have been something that jackass neighbor, Tom, said to her." Maybe he could go over to Tom's house and shake some straight answers out of him. He was debating that when an inspiration struck him. His head shot up. "I've got it. When I called the neighbor, I told him who I was, and he immediately went on a tirade. You could call him. Tell Tom you're a friend of LuAnn's, and you're looking for her. You might want to reassure him by mentioning the cat, Max, that LuAnn looks after."

Kayla nodded eagerly. "I like that idea. Bring up his number on your phone."

Jace punched in the redial button, tapped on the external speaker and handed the phone to Kayla. It rang three times then a male voice that Jace recognized came on.

"Hello?"

Kayla gave Jace a devious smile. "Hello, my name is Kayla…Smith. I'm looking for my friend LuAnn. We were supposed to go out to eat tonight, but she's not home. I know she looks after Max once in awhile, so I hoped you might know where she is."

"Well, she was home for about half an hour then she took off. I warned her about that slick lawyer Murdock, the one who attacked her, so I think she's hiding from him."

Jace gritted his teeth, eyes widening.

"A lawyer attacked her?" Kayla asked.

"Yup, no doubt about it. He left some pretty damning evidence behind."

Jace mouthed, *What kind of evidence?*

"Oh my goodness," Kayla said using a shocked tone. "What kind of evidence?"

"You better ask her about that. Not my place. I just hope she turns it over to the cops. She shoulda called them right away as it was."

"Murdock, you said. That name sounds familiar."

"Oh yeah, it was on the news awhile back. He got the broad who murdered her husband off *and* the drunk who put the old lady in the hospital. Oh, he's a shyster all right. I wouldn't even have known about it if the guys hadn't been talking about it at work."

Kayla held her hand up to stop Jace from blowing a gasket. "So you don't know any of the details except what you heard from them?"

"Nope, but that was enough to make me recognize his name when I saw it. She's a nice lady and should stay away from a decrepit bastard like him."

"So you found something—with Murdock's name on it?"

"Yup. Look ma'am, I gotta go. I'm running late for a dental appointment."

Kayla thanked him and closed the phone.

"What the hell is he talking about," Jace shouted, coming to his feet. "I've never even been in her house. How would he find something with my name on it? Unless Kastansa planted it, whatever it was."

"Calm down," Kayla said. "At least we found out why she ran."

Jace sat back in his chair, his chest heaving with anger. "We've got to find her. She's out there alone—an open target for Kastansa."

* * * *

LuAnn had sat for a long time at the turnout along the lake trying to decide what to do. She really wanted to go home, let Max in to comfort her and sit back and relax in front of an old movie.

But it would have been impossible to relax. Jace knew where she lived.

How could she have misjudged the man to the extent she had—enough to have sex with him? Or even worse, fall in love with him. He'd seemed so honest, so trusting. Even the way he related to a son that wasn't even his real son. It had been endearing to watch them together. And Dustin adored him.

Jace's betrayal gave her an overwhelming sense of anguish.

Having finally made the decision to talk to Jace's friend Logan, she was now back on the road heading away from Duluth following the north shore. She watched the billboard signs, still hoping to recognize the name of the bed and breakfast Logan's grandmother owned.

She also kept an eye on her rearview mirror to make certain no one was following her—something she'd never had to think about until a few short days ago. So far it seemed clear.

Then she spotted the sign—The Daybreak Inn—five miles ahead. Her heart started thumping at the thought of facing Logan. He was Jace's friend, but he was also a police detective. If she had to trust someone, it might as well be him.

Maybe, if they had an opening, she'd check in and get a room, talk to Logan in the morning. Give her time to gather her thoughts.

A few minutes later she pulled into the parking lot of The Daybreak Inn. The elegant colonial style building was nestled in a charming setting that blended woods with a marvelous view of Lake Superior in the background.

Taking a deep breath, she drew on her resolve and got out of the car. The front porch complete with wicker furniture, including a two-person swing, had a sign that read:

Welcome to Daybreak—walk right in

A tingling bell announced her entry, and an adorable tan and black pug-nosed dog met her in the foyer with exuberant licks.

From the adjoining room a friendly voice called out. "I see Pugsly has given you his stamp of approval. That's always a good sign. He doesn't greet just anyone." The voice came from a tall elderly woman who appeared to be in her late seventies. Her snow-white hair was back in a perfectly coiled chignon and a colorful apron covered her tidy cotton dress. She was so grandmotherly one couldn't help but fall in love with her on sight.

She extended an arthritic hand. "Welcome. You can call me Mamie."

Gingerly, LuAnn accepted the gnarled hand, smiling. "I'm LuAnn Barstow, happy to meet you, Mamie. And you too, Pugsly," she added, stooping down to rub the dog's ears. Pugsly responded with a quick slurp on her hand as his tail, curled tightly over his back, attempted to wag. When Mamie warned him to behave, he settled down on his haunches, his tongue hanging out to the side, to observe her.

"Cute dog," LuAnn said, straightening back up.

Mamie grinned. "Ain't he though. Just got him a couple of months ago. He guards the front door." She chuckled heartily. "You lookin' for a room?"

"Yes, if you have something available."

"Sure do, it being Tuesday and all. Most people come for the weekend and checked out yesterday."

LuAnn had a mental shock. Was it really only Tuesday. She'd spent a good share of last night wrapped in Jace's arms, either having sex or just holding each other and sleeping. She quickly shook that image off and followed the continuously chatting Mamie to a raised check-in desk just off the foyer. She was saying something about how the inn would be full by the end of the week because her grandson was getting married on Saturday.

"...so, how long will you be staying?" Mamie asked, handing LuAnn a short form to fill out.

"I'll start with one night and see how it goes. I'd rather no one knows I'm here if that's okay."

Mamie laughed. "Funny you should say that. It's the typical statement for a woman checking in alone. No problem. As long as you understand that if anyone else spends the night with you, it's extra."

With key in hand she headed for her room on the second floor, then turning back to Mamie asked, "Does Logan live here in the inn?"

Mamie gave her a puzzled look. "No, he lives in the large log cabin down by the lake—with his fiancé," she added then asked somewhat suspiciously, "You have business with him?"

LuAnn tried to give her a reassuring smile. "Sort off. I just need to talk to him. Do you know what time he goes to work in the morning?"

"He's off tomorrow. They're doing some wedding stuff. You want me to tell him you're here?"

LuAnn hesitated. Surely if Logan knew where she was, he'd be on the phone to Jace in minutes. Better if she caught him off guard then she could leave before Jace could get there.

"No," she said. "I'll catch him tomorrow when I'm ready."

She was surprised Jace hadn't called. Maybe she needn't have worried that Kayla would immediately hand the phone number over to her brother.

Another part of her wished she had.

Chapter Twenty

Armon Kastansa sat in his car and watched through the trees as LuAnn Bartow walked into The Daybreak Inn. She came back out a few minutes later and collected her bags from the car. He deduced that meant she'd checked in.

His nose was still swollen from when she'd kicked him. He could barely breathe through it and was certain it was broken. It had exasperated him to no end when Harridan put a stop to his plan to kill her. He'd looked forward to making her suffer before she died. With the kind of face and body she had, he could have a little fun with her before he did her in. He got stiff just thinking about it. And now it appeared she was alone; he didn't have that tough-assed Murdock to worry about.

It looked like an extravagant place to stay. Did that constitute spending a lot of money? On a schoolteacher's salary, that would be a *yes* he decided. He dialed up Harridan hoping he could get the green light to proceed with the original plan and get rid of her.

"Bart Harridan."

"Yeah, Mr. Harridan, it's Armon. I'm tailing LuAnn like you told me to. She's spending the night at a fancy bed and breakfast up on the north shore. Looks pricy. You wanted to know if she started spending money."

"What's the name of the place?"

"Daybreak Inn."

"Hell, I know where that is. Watch yourself. The owner's grandson is a friend of Murdock's, plus he's a cop. He lives in one of the cabins. Is Murdock with her?"

"Nope, haven't seen him all day. It appears as though they've parted ways. You want me to go back to plan A?"

Armon waited patiently while Harridan took his time answering. In the meantime he lit a joint he'd rolled earlier. He took a deep soothing draw, releasing the smoke slowly, forming perfect rings in the air. He liked to take his time when he did something he enjoyed. By the time Harridan talked, a good full minute had passed.

"Okay, if you can make it look like an accident or suicide. I don't want anything like a big fire that'll bring on a barrage of press coverage. That means nobody else goes with her—unless it's Murdock of course. Keep me posted. And don't get caught with your hand in the cookie jar. If you do, you know the drill—don't call me."

Don't call me, Armon mimicked after he hung up the phone. Rich bastards, they want you to do their dirty work as long as they don't get any muck on their own fingers.

If he had to be on his own, he might as well handle things his own way. He'd drive up the road and find a service station, shave his whole head, including the beard since that's the look he had on his alias ID. He would change clothes and clean up so he looked respectable. Then he'd use his businessman's persona and check in. Hell, he might as well get a little rest while he thought about how he was going to handle the situation. For sure he wanted to wait until he was certain Murdock didn't show. He doubted anyone would recognize him with a distorted swollen nose, no facial hair, and a smooth, shaven head.

* * * *

Two hours later Mr. and Mrs. Andrew Cardozo checked into The Daybreak Inn. Mr. Cardozo explained to the old lady in charge that his wife was traveling up from the Twin Cities and would be a couple of hours behind him. Then he asked if he could have his meals delivered to his room since he was uncomfortable eating around other people until the swelling from his bee sting went down.

Smiling sympathetically, she readily agreed to that arrangement saying her cook would be happy to accommodate him. She smiled broadly when he handed her a twenty-dollar bill for the extra trouble. He then had to listen to ten minutes of her extolling the amenities of the inn.

As he was preparing to leave, he asked if she might have a vase he could use for the flowers he'd bought for his wife to celebrate their twentieth wedding anniversary. She beamed at his thoughtfulness and hurried to find him a vase. While she was gone, he leaned over the register and noted LuAnn Barstow's room number. It was his lucky day. She was in 201 and he had 202.

The brochure in his hand said breakfast was at nine. When she returned with a decorative vase, he asked if they could get their breakfast at eight since they wanted to get an early start on their way up the north shore. She smilingly reassured him it would be no problem.

* * * *

Jace woke up, so that meant he must have fallen asleep sometime during the night. He came out to the kitchen to find Kayla making coffee.

"Don't you have to go to work?" he asked.

She shook her head. "I took the morning off. I wanted to see if I could do anything to help you find LuAnn. I'm glad you stayed. I guess I didn't want to be alone either." She gave him a quick once over. "You shaved, and you still look like hell."

He slumped down in a chair, put his elbows on the table and dropped his head in his hands, not moving until she set an aromatic cup of coffee under his nose.

"Here drink up. I want to run an idea past you."

"Shoot, I'm open to suggestions. No more calls, huh?"

"No, but here's what I've been thinking about. You said this mystery client of yours hired you to find LuAnn…then she's attacked in her home and something is left there to incriminate you. Could it be possible that you were his target all along?"

Jace didn't comment, but she definitely had his attention. He sipped the hot black coffee, his eyes fixed on hers. "Keep talking," he said quietly, not wanting to interrupt her chain of thought.

"What if—bear with me here because I'm just shooting from the hip—if you had a court case that went against something he believed in or offhandedly affected him personally in some way? What if his decision to hire you was predicated to get back at you for something you did in court?"

Jace's chest heaved with the effort of breathing. His sister had always been a mastermind at puzzles. She aced those ludicrous think-outside-the-box episodes in college all the time. What she was saying made sense.

He tried to recall his first meeting with Harridan. He'd been evasive right from the start, giving him bits and pieces of information, asking Jace to find a person who lived right in town. It was something his lawyer should easily have been able to do. Harridan had made it clear he wanted discretion, so Jace had rationalized that as the reason he wanted a stranger to find her. But what if Jace wasn't a stranger?

"Say something," Kayla said eagerly, interrupting his thoughts.

He lifted his eyes to hers. "I think you might be on to something."

She quickly took a seat across from him. "Give me some ideas. Let's brainstorm this thing."

Jace nodded slowly, thinking. They'd done this a lot as kids if they wanted to figure something out. "First of all, if what you're saying is true, he didn't pick LuAnn Barstow at random either. There must be something that connects us."

"Not necessarily," Kayla said. "He might have a separate issue with LuAnn and wants to—how do you say—kill two birds with one stone. Maybe if you were to tell me, in confidence of course, who your client is, we could come up with something."

"Bart Harridan."

Kayla's mouth fell open as she stared numbly at him. "*The* Bart Harridan?"

"One and the same."

"Oh my God. That brings up a stack of possibilities."

"Yeah. My two most controversial cases were the drunk driver and the Marley Jacob's murder case."

"The woman in the drunk driver case who ended up in the hospital—was it possible she was someone Harridan knew or was related to."

"Anything is possible but not that I'm aware of, besides that was almost a year ago. More likely it would be the Jacob's trial."

"Okay," Kayla said excitedly. "What kind of relatives or friends were in the courtroom at that trial? Do you remember seeing Bart Harridan there?"

"No, I'd have remembered that. Marley's mother was the most dedicated person. There were some others, but they came and went. She was there every day sitting right up front."

"Was she hostile or abusive to you?"

"No, she pretty much sat quietly holding a soggy handkerchief over her pale face most of the time, crying off and on. From what I remember Marley had a decent job and helped support her financially. It was the one thing about him that the jury took heart with. It portrayed him as a kindly man helping his mother."

"So how could he possibly be a wife-beater," Kayla finished for him.

"Exactly. Her testimony was highly damaging, especially since we had no solid evidence that Alexia was abused. We needed some proof, that's when I came up with the photos of her battered face."

"And the photos were actually from a car accident that happened while she was fleeing from her husband."

"Yes."

"So, what's the next step?"

"I guess I'll make a visit to both his mother Olivia, and his wife Alexia. Maybe if I drop Bart Harridan's name I'll get some reaction."

"My money is on the mother. The wife would have no reason to harbor ill will. You saved her from a long prison sentence."

"I agree, but if that doesn't pan out, Alexia might know if the family had any links to Harridan." Jace smiled at his sister. "Have I ever told you how much I appreciate you?"

"Not recently."

Jace glanced at his watch. It was only nine o'clock, too early to visit Olivia Jacobs.

"Why don't you try LuAnn's cell phone again? Leave her a message, assuring her you haven't told me her number. Ask her to call you back just so you know she's okay. Don't say anything about your call to Tom unless she calls back. She'll think you're just trying to cover for me."

While she did that, Jace poured himself a second cup of coffee. As he suspected LuAnn didn't answer Kayla's call, but she was able to leave the message.

"At least if she calls back," Kayla said, "we'll know for sure it's her number."

When Jace's phone rang a second later, they exchanged a hopeful look between them.

"Hello, Mr. Murdock." It was a female young-sounding voice. Definitely not LuAnn.

"Yeah, this is Jace Murdock."

"Well...ah...I understand you know how to find people. I...ah...need to find someone."

The woman sounded tentative, almost scared.

"Who do you need to find?"

"My mother."

Jace motioned to Kayla to fetch him a pen and paper.

"Okay, can you give me your name?"

"Well...okay...but you have to promise not to tell anyone."

He was getting the idea that he was talking to a very young person. He gave his anxious sister an ambiguous shrug. "I can do that. My work is always confidential."

"Okay...good...my name is Chelsea Harridan."

Jace very nearly dropped his phone. "Your father is Bart Harridan?" He asked even though he already knew the answer.

"Yes…yes…but it's real important you don't talk to him. I know you helped him find LuAnn, so I figure you must be very good at what you do."

This kid knew about LuAnn, now she had his full attention. "I'm not sure I understand." He said, "Correct me if I'm wrong, but don't you already have a mother?"

"She's not my mother," Chelsea said adamantly.

"You know that for sure?"

"Yes. I heard her say it…more than once." Jace glanced at Kayla who was listening to the one-sided conversation with a puzzled expression on her face. On the note pad he wrote *Chelsea Harridan*. When Kayla gasped, he held up a finger, motioning her to be patient and silent.

"Have you seen your birth certificate?"

"Yes…but I'm sure it's fake."

"Do you know your birth mother's name?"

"No. But you didn't know LuAnn's last name and you found her."

"How do you know about that?" Jace asked becoming more and more curious about this kid.

"I know lots of things. Like LuAnn is my mother's real daughter—I mean the mother who is not *my* real mother. I've been saving my allowance so I can pay you."

"Let me ask you this—how did you get my phone number?"

"My father's Rolodex. Please help me. I don't know anyone else who can."

Jace got the impression the child was close to tears. "I can't do miracles, Chelsea. I need something to go on. Like maybe your birthday and the hospital where you were born. And anything else that might get me started."

"I was hoping my birthday would be enough. I will be thirteen on the fourth of July."

"Well…that is unusual all right. Now if you know the hospital—"

"I don't. I'm sorry. I know lots of other things though that might interest you."

"Pertaining to your birth?"

There was a moment of silence on the line. "I—I should probably meet with you. I'll go to the Wendy's across the street from my father's hotel this morning at eleven o'clock. I can ride my bike there, and my father will be golfing then."

"Okay, Chelsea, I'll be there, but so I can get started, what is this other information you have?"

"I know my father paid to get you disbarred."

"What?"

"Mother's coming!"

Chapter Twenty-One

Jace stared dumbfounded at the dead phone. On the screen it read disconnected. He looked up at Kayla. Her wide eyes told him she read the shock on his face.

Mutely, he turned the notepad around for her to see where he'd written every word Chelsea had said in his clear concise handwriting.

Kayla read the notes, frowned, then read them again, obviously piecing in his part of the conversation.

"She knows her father paid to get you disbarred? Her mother's not her mother? LuAnn is her mother's daughter? Where is this all coming from?"

"I'm not sure."

"You think she's lying? Looking for attention?"

"No. The only thing I question is she thinks LuAnn is her mother's daughter. Either Harridan was telling the truth or Chelsea heard the message I left on his phone. That might mean she has a sophisticated way of eavesdropping."

"What message?"

Jace explained about the call he'd made to shake Harridan up.

Kayla massaged her temples. "What are you going to do?"

"I'm going to meet her."

"She's just a kid, Jace."

"Yeah, but if she can convince me she has reason to look for her mother, I'm going to try to help find her. How many babies you suppose were born in this area that year on the fourth of July? Five? Ten? Shouldn't be hard to find out."

Kayla glanced at his notes. "Chelsea said her father paid to have you disbarred. How on earth would she know that?"

"I don't know, but it puts a whole new slant on this fiasco. It certainly fits in with your theory about Harridan targeting me as well as LuAnn."

"Who would he pay to get that done?"

"Judge Porter. Devon overheard him asking Harridan for money. It seems the honorable Judge Porter has a gambling problem."

Kayla stared at him as though he'd taken leave of his senses. "For real?"

"Yup." Jace stood up and gave her a kiss on the cheek. "Right now I'm going to visit Olivia Jacobs. Keep your cell phone with you in case LuAnn calls."

"You want me to question Alexia?"

"Do you have time?

"I'll make time."

* * * *

An insistent pounding woke him up. Armon Kastansa's alias Andrew Cardozo charged to his feet ready to do battle. He'd been ducking bullets in the middle of a gunfight between the Russian mafia and Columbian drug lords.

Breathing heavily, fists clenched, he took in his surroundings and heard a female voice from the other side of the door. "Your breakfast is here Mr. and Mrs. Cardozo."

He managed to answer her, telling her to leave it outside the door.

Slumping down on the bed, he hung his head in his hands and tried to bring his heart rate down to normal. Damn, his brain hurt. He shouldn't have had those two extra joints before he went to bed. That bastard he met at the bar must have given him some bad shit.

He'd also partaken of several miniature bottles of booze they'd left in his refrigerator along with soda, candy bars, and salty peanuts and chips. They came with prices on them, and there was a can on top of the counter to deposit the money. He'd eaten all the snacks chuckling as he dropped two nickels and six pennies in the can.

Methodically, he focused his eyes on the bedside clock and swore again.

Last night he'd planned to take care of LuAnn Barstow. Slit her wrists, make it look like suicide. He'd just intended to rest his eyes a bit and must have fallen asleep.

He went to the bathroom, washed his face, groaning when he saw his craggy image in the mirror. He slipped on his pants and retrieved his breakfast by wheeling the whole cart into his room. Good smells came from the plates. For a moment he stared at the amount of food they'd given him then he remembered his *wife* was supposed to have joined him. He picked up one of the prissy china coffee cups, filled it from the supplied carafe, added a generous amount of cream and took a long life-restoring swallow. God he loved hot creamy coffee.

Contemplating the second cup, a marvelous idea hit him square between the eyes. Quickly he moved everything from the two trays to the table leaving the one cup with its fancy little saucer on a tray, taking precautions not to touch anything. After wiping down the cart to remove any trace of fingerprints, he filled the cup, then took a vial of powder from his satchel, sprinkled a heavy dose into the coffee and stirred it in. She'd only need to drink half of it to kill her.

He pushed the cart to the door, opened it to make sure no one was in the hall and hurriedly positioned the cart in front of room 201. He knocked firmly and called out, "Your coffee is here, Mrs. Barstow," before hastily retreating to his own room. As soon as he heard her door open and close, he retrieved the cart. Then smiling to himself, sat down to enjoy his double meal before Mr. and Mrs. Cardozo disappeared.

* * * *

LuAnn heard the knock on her door just as she came out of the shower. She'd had a restless night and was not looking forward to the day. Seeing Logan was going to be difficult at best.

Opening her door she saw the cart and managed a brief smile. They certainly knew how to take care of their guests here. She took the steaming cup and cute little saucer from the cart, went back in her room and locked the door. The coffee smelled heavenly. Disappointed not to find creamer or sugar, she took a sip anyway. It was horribly bitter and scalding hot. Grimacing, she guessed it was an exotic brand that was meant to taste that way. Sugar would have improved it, and cream or milk would have cooled it off, but she needed the coffee to get through the day. She took another sip, burned her lip, shuddered at the taste and set it aside. Maybe she could tolerate it after she'd dressed.

* * * *

Jace pulled up across the street from a moderately sized split-level house with a well-kept yard and lots of flowerpots. His first thought was if Marley Jacobs had been supporting his mother, she didn't seem to be doing too bad without his help. To his knowledge there was no life insurance.

Through the large front window, he could see her sitting in a recliner staring at a wall that probably held a television.

When he rang the doorbell, he heard what sounded like a small dog barking inside. Moments later, a strikingly beautiful Olivia Jacobs sporting a brilliant smile swung the door open wide, almost as though she'd been expecting someone. Jace recognized her features, but this woman with full makeup, her hair stylishly coifed, in no way resembled the dowdy sobbing woman who'd sat behind Marley Jacobs through four weeks of trial.

Her smile froze then turned into an instant scowl. "What are you doing here?"

Jace had the feeling this was not going to go well. "If you have a minute, I'd like to talk to you."

"Not even a second for you. Get of off my property and don't come back." That said, she slammed the door in his face. There was little he could do but turn around and walk back to his truck. He sat there drumming his fingers on the steering wheel thinking he should have gone to see Alexia and sent Kayla here.

He was contemplating the difference between this Olivia and the one at the trial when a black Mercedes pulled into her driveway. Quickly he slumped down in his seat far enough so he could still see who was driving the car.

The driver didn't get out; instead Olivia burst from the door, her wide smile back in place. She hopped in the car; it backed out and drove right past him.

Son-of-a bitch!

* * * *

Jace spotted Chelsea Harridan the minute he walked into Wendy's. She sat against the wall where she could see the front door, and when he stopped to look around, she smiled and wiggled her fingers in a little wave. She had long brown hair that curled at the ends. A colorful headband held it back from her face. He likened her flawless young features to a cherubic angel.

He walked over to her and held out his hand. "Hello, Chelsea, I'm Jace Murdock."

She put her small young hand in his and gave him an amazingly firm shake. He liked the kid already.

"Hello, Mr. Murdock. Thank you so much for coming. I was afraid you wouldn't show up since I had to hang up on you."

He took a seat across from her, noticing she had a large drink in front of her that looked like iced tea. "I understood—you didn't want to be caught talking to me by your mother."

"She's not my mother! My birth certificate says she is, but she isn't."

"You seem real sure of that."

"I am. They argue all the time. He tells her to quit drinking and to keep her voice down so I don't hear, but she never does. She says she doesn't care because I'm not her daughter. I play my radio loud sometimes so I don't have to hear them." Tears glistened in her eyes by the time she'd finished. She blinked them away as though embarrassed by them.

Jace found it interesting that she referred to her father as *he*. "How is your relationship with your father?"

She shrugged her small shoulders. "He rarely talks to me. The only rule he has is 'don't embarrass me.' As long as I don't do that, he leaves me alone. And my mother—Gladys—only talks to me when she's mad at me for not cleaning my room or running in the house."

It wasn't difficult to get a picture of this young girl's home life. His heart went out to her.

"Have you ever thought about going to a counselor at school?"

She gave a hissing snort. "And *embarrass the family*." She used her fingers to make little quotation marks. "Are you kidding? My father wants to go to the White House. I swear he named me after Chelsea Clinton."

"Do you have friends you can talk to?"

"I have friends." She gave him a little smile. "But they can't help me find my real mother."

"I need to ask you an important question, and I want you to be totally honest with me."

"Okay," she said with the eagerness of a child.

"Are you being abused, sexually or otherwise by either of your parents?"

At this she rolled her eyes. "No. That would mean they'd have to touch me or be in the same room with me."

Jace stifled the urge to smile. He really liked this kid and wondered how she maintained such an upbeat disposition considering the environment she was growing up in.

"What about meals. Don't you eat together?"

Again with the snort and eye rolling. "My father eats in his office, and my—Gladys—in the den. I don't remember ever eating with them—unless it was before I remember."

Frowning, Jace asked her where she ate.

"In the kitchen. Sometimes with Juanita. She's the housekeeper and also the cook. Other times she just leaves food for me, especially now that she doesn't like me anymore."

"Why doesn't she like you anymore?"

"I came home from school one day because I had a stomachache. It would have been all right except it was a Wednesday."

Jace gave his brain a cerebral shake. "What happens on Wednesday?"

My mother goes to play whist with her friends at the club, and Dad usually goes golfing, but he was home."

"Is that so horrible?" Jace asked, making a mental note that today was Wednesday. *Oh yeah, he goes golfing all right, in Olivia's hole.*

She actually snickered. "It was because he was…you know…with the housekeeper, in his office. I heard a noise, so I investigated." She made a disgusted face. "He really should have locked the door."

How could a child, seeing her father having illicit sex in his office, be so calm about it? He decided to bypass that for now.

"Doesn't it seem odd to you that your family doesn't eat together?"

"Of course it does. I didn't believe Gladys was my mother even before I heard her say it."

"Why is that?"

"My friends all eat as a family, plus they *do* things together; they laugh and kid around, tease each other and hug. At my house, nobody teases and nobody hugs—ever!"

"Do you believe your father is your real father?'

She lifted her shoulders. "I guess. Moth—Gladys—says I'm from one of his affairs."

"She said that to you?"

"No," she quipped, drawing the word out. "She'd have to talk to me to do that. She accuses him, mostly when she's drinking—which is a lot."

"I can understand why you're hoping you have a different mother."

"I'm not hoping I do. I know I do. I just need to find her."

Jace avoided telling her that if her mother gave her up it was probably because she didn't want a child. He was afraid she was setting herself up to be hurt or disillusioned or both. But…maybe he was wrong.

"I can't make any promises, but I'll do what I can to help you find her," Jace said.

"You found LuAnn…and you didn't know her last name."

"Now you're getting into a subject I'm a little curious about. How do you know about LuAnn? And even more pertinent is your comment about my disbarment."

She pursed her lips as though either uncomfortable or in thought. She took a deep breath. "I said that so you'd meet me."

"Then it isn't true?"

"Sure it's true. I wouldn't tell you a lie when I want your help. After all, I'm just a kid. Why would you bother with me? Would you have come if I hadn't said that?"

Just a kid…but a damn smart one. "I'm…not sure, but either way, I'm glad I met you."

She gave him a quick grin. "You're honest. I like that about you."

This time Jace didn't hide his smile. "You are a crafty little rascal."

Her grin broadened. "You tease. I like that, too."

"Now tell me what you know about my disbarment. I'm surprised you even know what it means."

"I didn't, but I looked it up in the dictionary. It means, *deprive of the right to practice law.*"

Right there Jace decided that if anybody in that family had a chance to get to the White House, it would be Chelsea Harridan. "So you heard your father say he paid someone to have me disbarred?"

"No Judge Porter said it."

Jace's stomach clenched. He tried to tell himself he shouldn't be taking a preteen's word for something this important. But he couldn't stop himself. "What did Judge Porter say exactly?" His voice sounded rusty to his own ears.

"Exactly?" She wrinkled her brow a moment then said, "they were talking about Dad loaning money to Judge Porter to go to Las Vegas, but Dad didn't think he'd pay him back so Judge Porter said, 'I trusted you to pay me when you asked me to fix it so Jace Murdock got disbarred'."

Jace's mouth went dry. If Chelsea Harridan was playing games with him, she was damn good at it. "Don't move," he said, "I have to get something to drink."

Before he could get to his feet, Chelsea pulled the straw out of her iced tea, removed the cover and slid it across the table. "You can have this. I don't like it."

He swallowed half the contents, set the plastic cup down and stared at her. "Are you certain you remember that correctly?"

"Positive. I knew you'd ask, so I listened to it several times."

Jace arched an eyebrow at her. "Are you saying you have this on tape?"

Her head bobbed up and down making her curls bounce. "Uh-huh."

"You tape you father's conversations?"

Her features fell. "Is that illegal?" she asked, making a pinched face.

"Ah...I don't think so."

She drew in a deep breath of air and huffed it out. "Whew, you scared me."

Her innocence amazed him almost as much as her cunning mind did. "Is there anything on that tape that might tell me where LuAnn is?"

"Kind of."

Jace put his elbows on the table and leaned toward her. "Please tell me what you know. I have to find her."

Her face pinched in thought. "I only heard my father's side of the conversation. The other guy said where she was then Dad told him to be careful 'cause the owner's grandson is a friend of yours and he's a cop or something. I don't remember the rest. I'd have to play it back."

Daybreak! She went to see Logan.

"I know where that is. I promise you, Chels, I'll find your mother. Right now I have to go to LuAnn. I'm afraid someone is trying to hurt her. Call me later, okay?"

"Sure." Her eyes were watery.

"Are you okay, honey?"

She nodded. "You called me Chels. No one has ever called me that."

Jace hesitated, reluctant to leave, but finding LuAnn was more urgent. He stood up, leaned across the table, grabbed the back of her head and pressed his lips on her forehead. "Call me when it's safe for you. Use a code name. Call me Doc."

As he left, his thoughts veered away from LuAnn long enough to think about the promise he'd made to Chelsea—he hoped he'd be able to keep it.

Chelsea watched him rush out the door, going to rescue LuAnn. Tears slipped from her eyes as she touched trembling fingers to her forehead. *And no one has ever kissed me before either.*

Jace hoped Chelsea understood why he had to go. That girl was one smart cookie, but she was playing with fire taping Harridan's phone calls. There'd be hell to pay in a king-sized bucket if he found out.

Wending his way through the construction in downtown Duluth, he yanked out his cell phone to call Logan.

His fiancée, Maggie answered, "Jace, I haven't seen you in ages."

"Yeah sorry, I've been a little preoccupied. Is Logan there?"

"Sounds like you're still a little preoccupied."

"I am. I'm on the way out there. If all goes well, I'll stop and see you."

"Okay, here's Logan."

"Hey buddy, what's going on?"

"I think LuAnn is out there. She ran off on me—"

"What did you do?"

Why the hell did everybody think he did something? Jace dodged a construction cone that had rolled into the middle of the road. "She got some misinformation, and she's convinced I was the one who broke in her house."

"Oh for…that's ridiculous."

"I'll explain when I get there; I'm about thirty minutes away. Can you see if she's at the lodge and if she's okay? I thought she came there to see you, but…I guess not. Please check on her…and don't let her leave until I can talk to her."

"I'll do what I can. Call you back in a bit."

Jace finally made it through the city and was heading north on Sixty-one when his phone rang. It was Kayla.

"Yeah, sis, what did you learn?"

"Not much, but Alexia thinks her former mother-in-law is having a thing with Bart Harridan. She wasn't sure but—"

"She's right, I saw them together."

"Well, holy crap. Does this get any more twisted? I guess I don't have to ask how your visit with Olivia went."

"She wouldn't give me the time of day. All but threw me off her property. I was sitting in my truck thinking about my next step when you-know-who showed up in her driveway."

"Huh. What about Chelsea. Was she lying?"

"I don't think so. She was taping her father's phone conversations." Jace swerved to avoid hitting a car that tried to cut him off.

"Gee-wiz. What if she gets caught?"

"Yeah. She knew where LuAnn went, too."

"By listening to her father?"

"Uh-huh."

"That means *he* knows where she is too."

"Exactly. She's at Daybreak. I'm about twenty minutes from there now. I think she went there to talk to Logan."

"Has he seen her?"

"No. I just talked to him. He's going to check on her."

Kayla sighed. "I have a bad feeling about this, Jace."

"Me too. I better get off the phone in case Logan calls. Are you at work?"

"Yes. I have appointments until four. Bye. You shouldn't be talking on the phone while driving. It's dangerous."

"Tell me something I don't know."

Jace wondered why LuAnn hadn't contacted Logan yet if her intentions were to see him. His imagination conjured up all kinds of grisly scenes.

With the road finally cleared of traffic, he pressed the accelerator to the floor.

Five minutes from his destination, his phone chirped. That particular ring meant it was Logan. He decelerated to answer it.

"Yeah, Logan. Talk to me."

"She's here, but she won't let anyone in the room. I tried the passkey, but she has the door barricaded. Mamie said she called down this morning and said she wouldn't be to breakfast because she was sick. What should I do? Break the door down?"

"No. At least if she's in her room, she's safe. I'm pulling into the parking lot right now. I'll talk to her."

* * * *

Chelsea had ordered some lunch at Wendy's then sat for a long time eating and thinking of Jace Murdock. Thinking about what a great father he would be. The way he jumped up to go when he figured out where LuAnn was. Just like a knight in shining armor going to rescue his princess. Would he be so anxious to help her if she was in trouble?

Sighing pensively, she realized she'd better get home before somebody missed her—fat chance. Hopping on her bike, she peddled the twelve blocks to her house, groaning when she saw a strange car in the drive, hoping it wasn't that creepy Kastansa.

She hadn't even shut the front door when her father's voice bellowed from his office.

"Chelsea? Is that you?"

"Yes, Dad," she answered, making a dash for her room.

"Come here immediately," he barked, thwarting her escape plan. He was using the tone of voice that said she was in deep doo-doo. Glancing at the hall clock, she noted it wasn't even two yet. What's the big deal? She quickly slipped her jacket off and tied it around her waist to hide her fanny pack. After adjusting things to make sure it was out of sight, she forced a smile on her face and walked into his office wondering what kind of blunder she'd made now. Seeing Kastansa hunkered in a chair did nothing to dispel her feeling of doom. She noticed his baldhead and lack of facial hair then ignored his malevolent smile.

Her handsome father had his arms crossed over his chest, and he glared at her like she was the scum of the earth. What could she possible have done—then she saw her tape recorder on his desk. Juanita must have found it when she was cleaning. And, of course, she'd go straight to her *master* with it.

Chelsea turned to flee, but Kastansa grabbed her around the waist and pulled her onto his lap.

She attempted to kick at him, but her efforts went unrewarded. "Let me go, you big, ugly bully."

"Chelsea!"

She froze at her father's harsh command. His eyes narrowed to malicious slits. "Get over here."

Kastansa released her, and she stepped forward on wobbly legs to stand before his desk. Fear crowded her mind as she waited for her sentence.

"What do you have to say about this?" he demanded, indicating the recorder with the cord painted white.

Her rapidly pulsating heart wreaked havoc on her brain, but she shrugged, trying her best to act nonchalant. "Sorry. I get bored sitting in my room. I was just messing around."

"How long has this been going on?"

"Just a day or two, I swear."

"And what about this?" he asked as he pulled something out of his drawer and threw it on top of his desk. It was a neatly bundled stack of hundred-dollar bills.

Chelsea made a little squeak. Her breathing became shallow, and she thought she might pass out—wished in fact she would. He must have torn her room apart. Her mouth moved as she tried to force words out of it, but no sound came out.

"What? Nothing to say for yourself."

She dropped her gaze to the floor.

"Look at me when I'm talking to you," he shouted.

She raised her head and managed to say, "I'm sorry."

"Sorry? That's it?"

He charged to his feet, and in less time that it took her to blink, slammed his hand across her face. She cried out and put a trembling hand to her flaming cheek, as he calmly sat back down.

"You devise a shrewd little scheme to extort money from your own father—and you're sorry?"

She had no answer for that as she attempted to check the tears sliding down her face.

His lips contorted into a loathsome sneer. "Where's the rest of it?"

Chelsea's fanny pack burned a hole in her stomach. She had taken the rest to pay Jace Murdock to find her mother. She certainly couldn't tell him that. But she had to answer him.

"I spent some of it and gave the rest away."

"To who?"

"Betty's father, Mr. Morgan, to pay his bills." She hoped he'd think of that as a charitable thing to do.

"I thought his wife was a big shot executive?"

"I made that up," she lied.

"Didn't he wonder where you came up with all this cash?"

Chelsea inwardly moaned. She was getting in deeper and deeper. Fortunately, as her teachers often told her, she had a quick mind. "I gave it to him anonymously…so he wouldn't feel bad about taking it."

"So you stole money from me to give away. Who the hell do you think you are, Robin fucking Hood? Who all have you told about this tape?" he asked, changing subjects.

She hoped that meant he believed her about the money. "No one. Truly."

"Truly? Huh. I swore whoever was blackmailing me was going to suffer a slow brutal death. I might be able to overlook that little sin, but taping my conversations is unforgivable." Chelsea started to shake, her body felt as cold as her father's eyes.

He glanced at Kastansa and said with the slightest hint of regret in his voice. "Take care of her. Make it look like an accident."

A desperate sound came out of her throat, and she might have turned to run but Kastansa's big hands gripped her upper arms in a cruel biting hold. She imagined him making an evil chuckling sound.

"Wait," her father said instilling some hope in her. "Where's your cell phone?"

Tears stung her eyes. If she gave him the phone, he'd know she'd call Mr. Murdock. Then he'd be in trouble.

"It's under my pillow," she said quickly, her voice shaking. "I always keep it there because sometimes I talk to Betty late at night."

"If you're phone doesn't show any unusual calls, I might reconsider your fate, but if you're lying to me, I'm going to take you apart piece by piece. Understand?"

Wordlessly she moved her head up and down.

He nodded to Kastansa, indicating the direction of her room.

Kastansa shoved her into the side chair next to her father's desk and strode out of the room.

"You had everything, Chelsea. A huge room with a big screen TV, a two thousand dollar stereo, all the clothes you could possibly want, your own phone, an allowance ten times what other kids your age get. What more could you possibly have wanted?"

Chelsea never imagined such intense fear was possible. She was in the middle of a nightmare. Her head throbbed and her arms hurt where Kastansa had pinched them. She was going to die. Her own father was going to have her killed. Her own father! Tears stung her eyes not because she was going to die but because nobody cared.

Through her misery she forced herself to think. This was her only chance to escape. Once Kastansa came back to report there was no cell phone in her room, her fate would be in his evil hands.

"What more did you want?" her father, his face puffed with fury, bellowed again.

"Love," she ventured weakly. "All I wanted was love."

As she said the last words, she put her hands on the arms of the chair, pushed herself to her feet and was out the door before her father could respond.

She raced through the sitting room, yanked the front door open and pulled it shut behind her. She'd made it halfway across the yard, heading for her bike before she heard him roaring, calling her names she'd never heard before.

For once in her life, she was thankful they lived on a steep hill overlooking the lake. She picked up her bike, shoved it down the driveway incline and hopped on peddling as though her life depended on it.

She glanced back to see both her father and Kastansa running behind her. Kastansa stumbled over his own big feet, crashing to the asphalt, bringing her father down with him. Amid the swearing she heard Bart Harridan's voice ordering her to stop.

Chelsea knew they'd be coming with cars, so she turned into an alley and kept peddling. With one arm, she cleared the tears from her eyes using her sleeve, as she went across lawns and through more alleys. No one was behind her yet, but from somewhere, the sound of screeching tires followed by a metal crunching crash struck terror in her veins.

* * * *

LuAnn's heart rate was traveling at super speed. She should have left this morning, but the bitter coffee had her feeling sick. It wasn't until she started vomiting that she realized it must have been poisoned. Mamie, she reasoned, had called her grandson, Logan, and he'd delivered the coffee. A male voice had announced its arrival. That meant they were all in on it.

The reason she hadn't left was not only because she was sick, she had nowhere to go. She'd dialed Kayla's number again but hung up before it rang. Who could she trust? She thought about calling Barb. Even Ron. But they'd probably think she was losing her mind.

And maybe she was. She'd cried until she was weak all the while wondering what horrific thing she had done to bring this down on her.

"LuAnn?"

The sound of Jace's voice brought her out of her self-pity but increased the panic surging through her like a freight train.

"Go away," she called out.

"I'm not going anywhere. So get over here by the door and talk to me."

She got up and sat in the chair braced against the heavy dresser she'd pushed in front of the door. In her hand she wielded the hammer she'd brought with her.

"I can hear you." She tried to convey confidence, but she sounded pathetic even to her own ears.

"Listen to me, LuAnn. I know what your neighbor, Tom, told you. He has it all twisted. Please…open the door, and I'll explain everything."

LuAnn's entire body trembled. She wanted to believe him, but the hammer was proof he'd been in her house. She brushed the tears from her eyes. "You must know you left something behind, Jace. You're name is on it. Tom wasn't fabricating that."

"Whatever he found, Kastansa had to have planted it. I was being set up. I'm certain Harridan was after me as well as you. I just haven't figured out why."

Could it be possible? She wanted to believe it…but there was too much pointing the other way. More tears stung her eyes

"Call Kayla," Jace said. "She would never lie to you."

"She's your sister—your twin. She'd say anything you asked her to."

"You obviously don't know my sister very well."

That was true at least. "Just like Logan is your friend. I was given poisonous coffee this morning. Fortunately I only took a couple of sips."

"LuAnn what the hell are you talking about? I didn't even know you were here until half an hour ago."

"And how did you find out—Logan?" She knew her voice sounded bitter, but she didn't care. She was angry now. Angry at him and all his many friends, and countless family members who'd do anything for him.

"Tell me what your neighbor Tom found, so I can try to explain."

"A hammer," she snapped. "He found a hammer with your name burned in the wood. And don't suggest this Kastansa person you made up did it, because it's an old hammer and the handle is well worn. That name was not etched in there recently."

"I didn't make him up, and I don't own a hammer with my name on it. Remember I told you my dad was a carpenter. It has to be his. How Kastansa got hold of it I don't know, but he left it there deliberately. Would I do something that stupid if I had attacked you—think about it? Besides if I wanted to harm you, I could have easily done it when you were passed out in my pickup."

She could have told him she wasn't unconscious while she'd lain on his seat in the pickup, but what purpose would that serve? Everything he said made sense, but he was a criminal lawyer. He knew how to argue a case. Is that what he was doing?

"Is Mamie there?" she asked.

"Yes. Yes, dear I'm here. And nobody on my staff delivered coffee to you. I'm certain it was the man across the hall. When my girl took his cart back to the kitchen, there was only one cup. He was delivered two. He supposedly had a wife joining him, but no one ever saw her."

LuAnn recognized the older woman's voice, and she believed her. She had to believe somebody.

"LuAnn? I love you, please open the door."

Jace's ragged voice sounded tormented. Was he a good actor too? His words tugged at her heart, but she still didn't fully trust him. On the other hand, she couldn't stay in the room forever, and other than the snacks left in the room, she hadn't eaten since yesterday. Her stomach hurt from vomiting and no substantial food. When they'd called to remind her she was missing breakfast, she'd been too sick to even think about eating. For the last hour she'd been fighting dizziness. Surely with Mamie there, Jace wouldn't try anything.

His pleading continued as she struggled to her feet, moved the chair then braced her body against the dresser to push it away from the door. It was heavy and had only budged a few inches when she had a stomach cramp and dropped to her knees then all the way to the floor. She sat there clutching her belly when she saw the door open as far as the dresser allowed.

A sudden movement on the floor in front of her caught her attention. Pugsly had squeezed through the opening and rushed up to her. He climbed on her lap and licked her face as though he knew she was in misery.

She threw her arms around the tan dog with the black pug nose, pressed her face into his chunky body and wept for all the wretchedness she'd suffered in the past forty-eight hours and beyond.

Logan had gone to get tools to break down the sturdy door when Jace realized she'd moved the barrier. After the dog slipped in, Jace wedged his body into the opening, using sheer strength to force it to give.

She was sitting on the floor with a strangle hold on Pugsly, weeping as though every burden in the world was on her shoulders. That damn hammer was clutched in her hand. The room reeked of vomit and sickness.

He dropped down beside her, pushed the reluctant dog out of the way and pulled her into his arms. He buried his face in her hair, whispering, "I love you, LuAnn. More than life itself. I thought I'd go crazy wondering where you were and if you were safe."

It took a good minute before she stopped crying and slowly put her arms around him.

"I thought…" She made a couple of attempts to talk until she finally got her emotions under control. "I thought you…wanted me …dead. And I couldn't understand why. I called Kayla but I—I just didn't know what to do. I was more hurt than scared. But I guess I should have been afraid. He would have killed me if there had been cream and sugar. As it was it was too hot to drink. By the time it cooled down enough I was already feeling nauseous. I took two little sips and was so sick."

"You want to see a doctor?" he asked.

She shook her head. "No…no I think I'm over the worst of it. I just need to eat something."

"What would you like?" Mamie asked. Neither one of them realized she'd come into the room.

"Anything but coffee." Her smile was weak, but it was there.

He got to his feet and reached for her. "Come on, I'll help you up. And give me that stupid hammer." He pulled it out of her hand and tossed it in a corner.

"I'm sorry I believed all that stuff about you."

He helped her over to the bed where he sat down with her.

"I'll go raid the refrigerator," Mamie said, squeezing back out of the room.

Logan appeared in her wake. He moved the dresser back against the wall where it belonged and came to squat down in front of her.

"You okay?"

She nodded, drying her eyes with a handkerchief Jace handed her.

"For the record, LuAnn, Jace is one of the most decent people I know. Whatever you heard about him had to be grossly off base."

Jace's cell phone rang. He pulled it out of his pocket and checked the caller ID. "It's Chelsea," he said, frowning. He hadn't expected her to call back this soon. "Wait until I tell you about Chelsea," he said to LuAnn, then opened the phone and said hello.

"M—M—Mr. M—Doc. Help me! He—he's trying to—to kill me."

"Chelsea, calm down. You have to stop crying. Who's trying to kill you?"

Both Logan and LuAnn watched him, listening on full alert.

"M—my father and Mr. Kastansa."

"Where are you?"

"In an alley…behind a dumpster. He's…he's looking for me. He—he hit me…hard. I think there was a c—crash. C—can you come get me?"

Sweet Jesus! Harridan must have found her tape.

"Listen, honey. I'm too far away. How far are you from home?"

"About four blocks."

"If you can give me your location, I'll call the police, and they can pick you up. Then I'll come get you."

"No! No! The police all know me, and they'd call my dad! Please no, I can't—I can't do that. Where are you, I can come there. I have my bike."

Jace swallowed the lump rising in his throat. "Listen, Chels. Do you by any chance know where the Pet Haven Veterinary Clinic is? It's on Flamingo Avenue just off of Superior Street about a mile from your house."

"Yeah, I know where it is. My friend Betty's father takes their cat there. I've been with them. Is that where you are?"

"No, but my twin sister Kayla is the veterinarian. You think you can get there without being seen?"

"Uh-huh. I can out run them on my bike."

Jace pinched the bridge his nose, attempting to squelch the feeling of panic. "Okay, but if they get close to you, start screaming, go into a service station or any business and scream. Call me back when you get to the clinic so I know you're safe. I'll call my sister; she can bring you to me."

"Okay."

"And buck up kid. You're tough. You can make it. Don't cry. You need to save your strength and see where you're going."

"Okay. Bye."

When Chelsea hung up, Jace experienced the most overwhelming sense of helplessness he'd ever known in his life.

He quickly explained his visit with Chelsea and the situation going on now to Logan and LuAnn.

"She wouldn't go to the police?" Logan asked.

"No, she thinks the first thing they'll do is call her father."

"Oh my gosh," LuAnn exclaimed. "That poor girl."

Mamie entered the room with a tray. "Why don't you all come next door to a clean room," she said.

Jace walked with one arm around LuAnn while he dialed Kayla's number with his free hand. An answering machine came on announcing that the clinic was closed for the day. He glanced at the clock. It was only three; she said she'd be there until four. A niggling of concern etched his brow. He set LuAnn free to sit down at the small round table to eat while Mamie fussed over her then dialed Kayla's cell phone.

"Where are you?" he demanded when she answered.

"Well, hello to you too."

"Kayla we have a problem. I sent Chelsea to the clinic. It's a long story, but if you aren't there when she gets there she may panic."

"I just left. My last appointment canceled so I thought I'd come out to Daybreak—see if there was anything I could do to help. I was just going to call you."

"Go back please, right away. Wait for Chelsea and then bring her out here with you."

Kayla did an immediate u-turn and headed back to the clinic while Jace gave her a brief explanation, warning her to be careful. At ten after three she pulled up in the parking lot. After sitting there a few minutes, she got out of the car and look up and down Flamingo Avenue all the way to

Superior Street. Since she saw no sign of Chelsea, she decided she may as well go inside and find something to do while she waited.

As she unlocked the door she heard sobbing coming from the side of the building. Her heart quickened when she saw the child huddled behind the bushes, her arms around her bike.

"Chelsea?" Kayla called out.

The girl looked up at her with wild, startled eyes. She looked on the verge of fleeing. "I'm Kayla," she said quickly. "Jace's sister."

Chelsea didn't move, but she spoke. "He said you'd be here and when you weren't, I didn't know what to do. He told me not to cry, but I'm having a hard time."

Kayla went to her, knelt down and gathered the girl in her arms. "It's all right. You're going to be okay." She helped Chelsea to her feet and led her toward the Land Rover.

"Can I bring my bike?" she asked pleadingly.

"Of course, why don't you hop in the car while I load it?"

Chelsea bobbed her head solemnly then stepped out of the bushes and waited for Kayla to extract the bike. A car drove by going at a snail's pace. Chelsea shrieked and then threw herself back at Kayla. "Get down, it's my father. He must have followed me."

Kayla dropped the bike, grabbed Chelsea, and together they ran to the back of the building, then up the short hill behind it. They climbed over a four-foot wall heavily covered with wide-leafed grape vines. On the other side they crawled beneath the thick overgrowth. Peering through the leaves they both watched as Bart Harridan pulled in beside Kayla's car. He got out of his vehicle and started looking around. Then he looked inside the *unlocked* Land Rover and obviously spotted her purse on the seat. With a grim smirk on his face, he walked around the side of the clinic. Chelsea made a panicked sound when he spotted her bike.

"Don't move, don't breath," Kayla warned in a whisper. "Even if he looks up this way. We're hidden by the vines. He'll only see you if you move."

Chelsea gave a jerky little nod so slight her head barely wiggled. Kayla wondered if Chelsea's heart was racing as fast as hers. She suspected it was—possibly even more so.

Harridan lifted up the bike just as Kayla's phone rang. Silently swearing, she pinched the mute button through her jeans pocket. Out of the corner of her eye, she saw Chelsea unzip her fanny pack and do the same thing to her own phone all the while not moving her head. Smart girl, Kayla thought.

The ringing sound quit, but Harridan had stopped and turned toward them. He surveyed the hill for a long time. For a moment it seemed as though he looked right at them. Kayla was proud of the brave little girl beside her—she didn't move so much as a hair. Then he looked at the bike again examining it as though to assure himself it belonged to his daughter.

Kayla had a sudden thought. He couldn't have followed Chelsea to the clinic or he would have arrived before Kayla did—he must have known she was Jace's sister and came for that reason. Of course he'd recognize her name; *Kayla Murdock, Veterinarian,* was stenciled in huge letters on the front door.

Her theory was confirmed when he dropped the bike and started walking through the brush below them.

Chapter Twenty-Two

"Neither one of them is answering her phone," Jace complained. "What in God's name is going on?"

"Give them a few minutes," Logan suggested. "Stay off your phone, in case one of them tries to call."

Jace wondered if he had inadvertently put Kayla in danger. "Kayla for sure would have left a message. I have a bad feeling about this." He got up and started pacing.

"That's it," Logan said. "You stay off your phone. I'm calling the squad car on duty in that area. At least they can drive by and let us know it anything suspicious is happening. And don't worry about them turning Chelsea over to Harridan. I'll warn them against that."

"This is entirely my fault," LuAnn said, dabbing at her eyes again.

Jace stopped pacing and came to sit back down beside her. "How do you figure that?"

"It was me they wanted to kill."

"He was after me too, LuAnn. And we still don't know why he wanted either one of us. And you sure as heck had nothing to do with Chelsea taping her father's conversations."

"I'd just feel awful if anything happened to that little girl or your sister."

"No more awful that I'd feel. Remember I'm the one who told Chelsea to go to Kayla."

"But what other choice did you have?"

"Maybe I should have called the police right away."

"Wouldn't have worked," Logan said, snapping his phone shut. "If she was afraid of them, she wouldn't have exposed herself. It'll take a few minutes for them to get there. They're all at an accident scene. The ambulance just left. Some guy ran a red light and got broadsided. Say come to think of it, that's only a few blocks from Harridan's place. You don't know an Andrew Cardozo, do you?" he asked Jace.

Jace shook his head. "No can't say I—"

Mamie's laughter interrupted his thoughts. "That'll teach that reprobate for messing with one of my guests."

"What are you talking about?" Logan asked his grandmother suspiciously.

"He's the man who checked in across the hall from LuAnn. The hairless guy who poisoned her. The same one who supposedly had his wife coming to meet him for their twentieth wedding anniversary. Lied through his teeth, he did."

"You mean hairless, as in bald?" Jace replied.

"Yup as an eight ball," Mamie said, grinning. "No hair anywhere on his head."

"A different identity?" Logan suggested.

"What did he look like otherwise?"

Mamie shrugged. "Big guy. Business suit. Walked like an ape."

"That's him," Jace said quickly. "Son-of-a...gun," he finished, glancing at the older woman. "Kastansa, how bad is he hurt?"

"Should be pretty bad," Mamie said, chuckling.

Logan gave his grandmother a look. "Tell me you didn't?"

Mamie threw her hands in the air. "Do what?"

"Do what?" LuAnn repeated impatiently when Logan didn't answer.

"Grandma Mamie has this little thing she does—"

"It's not a *little thing*," Mamie protested.

"She sticks pins in Voodoo dolls," Logan muttered.

"And it works too," Mamie insisted. "I stuck him with five. That's the most I've ever used on one person. But he really pis...teed me off."

Logan sighed. "Grandma Mamie, if I really believed that, I'd have to arrest you."

She scoffed at that.

Jace looked at his disgusted friend. "What kind of shape is he in?"

"Doubtful he'll make it."

Mamie snickered knowingly all the way out of the room, saying she had to see about the girls getting supper prepared.

Logan shook his head then answered his ringing phone. "Yeah Spence, did you get there?"

"Yup, Kayla's Land Rover is here and so is a black Mercedes. What do you want us to do?"

Logan held the phone aside and explained what he'd learned. "You're the lawyer," he said to Jace. "What do you think? Do we have enough on him to pick him up?"

Jace shook his head. "Not without Chelsea. But maybe we have enough to get a search warrant. He might still have the tape. But tell them not to leave until they find Kayla and Chelsea."

Logan relayed Jace's message. Then stressed his own orders. "Do not leave there until you find them, Spence. Call me as soon as you do."

* * * *

It had only been fifteen minutes, but Kayla felt like she'd been holding her breath for an hour while Harridan searched for them, at one point walking within three feet of their hiding place.

He continually called, "Chelsea come on out. I'll take you home. I promise I won't hurt you."

He suddenly stopped walking and faced the parking lot. Then she saw the patrol car parked next to his Mercedes. She breathed a prayer of thanks but didn't plan to move unless she saw the patrol car trying to leave. She didn't want Harridan to see Chelsea.

* * * *

Harridan talked to the officers then, clearly unhappy about the situation, got in his car and left. She recognized Spencer Anderson as he walked toward the side of the clinic. She took Chelsea's hand and stood up. "Holy cow, Spence, am I glad to see you."

Spence gave her a broad smile. "Happy to see you too, Kayla. What the hell's going on? Is she really Bart Harridan's daughter?" he asked, glancing at Chelsea.

When he said that, Chelsea released Kayla's hand and tried to back away.

Kayla grabbed her quickly "Its okay, sweetie. Spence is a good friend of mine. He's here to help us."

"That's right," he said, smiling at Chelsea. "Duluth's finest at your service. But I still have to ask. Harridan seemed to think you might have been abducted, Chelsea. Any truth in that? Is Kayla abducting you?"

Chelsea smiled up at her new friend. "No, sir, she saved my life."

* * * *

"Hey, Logan. We found 'em. She's on the way out to you. We'll shadow them for a ways to make sure that joker isn't following."

"Good job, Spence. What's the word on Cardozo?"

"In surgery as far as I know."

"Okay, thanks, buddy."

"No thanks necessary just send flowers. And tell Jace to put a good word in to his sister for me."

"He heard you, he's listening on speakerphone."

Spence laughed and hung up.

"Praise the Lord," Jace said. "Now we can relax."

Logan stood up to leave. "I better go see how Maggie's doing. She's supposed to pop in another month, and she's been having back pains. We just hope she won't go before the wedding on Saturday."

"That would kind of throw a monkey wrench in your plans. You'd have to get married at the hospital."

"She's going to be mad as hell when she hears about all the excitement she missed. That might just do it." Laughing,

Logan walked out the door, locking it behind him, leaving Jace and LuAnn alone at last.

Jace put an arm around her and took her hand. "How are you feeling, sweetheart?"

LuAnn put her hand over his and squeezed. "Much better since I ate and even better since the police called. But maybe you should call Kayla just to be sure they're safely on the way."

Jace agreed, dialed her number, talked to her for a few minutes then hung up.

"She's on the way. Chelsea's with her. What a delight that little girl is. I can't wait for you to meet her."

They were silent for a while, just content to be together.

He turned her to face him. "We haven't had a chance to talk, so I want to make sure you understand the truth about the things Tom told you."

She gave a deep profound sigh. "He said you got a drunk driver off who put an old lady in the hospital."

"That was one of the cases I truly regret. I got him off because the lady suffered a heart attack when he crashed his car in front of her. She had a preexisting heart condition and had forgotten to take her medication. Granted, the crash brought it on, but any excitement at all could have done that. Plus she made a full recovery. The kid, he was only twenty-one, swore he'd never drink again."

"So no one was hurt. Sounds like you did your job."

"Except it didn't end there. Six weeks after the trial, he had a head-on collision with a car full of teens. Two were seriously injured. One lost a leg. His blood alcohol level was 0.19, more than double the legal limit. I know I did my job, but it doesn't keep me from feeling responsible."

LuAnn put a hand on his arm. "We're all human," she said. "Most of us try to do what's right, but we can't always predict the outcome."

"I find that to be true more often than I like," Jace said rubbing a hand over his tired eyes. "The other case you might have heard, it was on the front page for several weeks. A woman killed her husband. He was abusing her, but I had no proof. His mother gave a damaging statement claiming, in a nutshell, that he was the world's best son. Just from talking with the wife, I knew that was far from true. I couldn't see her going to prison for twenty years for doing what she thought she had to do. I got my hands on a photo that showed her face all battered. Problem was it happened when she had an accident while trying to escape him. That little stunt got me disbarred. I likely could have contested it and won, but I was ready for some time off from the criminal justice system. Through Chelsea I discovered I was illegally disbarred. I know it had something to do with Bart Harridan, but I haven't figured out his connection."

"I'm sorry I mistrusted you," LuAnn said.

He took her in his arms. "How about we go on from here. Leave the past behind us. I meant it when I said I loved you. I think I fell for you the first time I saw you walking into Applebee's on Sunday."

Her eyes sparkled again. "I love you too, but there's something I have to tell you. I don't want any more secrets between us."

"If you're talking about Becca," he said. "I already know."

"But how…she doesn't exist. I made up the name."

He took her hand and kissed it. "When you ran away, I suspected it had something to do with Becca, so I went to see Hank Jamison."

Her mouth fell open, and her eyes were wide as saucers.

"Don't hate me for that," he said quickly. "I was desperate when I couldn't find you. And you should know that he doesn't harbor any ill will toward you. One of the first things he told me was he blamed his son far more than he did you. In his words he said, 'Neil was older and should have known enough to use birth control.' He's a broken man, honey. He hasn't gotten over the loss of his son, but he said you have nothing to fear from him."

LuAnn dabbed at her red eyes. "Thank you. You can't know how much that means to me. I've been tormented for thirteen years. I don't think I'll ever get over it either. I gave her the name Becca just so I could identify with her. I'm glad it's out in the open and you know. For all these years the only people who knew were my father and my grandmother—and she'll probably hate me until the day she dies."

"She is a crabby old fart, isn't she?" Jace said, smiling.

LuAnn laughed too. "That's putting it mildly. Can we just lie down and hold each other for a while?"

"I thought you'd never ask."

* * * *

Bart Harridan knew where they were headed. He waited for them ten miles out of town. He wasn't sure what he could do when they passed him, but he'd decided he had to try. Maybe he could run them off the road. Where the blue blazes was Kastansa when he needed him, and why wasn't he answering his phone?

If he ran them off the road himself, the finger would point directly at him. Especially since the police had shown up at that damn clinic.

He still couldn't figure out where they were hiding. He knew damn well they were right there watching him look but danged if he could find them.

While he sat there waiting, he thought about his dilemma. Actually, Chelsea was the only one who knew anything, and he had the tape, so she had no proof. Why not just go home. Let her go wherever the hell she wanted. His life would be less complicated without her.

He couldn't believe that little witch had blackmailed him—and gotten by with it too. If Juanita hadn't found that recorder, he may never have known. He'd been so furious he'd torn her room apart, mainly to see if she had any other tapes hidden. When he'd found the money taped under the dresser he about shit his pants. If she had been there, he'd have literally ripped her to pieces, he'd been that furious. She'd put him through hell then gave the money away. Stupid. Stupid. Stupid.

Love. She'd said. She wanted love. Hell he grew up without love and look how successful he'd been. The little brat didn't know how good she had it.

When the Land Rover finally drove past him, his adrenalin kicked up. He was second guessing himself when he spotted the patrol car following her.

Crap. He recalled James bond's famous words, *live to die another day.*

He may as well go home and destroy the evidence.

Chapter-Twenty-Three

Jace woke up in a panic. An hour had passed since they'd fallen asleep. Kayla should have been there long ago. He eased himself off the bed so as not to disturb LuAnn. After what she'd been though, she needed her rest. He didn't want to leave her, but he had to check on Kayla and Chelsea.

Laughter from the sitting room drifted his way as he came down the stairs. That gave him a major dose of relief. He spotted Chelsea first. She sat on the carpeted floor entertaining Pugsly with a ball.

"Mr. Murdock," she shouted. She leaped to her feet and threw herself at him. He caught her up in a giant bear hug. Over her head he saw Kayla's smile.

Chelsea was quick to start explaining. "We had to hide in the vines 'cause my dad was looking for us. Kayla saved me."

Jace set her back on her feet then noticed the large bruise on her smooth cheek. He touched it. "Is this where he hit you?"

She nodded solemnly. "I don't ever have to go back there, do I?"

"No!"

Jace smiled at the chorus that came from Mamie, Logan, Maggie and Kayla before he even had a chance to speak.

"Absolutely not," he said, hoping this wasn't going to be another child whose fate he had no control over.

Kayla got up to give him a hug. "You owe me big time, brother."

He kissed her on the cheek. "Name it, sis, this time you've earned it."

"That's no fun. You're supposed to give me an argument."

When they separated, Chelsea went directly to Kayla's side and was welcomed by an arm around her slim shoulders. Her face beamed with happiness.

"How's your woman?" Kayla asked Jace.

"Sleeping, but I think she'll be fine. Did they clue you in on what went down here?" He nodded toward the group filling the room.

"Uh, huh. Now, let me tell you all about our escapade."

"First get me one of those beers." He indicated a bottle in Logan's hand. Logan sat on the loveseat with an arm around, Maggie, his very pregnant wife to be.

"I'll get the beer," Chelsea said. "I know where it is."

Jace walked over, bent down and gave Maggie a peck on the cheek. "You certainly are looking…fit."

Maggie pretended to scowl. "You were going to say 'fat' weren't you?"

"Do I look stupid?" he said, giving her round tummy a pat.

"Can I answer that?" Kayla quipped.

Chelsea bounced back in the room with his beer. He thanked her, twisted the cap off, took a deep swallow and sat down on one of the sofas. Kayla occupied the other end and Chelsea quickly plopped down between them.

Mamie smiled from her usual position in a cushioned recliner. "That young lady certainly knows her way around here."

"She's smart, too," Jace said, giving one of her long curls a tug. "Okay girls, tell me what happened." He looked at his sister and the imp between them who appeared anxious to share their adventure.

Chelsea started with her encounter at home. "They were waiting for me when I got home from Wendy's…"

Jace had a hard time identifying this exuberant girl with the sobbing child who'd called him earlier seeking help. *Kids were so resilient,* he thought thankfully. But he was confused too. How could this young girl talk so unemotionally about her father, who'd attacked her—as though he was a stranger? He caught his sister's gaze over the top of Chelsea's head and understood that she shared his thoughts.

"...and when I got to the clinic and she wasn't there, I really got scared. I hid in the bushes just knowing he was going to find me. And he would have too if Kayla hadn't come. When he showed up, we ran up the little hill and hid behind a wall under the vines. Kayla told me to be still and not move when he walked around looking for us. And then her cell phone rang..."

Jace glanced at Kayla. He knew it was his call that almost gave them away. She confirmed it by raising her eyebrows and nodding.

"...and he must have heard it because he climbed over the wall. I thought he would be able to hear my heart pounding I was so scared...then he started calling my name over and over saying he wasn't going to hurt me. I knew better though because he was really angry about the tape, even more than the money."

"What money?" Jace asked, confused. She hadn't mentioned money before.

Chelsea's cheeks turned pink, and she made a grimacing face, almost as though she hadn't meant to tell that part.

Jace leaned forward so he could look at her. "What money?" he repeated.

Her features tightened, and she lifted her shoulders holding them that way for a moment looking like a turtle trying to escape into its shell.

"Come on Chelsea, tell us about the money," Kayla said. "Remember we care about you. We're not the enemy."

Her Adams apple bobbed up and down as she swallowed. "Well, a few days ago I sent him a note—"

"Your father?" Jace asked.

"Yeah. I told him to leave money in a trash can in the park behind our house or I would expose him."

"Expose what?" Jace asked. "Something from the tape?"

"No, I hadn't bought the tape player yet, but before I did, I listened at the cold air duct in my room. It's right above his office."

She got startled looks from everyone in the room. "I wasn't really being bad," she replied quickly. "Mostly I was just bored." She grinned. "I felt like a spy, that's how I got the idea to buy the recorder, so I could be a real spy. I wasn't trying to be mean or anything."

Jace shook his head. She had a clever innocence about her that was almost humorous. "So…if you didn't have the recorder yet, what were you going to expose?"

"Nothing in particular. I just knew the way he talked he was guilty of something. Especially when he talked to Mr. Kastansa. That was always interesting listening."

Jace tried to hide a smile. "Once they talked about this Jack guy. I think Mr. Kastansa killed him with fire or something…"

Jace's smile faded in a hurry. Jack? Jack Randall? Was that the missing link to LuAnn? But that still didn't explain why Harridan would want to kill LuAnn all those years later. Jace polished off his beer and glanced at Logan. He could almost hear the gears grinding in his friend's head.

"…I wrote it all down in my dairy," Chelsea added. Her brow suddenly wrinkled. "Oh my gosh. I bet he found that too."

Kayla noted their exchange. "How much money did you ask for?"

"Only ten thousand dollars."

Jace nearly choked on his last swallow of beer. She was blackmailing her own father. "Why did you want ten thousand dollars?" he asked incredulously.

Chelsea ducked her head and didn't answer.

"Why did you need that much money?" Kayla prompted.

"To pay Mr. Murdock," she said barely above a whisper.

But they all heard it, because four sets of eyes instantly honed in on him.

"Okay, brother dearest," Kayla said, furrowing her brow, "your turn."

Jace took a very deep breath. "My business with clients is strictly confidential. You can tell them if you want to, Chelsea. I won't." The hostile stares softened when they turned from him to Chelsea.

"I. . .I asked him to...to find my mother."

"But. . .don't you have a mother?" Logan asked.

"Gladys is not my mother," Chelsea said sharply.

Jace leaned forward to look at Chelsea. "I believe her."

"We met for the first time today at Wendy's. That's where I was when I came home to find my dad all up in the air."

"How did you choose Jace?" Kayla asked.

"Because by listening to my father, I knew he found LuAnn. She's sort of my sister." She suddenly looked around frowning. "Where is LuAnn?"

"Upstairs sleeping," Jace said. "She's not your sister. You must have heard the message I left your father."

Chelsea snickered, "Yeah, I had it on the tape."

"I meant that for your father." To the others he explained. "When Harridan first contacted me, he asked me to find LuAnn, saying she was his wife, Gladys's, daughter. I knew he was lying, and I wanted to shake him up. I hoped his wife would listen to the message. I never intended you to hear it," he said to Chelsea. "LuAnn was actually with me when I made the call."

"Did someone mention my name?" a voice said from the stairs. Jace's heart swelled when he watched the love of his life descend the stairs. She looked as beautiful and regal as a princess. He stood up, met her at the bottom step and took her hand.

"Hey, sweetheart, come and meet Chelsea and Maggie.

Chelsea bounded to her feet. "Are you LuAnn? You are so pretty, just like I imagined you would be."

Chapter Twenty-Four

"And you must be Chelsea?" LuAnn said holding out her hands. "I've heard a lot about you."

Chelsea ran into her arms. "I really wanted you to be my sister.

"Sorry, honey," LuAnn said. "But we can be friends, can't we?"

Chelsea nodded vigorously, a broad smile on her face.

A serving girl walked in and announced that the evening meal was ready.

Everybody stood up and Kayla said, "Come on Chels, you're going to have to tell your story all over again for LuAnn."

LuAnn felt marvelous. The rest she'd had did wonders for her system and her mental health. She looked around the table at all her newfound friends laughing and chatting. Jace sat next to her, looking at her with adoring eyes, his hands continuously roving beneath the table. And Chelsea had grabbed the seat on the other side apparently not ready to give up the idea that LuAnn was her sister.

With all the happiness surrounding her, LuAnn decided she couldn't be more content. She had one moment of consternation when Maggie stood up holding her protruding belly. It was a disquieting reminder of the one aspect of her life that hampered her total serenity.

Becca.

Chelsea gave LuAnn an abbreviated version of the excitement at the clinic. Obviously the second telling was done with more enthusiasm as Chelsea embellished on each scene. She had everyone laughing with her animations.

"Did you really charge her ten thousand dollars to find her mother?" Maggie said to Jace accusingly.

He snorted. "Chelsea, how much did I charge you?"

Chelsea giggled. "Nothing—yet." Then she looked around the table. "I didn't have much information for him though. All I know for sure is that my father brought me home for Gladys, but she didn't want me. She insisted I came from one of his affairs. I was only eleven then, so I had to ask my teacher what an affair was. Mrs. Mlynek seemed kind of shocked, but she explained it to me."

Without missing a beat, Chelsea smiled up at Jace. "He asked me all sorts of questions, like what hospital I was born in and when is my birthday, stuff like that. All I knew was my birthday, and I actually thought that would be enough. After all how many babies are born on the fourth of July?"

LuAnn dropped her knife in her plate with a loud clatter. At first she couldn't breathe then she felt like she was hyperventilating.

She looked at Jace. "Becca was born on July fourth."

A hush fell across the table.

Jace looked at her with profound sadness. He put his arm around her. "Honey, you know Chelsea can't be your daughter."

"Why are you so sure?" she choked with a hint of anger.

"Because Hank Jamison told me what happened."

"What happened?" she repeated numbly.

All eyes, including a suddenly frozen Chelsea's, were trained on him waiting for an answer. "I'd rather not say it in front of everyone."

"Tell me what he said! I don't care anymore who knows."

Jace's jaw clenched. He shifted his weight around in his chair as though he'd suddenly become extremely uncomfortable. "Jamison told me he went to your house after he thought your baby would have been born. Jack, your father, told him you'd had an abortion."

LuAnn's dark brown eyes registered shock and anger. "That's not true! I gave birth to my baby. I was only fifteen, so my father forced me to give her up. He said he'd throw me, and my baby, out in the street if I didn't. He made me sign some paper. He tore her out of my arms and walked out of the house. I never saw her again."

She looked at a mesmerized Chelsea. "Are you sure your father is your real father?"

She shook her head mutely then found her voice. "I—I don't know. His name is on my birth certificate, same as Gladys's. He never said he wasn't my father, like Gladys did." Chelsea's face screwed up in thought. "Actually, he never acted much like a father though. Even when I was little, he never tossed me in the air or teased me or tickled me like Betty's father does to her and her brother."

"You know," Logan said. "A DNA test could prove it."

"I doubt we need to resort to that," Jace said. "Hear me out. Chelsea said her father talked about killing a man named Jack in a fire."

LuAnn gasped. "You think he murdered my father?"

"Yes, I do. And that would explain why I couldn't find any trace of this lottery he supposedly won. My guess is Bart Harridan paid him that money for your baby."

"How would Jack and Harridan have gotten together on a deal like that?" Logan asked.

"Jack worked for Otis. Otis serviced the elevators in Harridan's hotels."

LuAnn was blinking rapidly. "So why would he kill my father?"

"Didn't you tell me your father spent all the money and then he died?"

LuAnn nodded not daring to hope he was right.

"Again I'm guessing, but it's all starting to fit together. When Jack ran out of money, he must have gone back to Harridan asking for more."

"So Harridan had him killed," Logan supplied.

Kayla stared from Chelsea to LuAnn. "They do resemble each other. But why after all this time did he want to kill LuAnn too."

"I think I know," Chelsea said, her face reddening. "I never heard LuAnn's name mentioned until after I sent my father that blackmail note. He must have thought it from was LuAnn."

Jace smiled at her. "You are one clever young lady, Chels."

"Then it's all my fault you were almost killed," Chelsea said tearfully.

LuAnn threw her arms around her daughter. "But if you hadn't done that I never would have found you."

Tears trickled down Chelsea's face. "You really think I'm your daughter?"

"Yes I do sweetie, yes I do," LuAnn said through her own tears.

Everyone around the table unanimously agreed.

"Damn, Jace," Logan said. "You really need to get back into law. You sure know how to put a convincing argument together."

"According to Chelsea, Bart Harridan paid Judge Porter to get me disbarred."

"Why would he do that?" Kayla interceded looking to Chelsea for an explanation.

Chelsea sniffed and wiped the happy tears from her eyes. "It was on the tape. He said, 'I trusted you to pay me when you asked me to fix it so Jace Murdock got disbarred.'"

When she wiggled her little quotation fingers, Logan's eyes widened. "You remember that word for word?"

"That's exactly how she quoted it to me." Jace said, chuckling. "LuAnn's girl is one smart cookie."

The reference to being *LuAnn's girl* brought a smile as wide as the lift bridge channel on Chelsea's face.

"Damn," Logan muttered. "Too bad Harridan will have destroyed that tape by now."

Chelsea giggled. "It doesn't matter, I have a copy."

"Where?" both men asked at the same time.

Chelsea jumped off her chair and raced into the sitting room. Three seconds later she was back with her fanny pack. She unzipped it and dumped a cell phone, a tape and a stack of hundred-dollar bills on the table beside her empty plate.

Silence filled the room.

"Oh, my God." Kayla breathed.

Chelsea picked up the money and handed it around LuAnn to Jace. "This is yours for finding my mother." She looked up at LuAnn who circled her with an arm and a squeeze.

Jace picked up the money and handed it back to her. "I'll trade you for the tape."

"Don't do it, Chels. The tape is worth more."

Jace gave his sister a mock menacing glare. "For crying out loud, we shared a womb. Whose side are you on?"

"The female side."

Chelsea giggled. Everyone else laughed.

Chapter Twenty-Five

While Mamie hunted up a tape player, Jace excused himself to make a call to Superior, Wisconsin.

Ten minutes later, they were all hunkered around the coffee table listening to the tape.

Several times Jace stopped it, rewound and replayed. Eyes widened and jaws dropped at what they heard. Logan just kept shaking his head in disbelief.

One statement had them all staring at each other in shock. It explained the final missing piece to the puzzle. Jace replayed the proclamation, made by Judge Ramous Porter as he talked to Bart Harridan.

Well, I still need that stake. I swear I'll pay you back in three days. You can trust me just like I trusted you to pay me when you asked me to fix it so Jace Murdock got disbarred. I put myself on the line for that you know; I had to call in a lot of markers. What he did wasn't all that unheard of and it wasn't grounds for disbarment.

Bart Harridan's reply was the coup de grâce.

That son-of-a-bitch got Alexia Jacobs off for murdering my son. And those damn women advocates were prepared to give him a fucking medal.

When the tape ended, Logan and Jace exchanged looks.

"Sounds to me," Logan said, "like I can get a couple of arrest warrants written up."

"And it sounds to me," Mamie mumbled, "like I may have to get out my pins and dolls."

That declaration was followed by rolling eyes and an insistent knock at the front door.

"I'll get that," Jace said jumping to his feet.

Mamie frowned. "Who could that be?"

Jace came back moments later followed by an attractive man in his late fifties. Jace stood aside to make the introduction. "This is Hank Jamison, Chelsea's grandfather."

Jace motioned Chelsea forward. She came to her feet and slowly walked to stand in front of the imposing man who strangely with his good looks and tall stature reminded her of Bart Harridan. But the gentle look on his face and kindly moist eyes were a sharp contrast to the man she'd called father for almost thirteen years. Grandpa Hank, as she would soon learn to call him, held out his arms to her and she stepped into them.

Emotion ran as thick as honey in the moist eyes of the spectators.

* * * *

"Chelsea, can I ask you one question?" Jace said sometime later.

She looked up from the floor where she was playing with Pugsly at the feet of her mother and new grandfather. "Sure. What is it?"

"Remember when you called me to meet you at Wendy's and dropped that bombshell on me about Judge Porter?"

"Yeah?"

"You had to hang up because your mother was coming? Was that true?"

Chelsea stared up at him a moment before she spoke. She pulled Pugsly on her lap and gave Jace a crafty grin. "I refuse to answer on the grounds that it might incriminate me."

The End

About the Author

Born and raised on a North Dakota farm, Jannifer Hoffman started writing at the age of twelve, creating novels in her head while walking home from a one-room schoolhouse. A lifetime avid reader, she began writing in 1974 after reading *The Flame and the Flower* and *Sweet Savage Love*. After completing two historical romances, *Ceremony of Deception* and *Silver Shadows*, Jannifer decided to try her hand at contemporary romance. *Bittersweet Memories* is her eighth completed novel.

She readily admits it took thirty years of hard work, writing classes and writer's groups to finally realize what "serious writer" meant.

Her limited free time is spent sewing for a boutique and enjoying her family including three children, five grandchildren, and a special man who has been her partner for some twenty-five years. Jannifer lives on a lake in northern Minnesota during the summer and migrates to Yuma, Arizona for the winter.

Visit her website at www.janniferhoffman.com

Want to read more from Jannifer Hoffman?
Now Available from Resplendence Publishing:

Secrets of the Heart

Nicole Anderson owns a successful costume design business, has a wealth of small town friends and sleeps in a lonely bed haunted by demons from the past. She's convinced herself her life is exactly the way she wants it and has shot down every marriageable man within a fifty-mile radius.

When Hunter Douglas is assigned the task of delivering a deceased friend's children to their aunt, he must first convince the belligerent Nicole Anderson that she actually *had* a sister. Though forced to take his two charges to Minnesota, Hunter fully intends to persuade Ms. Anderson to allow the children to return to New York with him—without sharing his own little secret. The last thing he wants to do is fall in love with a woman who lives in a small Midwest town with neighbors who seem to know every move he makes.

As the heat index between Nicole and Hunter rises, a bizarre puzzle begins to unfold involving false birth certificates, a stolen suitcase, odd pictures, an elusive stalker and a grandfather's legacy that could turn deadly.

Secret Sacrifices

Driver Jamie LeCorre, competing in the male dominated Stock Car Racing field, needs a tape that will exonerate her from a deadly crash. Weary of dealing with domineering, chauvinistic males, she is suddenly attracted to just such a man. A man who can get her tape.

Quint Douglas has sworn off high profile, overly intelligent women. He discovers the blond bimbo of his dreams trying to change a flat on a pink BMW. Offering help, he uses a bit too much attitude and is shot down. Yet, Quint still tries to win her over in spite of his deep-seated fear of speed.

Together they enter the tight knit Stock Car Racing world to investigate an old murder, a new body and a highway collision—all tied together with too many suspects. Quint tries to keep Jamie from being the next victim even as she races around the track at 180 miles an hour, pursued by those who would like to see her eliminated, in more ways than one.

Rough Edges

When Julia Morgan M.D. miscarries twin girls, she divorces her husband, believing he is to blame. He forces her out of her position at the hospital and threatens her credibility as a doctor if she attempts to practice medicine. Without mentioning her medical degree, Julia accepts a position as nanny on a Colorado ranch 900 miles away.

Dirk Travis is in trouble. His wife has gone missing, and his housekeeper is threatening to quit. He is in desperate need of a reliable person to look after his four-year-old twins. Even though Julia appears to be the answer to his prayers, he can't help but think she's a bit too perfect.

Both insist their relationship will be business only. While those plans start to go awry, other things begin to happen. People are getting killed and Dirk is the prime suspect, but that doesn't stop the heat index from rising between Dirk and Julia, even as she appears to be the next target.

Blood Crystal

When a priceless crystal is stolen and five international agents killed, rookie agent Dani Lovato is sent undercover into the clandestine world of precious gems to retrieve it.

Stephen Douglas returns from Afghanistan, a wounded war hero, to find the life he left behind in shambles. Depressed and hitting rock bottom in an LA jail, he's offered the chance to be released with a clear record. All he has to do is show up at a warehouse and pick up the sheriff's daughter who is stranded and in harm's way. What sounds like a simple venture turns into an escapade that becomes the ride of his life.

Thrown together, not trusting each other, Stephen and Dani embark on a cross-country mission to return the Blood Crystal from the bowels of LA to its rightful owner in Washington D.C. Along the way, they discover there is a thin line between the good guys and the bad guys, and staying alive becomes more challenging with each perilous turn. Sparks fly between them in more ways than one as Dani accidently learns the startling secret of the Blood Crystal.

Random Fire

Katie Benson wants to get pregnant. She doesn't want or need a husband, but since she has to name the father to get her inheritance, she's hunting for a live donor. While visiting a friend's home in northern Minnesota, she spies a lone fisherman out on the lake and decides he would be the ideal specimen. Now all she has to do is convince a stranger to cooperate without cluing him in on the plan.

Virgil Douglas is nursing yet another failed relationship. What was it with women anyway? They couldn't seem to understand that he liked his uncomplicated life just the way it was—no wedding ring, no babies. But when he rescues a woman from drowning, he starts to reassess what he wants in life.

And then she disappears…

Edge of Daybreak

THE ESCAPE

After her husband is murdered, Maggie Carpelli discovers her father-in-law may be involved in a multi-million dollar investment scheme. He'll stop at nothing to prevent this information from getting into the wrong hands. He is out for blood…hers. She has to disappear without leaving a trail. The perfect escape presents itself in the form of a man-in-distress.

THE BARGAIN

After spending two years in an Arizona prison, Logan Rydell is headed to Minnesota on a
mission to clear his name. Trouble is, he's low on funds and out of luck…until a classy lady appears and makes him an unbelievable offer.

THE PURSUIT

Maggie puts her life in the hands of a ruggedly handsome stranger who has as many secrets as she does. Fighting a growing desire for her mysterious companion, Maggie keeps an eye on the rearview mirror, and Logan tries to understand why a once married woman can't say the word sex out loud…and who is chasing her?

Also Available from Resplendence Publishing

The Gladiator Prince by Minnette Meador

Centurion Series, Book Three

Prince Thane is the last surviving royalty of the Trinovantes Tribe in Roman Britannia, having surrendered to the Romans to save his two young daughters, whose identities he sacrifices his freedom to protect. He is condemned by Nero himself to become a gladiator, to fight until he dies in the arena. When his two daughters are taken in a slaver's raid, Thane escapes to find them.

Phaedra holds a terrible secret that would mean the death of her younger brother. Her only hope is to force the gladiator to protect them as they flee to Rome. He reluctantly agrees.

Little does he know that the beautiful Syrian woman holds not only the key to his passion, but a secret that triggers a disaster that ignites the world. Will this spoiled willful girl betray him in the end or sacrifice herself to save them all?

Taming the Princess by Temple Hogan

From the Sea Series, Book Two

Exasperated by his spoiled, arrogant daughter, Gillian, and her refusal to pick a husband from all the noblemen who plead for her hand, King Darragh decrees she must marry the very next man who comes to the castle. Princess Gillian finds herself married to Padruig Tierran, a lowly fisherman from a distant land. After a hasty marriage, she is whisked away to his fisherman's croft, where she must learn to cook and clean, none of which she's successful at. But Padruig has many lessons to teach his new wife and Gillian proves to be an avid pupil.

The Virgin Pirate by Temple Hogan

Book One in the *Pirate's Booty* Series

Born to a life of piracy, Nellie Bouchard knows no other life, but she longs to find a world beyond the ruthless violence and danger. Her wish is fulfilled when she captures Lord Trey Carlyle. Mesmerized by his masculinity and raw sexuality, she insists he teach her the secrets between a man and woman. Long tropical nights and sun-drenched days aboard her ship allow him to show her every aspect of sexual encounters while she teaches him about love. But he's her captive and she's a pirate with a price on her head. Their future might mean separation…or death.

Glass Slipper by Abigail Barnette

Naughtily Ever After, Book One

When Julien Auvrey promises to help his goddaughter snag a prince, he has no idea that the squalling infant he held in his arms nineteen years ago has turned into a beautiful young woman. Once he sees Joséphine, he knows that she's just what the prince wants in a woman…and just the type of woman that Julien wants in his bed. But Julien is a life-long bachelor, and Joséphine deserves more than just a brief affair. With his help, she'll blossom into a wife fit for the prince—in and out of the bedchamber.

Joséphine Thévenet wants nothing more than to be quit of her father's crumbling house, her stepmother's temper, and her two obnoxious stepsisters. Notorious seducer Julien

Auvrey appeals to her desire for escape, and plenty of her other desires, as well. When etiquette lessons turn to carnal instruction, Joséphine fears she will lose her heart before she can win the prince.

Julien can't deny the raw heat between him and Joséphine, but he also can't deny the promise he made to her father. To possess Joséphine, Julien must betray his friend, and give up his own life of indulgence. Can he truly ask Joséphine to turn her back on the chance to be princess for nights of endless pleasure? Can he trust himself to love her as she deserves?

Tutoring Miss Molly by Lyn Armstrong

Desperate to help her sick aunt through another brutal winter on their meager farm, Molly Cambridge will do anything to survive. Even if it means becoming a courtesan at the scandalous Harmon Manor. To catch the eye of a wealthy benefactor, she must learn the art of carnal pleasure from a resentful Marquess. Yet her traitorous heart cannot resist the handsome tutor that harbors secrets that may destroy them both. With attempts on her life and time running short, love is a luxury a courtesan can ill afford.

Bored with the spoiled, decadent lifestyle of the infamous sex society, Lord Devlin Harman has little time for courtesans and their cunning wiles. Blackmailed into tutoring an inexperienced courtesan, he is determined to show the farm girl the error of her ways. However, a unique beauty exists beneath the mud-stained rags, causing his jaded heart to melt and his flesh to burn for her touch. If she does not become the chosen courtesan at the mistress auction, he must marry a devious aristocrat by spring. Can he let Molly be a courtesan to gain freedom from his marriage contract? Or will he sacrifice everything for a farm girl?

Infernal Devices by Abigail Barnette

The Two Aces. Victorian London's most salacious secret, the club is a place where erotic fantasies are played out among clockwork automatons and aether powered machines. Where nothing is off limits and the pleasures are as wicked as the imagination will allow...

Permilia Deering goes to The Two Aces looking for the sexual excitement that she knows she will not find with the man to whom she is affianced, notorious cold-fish Wallace Sterling. On her first visit to the club, she meets the Ace of Spades, a masked stranger who drives her to heights of passion she's never dreamed possible—and makes her seriously reconsider becoming a mannerly society wife.

When Wallace Sterling first glimpses his fiancée standing outside The Two Aces, he assumes she's uncovered his secret identity—the Ace of Spades. But Permilia has no idea that her intended is living a double life, and Wallace worries that he'll be out of the picture once she gets a taste of what the Ace of Spades can offer her...

Chasing Temptation by Regina Carlysle

London's Haute Ton calls her Miss Temptation. But Elizabeth Grayson can't be bothered by society's diversions while seeking justice for her murdered sister. She is a woman on a dangerous mission. Now is not the time for mindless social engagements or courtships from men she has no intention of marrying. However, Christian Delaford is no ordinary man. He stirs her like no one she has ever met before. His eyes speak of sin and tangled sheets. Of decadent nights spent in his arms. Far too diverting for her peace of mind.

Christian Delaford, the Duke of Haverton, must be married

by midnight of his birthday or forfeit his heritage to a distant relation. After years of living a hedonistic life in the Orient, the thought of binding himself forever to an insipid English Miss fairly curls his toes. London's current 'diamond of the first water', however, changes his mind. In Elizabeth, he finds a bold and daring woman who harbors a terrifying secret. He vows to chase Miss Temptation, to the ends of the earth if needs be, and save her from the forces that would tear them both apart.

Unmasked by Genella deGrey

Venice, Italy, 1795 - Gwendolyn Rawleigh longs for adventure, but has fallen into a clandestine, carnal game of instruction with an intimidating stranger who insists she must embrace this new found tuition before she can proceed.

Marcello Verdante finds the alluring Miss Rawleigh irresistible. However, he must remain anonymous for her safety as well as his own.

Ellie Appelton wants so badly to emulate Gwennie's sophistication, but is afraid of where her own wicked thoughts may take her. She finds her liberation in a close, intimate friend . . . her impromptu Chaperone.

Never in his wildest dreams did Preston Rawleigh think to find himself attracted to his sister's innocent best friend . . . Then again, the magical wonderland of Venice can reveal secret truths even a masked reveler cannot hide.

Come spend a few days exploring the sensual mysteries of Carnivale -

Some will be pursued, most will be caught, and all will be Unmasked.

Find Resplendence titles at these retailers

Resplendence Publishing
www.ResplendencePublishing.com

Amazon
www.Amazon.com

Barnes and Noble
www.BarnesandNoble.com

Target
www.Target.com

Fictionwise
www.Fictionwise.com

All Romance E-Books
www.AllRomanceEBooks.com

Mobipocket
www.Mobipocket.com

1 Place for Romance
www.1placeforromance.com

Made in the USA
Charleston, SC
15 May 2012